HEDGES

Other Books by
ELIZABETH STANCY PAYNE

LIGHTS ALONG THE LEDGES
FATHOMS DEEP
ALL THE WAY BY WATER
SINGING WATERS
HEARTHSTONES
PAINTERS OF DREAMS

HEDGES

By ELIZABETH STANCY PAYNE

A. L. BURT COMPANY
Publishers   New York

Published by arrangement with The Penn Publishing Company

Printed in U. S. A.

COPYRIGHT 1929		MANUFACTURED
BY THE		IN THE
PENN PUBLISHING		UNITED STATES
COMPANY		OF AMERICA

HEDGES

Published October 1929
Second Printing before Publication
Third Printing November 1929

For

M. K. H.

CONTENTS

CHAPTER		PAGE
I.	MARCH SUNLIGHT	11
II.	DAFFODILS AND DESIRES	24
III.	WHAT PRICE SOLITUDE?	37
IV.	APRIL INDECISIONS	51
V.	WON'T YOU WALK INTO MY GARDEN?	58
VI.	APPLE BLOSSOMS FROM KITCHEN WINDOWS	70
VII.	CONSIDERING VALLEY LILIES	83
VIII.	LILACS IN THE RAIN	98
IX.	A DREAMER IN THE DUSK	110
X.	BROOKS AND BUTTERCUPS	122
XI.	ON BIRD BATHS AND HOME TRUTHS	139
XII.	CHURCH BELLS IN THE VILLAGE	151
XIII.	JUNE MOONLIGHT	165
XIV.	AFTERNOON OF AN AUTHOR	180
XV.	MISUNDERSTOOD HUSBANDS	192
XVI.	AUGUST INTRUSIONS	196
XVII.	LEAFY SHADOWS	212

CONTENTS

CHAPTER		PAGE
XVIII.	SUMMER LIGHTNING	225
XIX.	BITTERSWEET AND BUTTERNUTS	238
XX.	FROST	256
XXI.	IN THE TOWN TRADITION	272
XXII.	EAST WINDS BLOWING	283
XXIII.	CHRISTMAS CANDLES	297
XXIV.	SNOW AND FLAME	309
XXV.	IN THE GRIP OF WINTER	318
XXVI.	JANUARY STARS	330
XXVII.	TWO BY THE FIRE	339

HEDGES

*OH, I would make tall hedges grow,
    To shut me in, from pain —
A place that only I should know,
Where I could watch my roses blow,
My own tree shadows come and go,
My winter garden, soft with snow,
    My lilacs in the rain!*

HEDGES

CHAPTER I

March Sunlight

DURING that interval before the pointer of the office clock made its slowest but most attractive leap — from one minute of five to five — a sunbeam, streaming dust-freighted under a window shade, touched the hands of a girl who was setting her desk in order preparatory to leaving it for the day.

Her hands had been moving methodically, tucking slips of memoranda into desk drawers, capping the inkwell, replacing folders in a file at her elbow — accurate, unhurried movements of a conscientious worker to whom her work and its tools had dignity and significance. Outside her ground-glass paneled cubicle — a place of cherished privacy — five o'clock sounds could be heard: pushing back of chairs, bang of typewriter-weighted desk lids, slamming of desk drawers, almost the snap of vanity boxes as small mirrors were passionately consulted to make sure faces were there, fair and agreeable to behold as they had been when last envisioned. By the time the office clock had made its next leap — from five to one minute past — the outer office was deserted. But within the glass-paneled cubicle Miss Gail Ormsbee sat staring at the dusty sunbeam that touched her hands.

Twice a year, in March and in September, that five o'clock sunbeam visited her desk. In summer, the sun was too far north and in winter, too far south for stray beams to creep between tall structures and slant into the room at just that angle. The sunbeam's appearance heralded commencement of a new season. Suggested change. And imminence of change caused stirring of restlessness. Between the end of one definite period and the beginning of another you felt anything might be on the way — maybe better, maybe worse, but at any rate interruption of routine. Usually things went on in the same old way. But the semi-annual sunbeam had for how many years — three? four? five? — shot in at that window with its enlivening suggestion of time passing and a new season begun.

Today, however, Miss Gail Ormsbee smiled contentedly at the sunbeam. Today it stirred no lurking restlessness; brought no melancholy reminder of monotony. Next time it slanted under that window shade and touched busy hands at that desk — they would not be her hands.

But she went on tidying the desk. She was a neat and systematic person. She closed the heavy lid carefully, not to jar the typewriter; slipped her French-American dictionary in the rack beside her *History of Costume* and *Who's Who Among Couturiers*, indispensable accessories of daily labor. For she was expert fashion copy writer for a trade journal which supplied (as a side line that got rid of expensive photographs made for its illustrations) syndicated fashion copy to a vast number of small newspapers throughout the country.

And like most expert fashion copy writers, Miss Gail Ormsbee was, in personal attire, quite a plain, unarresting sort of person. Any flapper stenographer in the outer office could have told her a lot of ways in which she might improve herself. Her serge skirt, for instance, might have been shorter — for she had really good knees as well as nice ankles. Her collar, instead of being pinned with a stern little brooch, might have flared a bit — because her throat was white and young and lovely. And with that severe, brushed-back haircut that showed forehead and ears and the shape of her neat little head, a pair of swinging earrings would have given some style. As any flapper could have informed her, a boyish haircut positively demands feminine ear ornaments to give it proper piquancy. And by the same token no boyish haircut should be accompanied by low-heeled shoes. Comfortable or not, they failed to lend the haircut that zest which tall-heeled slippers would have supplied.

All in all, the outer office decided, in gossip confabs in the washroom, Miss Ormsbee, who did editorial work in her precious private cubby-hole and undoubtedly had brains, (as far as that went) had been gifted by nature with real points and it was a crime the way she neglected them.

And in a way, they were right. The small head with its thick, austerely clipped hair had an aristocracy of its own, but the hair — a light, sunny brown — was too lovely to be cut that way. The straight nose would have been saucier a bit more tilted. And the wide-apart eyes, gentian blue and shaded with double fringes of black lashes, had no coquetry because of straight black brows under which they looked with uncompromising directness and occasional severity at a frequently aggravating world. The close-pressed lips did not smile enough. When they did, and a dimple flashed out at one side, you realized that Miss Gail Ormsbee had the makings of a very pretty girl — if only she would concentrate on it and not so earnestly on other things.

You got the impression that here was a young woman to whom life had brought problems and even vicissitudes and that in combating and conquering she had acquired a forthrightness that had somehow throttled down the femininity that would have been more appealing. A pity too, for she was only six-and-twenty. Except for something youthfully wistful in the black-lashed blue eyes, something quick and springing about the movement with which she left the desk chair and crossed the room, she might have been a competent business woman in the thirties.

Standing at the door of her partitioned-off cubicle, serviceable little felt hat down over her eyebrows — not a trace of tilt in it — plain and capacious handbag swinging from her arm, she surveyed the neat desk and tidily pushed-in chair and the meticulously adjusted window shades; and in her look, had you been a discerning person, you would have glimpsed something of the look of the "lifer" taking a last survey of his cell on the day of liberation.

"Two weeks ought to be enough notice to give them," thought Miss Ormsbee, preparing to close the door upon her sanctum. Then she went back, gathered up a cluster of jonquils from the glass on her desk, and as she passed through the outer office handed the flowers to a scrubwoman who was stooping over a pail.

"I bought them this noon. Take them home with you, Mrs. McGuire."

The scrubwoman wiped sudsy hands on her apron. "Thank you, Miss. They'd make you think o' spring, wouldn't they?"

"And a garden!" Under the serviceable hat Miss Ormsbee's blue eyes had a sort of shine in them. "A spring garden, Mrs. McGuire. With tulips too. And iris. And lilacs..."

The scrubwoman carefully wrapped the jonquils in a tag of newspaper snatched from a scrap-basket. "I'm not knowin' much about spring gardens an' that's the truth. But I 'mimber apple blossom time whin I was a gurrl. Back in the owld counthry, it was." She got down on her knees again and reached for her scrubbing brush. "Thank you kindly, my dear. They'd a' lasted y' another day in yer office."

The quick, lovely smile that made Gail Ormsbee suddenly ingenuous and young was her only answer to the old Irish woman. When there is within, a swelling, secret joy, it has to be shared with somebody — the smile said that.

"Guess she got a raise," opined the elevator boy who let her out on the street level. "Good lookin' skirt if she'd grin like that oftener."

Glaring and hot out in the street. One of those unseasonably warm days in March that make winter furs suddenly intolerable. Garish light blazing on asphalt. Dirty papers blowing about. Men with hats pushed back from damp foreheads. Women already in those lighter colors that in cheap materials lend a so much tawdrier effect to a crowd than even the poorest winter garments of darker hue. People swarming on the tops of busses. Baseball news blaring from radios in shop doorways. The city was so ugly at this hour, in spring. All the decent reticence of winter vanished. The noisy and shoving element not hiding within walls to keep warm, but released into the streets.

Miss Ormsbee, threading her way across town in the throng of wage-earners that moved eastward and westward on the pavement, wondered if among all the thousands who poured out of offices and warehouses and shops, there were even half a dozen to whom occurred sentimental regret for the poetry of winter dusk. Probably not; to most of these toilers elbowing one another to reach subway and "el" steps, there was joy in the knowledge that soon the daylight-saving arrangement would leave the sun still higher when they emerged. At this hour in December one would emerge into fairyland. Windows of tall buildings would be rows of jewels against the dusk, traffic lights and lamps of taxis, colorful fireflies ceaselessly in motion. Limousines would be rolling up the avenue past shop windows brilliant with light and color and beautiful wares. And the crowd would melt into the dusk; it would not be strident and oppressive as it was now, but entirely unirritating, its elbowing and philandering and gum chewing veiled by kindly darkness.

Fun, to walk home from work in winter. You could sleuth along, lost, yourself, in the dusk. Nibble chocolate. Tuck hands in coat pockets. Wear your comfortable old galoshes. Observe without being a target for observation — that complete delight of the city saunterer whose pleasure in outdoor strolls is contemplative, not gregarious.

"Well, thank goodness," remembered Miss Gail Ormsbee, "I shall soon be out of all this."

She was gazing into a window that offered attractive display of garden hose, lawn mowers and watering-pots when her elbow was firmly gripped by a pedestrian coming up from behind. A pleasant masculine voice remarked:

"Howdy?"

After the first jump she looked at him with disfavor. (Elbow-grabbing savored of ownership. To be discouraged.)

He swung into step with her. "What's the rush?"

"Rush —?"

"You didn't wait for me."

"Do I have to?"

He had her elbow again, piloting her expertly through a gap in humans congregated at a crossing and getting her safely across between the shriek of the traffic whistle and the start of juggernaut cars around the corner. Sanctuary of the opposite curb having been achieved, he remarked, "When a lady sends a gentleman a note —"

"Oh — the note!" She remembered, smitten.

"— When, I repeat, she sends a gentleman a communication expressing regret that she cannot dine with him even to celebrate his safe return from a week's sojourn in the howling hinterland of the middle-west; but offers by way of salve to his bruised sensibilities an interview after office hours if he finds it convenient to hang around —"

"I'm sorry, John. I clean forgot."

"Forgot, did you? Must be some stirring news you have to impart. The P.S. I recall had something about news —"

"Tremendous." Her blue eyes lifted to his with swift upflinging of black lashes. He loved that swift, direct glance of Gail. When the dark lashes flashed up, revealing that deep blue within their shadow, it always made John Ingram think of sudden glimpse of still water reflecting the sky in some woodsy place.

"They gave you a raise," he guessed.

"Nothing like that."

"Then the short story has been accepted."

Something of starriness went out of the blue gaze. "No. It came back."

"Well, I've told you, many's the time, that as long as they come back there's hope for a writer. It's only after they cease coming back he needs to watch his step. You're working up now; don't get anxious to begin the downward slide too soon."

The rare, bright laugh with its dimple and flash of beautiful teeth illuminated Gail's face. "A long way to go — before we reach that dangerous peak."

"You're on the way. About this tremendous news now —" he stood still abruptly. "Look here, you're not — It isn't some chap, is it, Gail?"

The dimple disappeared. "Chap! You know very well, John Ingram, I've no interest in such frivolities."

He looked relieved. "A lot could happen in a week when my eye wasn't on you. Well, then —" He registered apprehension again. "You haven't been offered another position? You are not giving up your work on the Buyer and Retailer?"

"No — not exactly."

"More and more reassuring. If she isn't going off with a wealthier feller and doesn't contemplate forsaking the roof that shelters our mutual labor, the big news doesn't seem to threaten our own comfortable routine. We old folks do detest change — and so why can't you have dinner with me in the good old way and tell me all about it while we eat?"

They had arrived at her doorway and he grinned up at her as she paused, two steps above him on the flight that led up to an old fashioned vestibule. An ultra respectable brownstone boarding-house in the East Thirties. Dozens like it between Madison and Lexington, and most of them populated by successful business women.

He had removed his hat and, standing thus above him, she could look down on the sleekly brushed light brown hair thinning a bit at brow and temples. John Ingram was not a tall man but his slim erectness and a certain grace of carriage suggested greater height than he possessed. There was about him also a suggestion of self reliance and capacity for meeting situations. A man yet below his middle thirties, with lines of reticence about a good mouth, and gray eyes you instinctively liked. Here was a pleasant chap, you concluded. College background undoubtedly. The kind of chap who wore good clothes and employed good manners because he'd been bred to them. Older than his years because of some faithfully carried responsibility, but the sort of chap who, though he wouldn't shirk a real issue, mostly met life with philosophical good humor.

"How about it?" he urged.

"About what?"

"Dinner."

"Not tonight, John."

"Why not — you cold-hearted woman? When I'm back from a lonesome middle-west jaunt and yearning for sympathetic welcome home —"

"You know why not." She gave him a straight man-to-man glance — slightly impaired by the up-flinging of dark lashes.

"You're afraid I'll propose again," he challenged. "All right, I promise not to, this time — though it's no crime."

"It spoils things," she retorted. She was getting out her latchkey. "Here we have been working in the same building for five years —"

"Six," he corrected. "Don't forget that first year when you were doing shorthand and taking my dictation —"

She remembered; and how he had gotten her on the editorial staff of the Buyer and Retailer upstairs when he had discovered her knack with words and phrases. But she continued relentlessly: "You begin by asking me to go to some lectures, instructive for my work. I go. Then you ask me to go and hear some good music. Then you edge in a theater. And next time we have dinner beforehand. And then it gets to be a regular habit once a week: dinner and theater. Not that I didn't enjoy it." She was honest about that. "Not many theaters come my way — and when you board you do relish decent dinners."

"Don't think I did it just to feed you —"

"Then," she pursued, "you take to sending me books because you find out I'm buying books with the dinner money I've saved —"

"Might call it our Book of the Week Club." He chuckled. She did not smile. Gail Ormsbee, in earnest, had no time for inconsequent mirth.

"And then I have to send you some books: to get even for all you are squandering on me. And we discuss the books over the dinners. Everything going pleasantly; we have nice pally times. Just as two men might, who worked in the same building —"

"Just exactly!" inserted Mr. Ingram.

"And then —" her tone was accusing — "you take to proposing to me. Why couldn't you be satisfied the way things were? I don't want to get married."

The chuckle was reflected in his eyes by a twinkle. "You have to get married sometime."

"Do I? You don't have to decide that, do you?"

"And you told me yourself, lady, on one of those occasions you so deplore, that there was nobody you'd rather marry . . . because we have similar tastes —"

"Except for one thing," she reminded him pointedly.

"Two," he amended. "They'd do you good." He grinned at her.

"You are to decide that also, are you?" Suddenly she smiled, black lashes crinkling around wide-apart blue eyes. "It's no use, John dear. I've my own work to do. For pity's sake let me do it in peace. I've a chance now —"

But he was glancing over a shoulder at a big car

drawing in at the curb. "My honorable boss," he murmured.

The man who was driving hailed them genially. "Not butting in, am I? Followed you two over here. If you're on your way out to our neck of the woods, John, hop in; I want to talk over that Clark and Seebold crane advertising." Then, noting Mr. Ingram's tentative glance at the lady, "A date? Sorry —"

"Not at all," declared the lady. "He was only strolling across town with me; I've a dinner engagement of my own. John's excused, Mr. Atchison. Take him along to that neck of the woods you are both so crazy about."

She ran up the steps and inserted her latchkey in the door; waved a friendly hand and in a second was inside the house.

"Fine girl," said the editor of The Engineering and Structural Review.

"One of the finest," agreed his associate editor.

"Dependable."

"Absolutely."

"Ambitious too, I imagine. Might do something better than that fashion copy."

"A whole lot better," said John Ingram.

His chief slewed an eye around at him. But one had to keep eyes ahead in city traffic. Presently Warren Atchison appended, "Always seemed to me a very self-contained young woman. Not much come-hither about her. Good looking girl too. Sort of a pity."

His passenger offering no reply to this there was no further conversational exchange until the car swung into the plaza before the ferry house. Then the chief inquired casually:

"How are the youngsters?"

"Fine and dandy," responded his associate editor. And added, "They're a couple of tykes. Getting to be more of a handful every day."

CHAPTER II

Daffodils and Desires

THE sun that had, at five o'clock, revealed downtown streets in glaring ugliness, slanted at six into an uptown studio window and made a picture of a girl sitting on a couch. The girl had on a yellow smock and beside her on a little table were yellow daffodils in a copper jug. Her hair was pale corn-color, fluffed about her face. She had amber eyes and little amber freckles across the bridge of a piquant nose. And on one of her cheeks was a splotch of pure gamboge from the paintbrush too hastily tucked behind an ear.

With all five fingers she held a cigarette by its end, like another paintbrush, and made a sweeping, obliterating gesture in the air.

"Hedges!" she said. The gesture painted them out at one stroke.

Miss Gail Ormsbee who was reclining in the only comfortable chair the studio afforded, nodded with equal firmness.

"Tall hedges — so nobody can see over them." Arms behind her head and slim ankles crossed on a footstool (as one sits, contentedly relaxed, in the company of good friends) Miss Ormsbee continued in dreamy self-absorption:

"And casement windows looking out at the back on a garden."

"The kitchen would be at the back," reminded a

brisk voice from an adjoining room whence came rattle of crockery and enticing smells.

"Well, a kitchen can have casement windows," Miss Ormsbee stated. "There'll be jonquils and tulips and iris in the garden. And later on, roses — little yellow ones on bushes and red ones on a trellis. And after that, hollyhocks, and bachelor buttons and poppies — the way they plant them at Gloucester, so they come up a mass of blue and pink . . . And then zinnias and marigolds and those little rusty chrysanthemums that smell so nice in autumn." Her eyes had a far-away look. "I can see them all —"

"So can I," said the yellow-smocked artist. "And you, down on your knees, pulling up weeds. And slapping at mosquitoes. Of course there'll be mosquitoes, there always are."

"In spring —" Miss Ormsbee's eyes had the far-away look — "there will be lilacs!"

The occupant of the couch cast herself backward on the cushions. "Lilacs! You pathetic old maid — sentimentalizing about lilacs. What do you think you're going to be doing when you aren't plucking lilacs and picking bugs off rose bushes?"

"Writing."

"Don't think it," called the brisk voice from the other room. "What she'll be doing, Arlene, will be dusting and mopping floors and scrubbing out the gas oven. And stalling off neighborly ladies who drop in of a morning. Social sort of people never have any respect for a writer's working time."

In the doorway appeared a stocky little person with a bread knife in her hand. Her tailored skirt and blouse were protected by an unhemmed length of dish toweling pinned on here and there. She had keen gray eyes, made the keener by horn-rimmed glasses and her thick dark hair, cut short and unwaved, was sprinkled with gray.

"If you want to write, Gail Ormsbee," this one advised, "do it right here in New York. In a tenth storey room where you won't hear the noises for the din. Elevated trains won't bother you half so much, believe me, as lawn mowers whining under those casements, and blue jays screeching in those hedges you talk about —"

Gail looked at her wistfully. Hilda Braithwaite might have been expected to understand. Hilda had been grinding out copy for years and years in an office.

"It isn't just the writing, Hilda —"

The keen gray eyes looked at Gail affectionately. "Of course it isn't, honey. I know what it is, all right. You've got a domestic fixation and you think you have found a way to indulge it and do your job too. If you were forty it might work out, but I think you are making a mistake now. You'd much better —"

There was an ominous hissing behind her and she vanished. Arlene West on the couch, lighted another cigarette and said plaintively, "If any gone and forgotten godmother suddenly surprised me with five thousand dollars I'd never be mad enough to bury it — and me — in any mausoleum at the back of beyond. Why, holy cats, Gail could take a round-the-world cruise in a stateroom all to herself! And have enough left to furnish a nifty little one-and-bath and live the life of Reilly right here with the rest of the crowd! She thinks she wants to live the simple life because she's fed up with an office. Spring always makes people feel like that. Don't I, myself? Look at the way I slaved over those window boxes last year for the sake of a few feeble petunias —"

"Poor things. I remember them," inserted Miss Ormsbee.

"Well, I worked off my garden urge on those window boxes, just as Hilda, there, takes out her domestic urge in that kitchenette of hers. Why can't you? I'm talking for your own good, you poor simp. How'll you feel when you wake up and find the five thousand and yourself buried under six feet of January snow, behind those casements — and nothing to do but write?"

"Dinner in two minutes," called the brisk voice of Miss Braithwaite. "If anybody has set the table."

The girl in the yellow smock leaped off the couch, dragged out a folding card table, tossed on it a square of green oilcloth and then slapped on the oilcloth several plates of Italian pottery, odd knives and forks, and salt and pepper holders representing respectively a bright green toad and a deep pink owl. And finally scattered paper napkins here and there. Then she carefully carried across the room a bowl of white narcissus and set it in the center of the board.

"All ready," she called cheerily. "Everybody bring along something to sit on."

While the artist was absent, fetching a bottle of water from the icebox, Miss Ormsbee's hands hovered deftly over the table. Immediately silverware tidily flanked plates. Triangles of paper napkin lay accurately in place. The toad and the owl became orderly and not helter-skelter. This was entirely for her own satisfaction; nobody else, she knew, would notice the improvement.

Hilda Braithwaite appeared with steaming frankfurters and potato chips from the delicatessen, a really delightful salad with roquefort dressing, and a glossy apple pie from the baker's — the last, as dessert, finding temporary refuge on the couch. It was remarkable what you could do with a two-burner grill and a lapboard balanced on top of a bathtub; in Arlene's studio six had dined sumptuously more than once. The three now made a merry meal of it and when the day's humidity culminated in an electric storm that darkened the room, the artist fetched tall white candles which glimmered poetically at either side of the bowl of narcissus.

They lingered contentedly over Hilda's excellent coffee. To these three good pals the fortnightly feeds at Arlene's studio were happy occasions. Hilda reciprocated with Sunday suppers at her two-and-bath on West Fiftieth street. And Gail extended hospitality at a pet restaurant of theirs on West Eighth where tables set cosily between high-backed settles insured jolly privacy for a little dinner party.

Hilda Braithwaite had a real apartment with a kitchenette and a gas oven. And she was a natural-born cook. Nobody could match her when it came to raised biscuit and tenderloin steak with mushrooms. She even had a knack with lemon pie. More than one masculine guest had been heard to remark at one of Hilda's suppers that her talents were wasted in a literary career. But they asserted it to the assembled company only. None of them, she complained, took her aside and talked about it. Hilda was too chunky and too downright and too rapier-tongued to attract romantic admiration. Good cook or not, she protested, she hadn't a chance. No man with a soul above eating yearned for a wife whose indefatigable sense of humor would see right through him and turn his funny side out for other folks' delectation. Hilda's own funny side was also frequently called to the attention of chortling beholders — a fatal habit, admitted Miss Braithwaite, and death to romance.

She was employed in a publishing house and did blurbs for book jackets; taking a turn at manuscript reading when things were rushed. Evenings, she wrote book reviews for a weekly journal and had, always, under her arm some new novel which she skimmed, going home in the subway or while waiting for her meal in a restaurant. In her office capacity she was tender toward fledgling authors, giving a good word where she could; and in her book reviewing job, ruthless toward arrived authors. "Take 'em down and they'll try harder next time," she asserted. "But give 'em the least puff and they'll be so inflated they can't see their own futilities." The incessant acrobatic effort necessary for puffings (in the jacket blurbs) and deflations (in the book reviews) made it impossible to do sincere and earnest literary work of her own. But she had a book to her credit: a collection of mirth-provoking essays on the experiences, pathetic, ridiculous and harrowing, of an unattached female with sociable instincts in a world where social diversions were arranged for pairs.

These skits had been gathered together under the title: *One Without* and the book had enjoyed quite a vogue the preceding winter.

She was older than Arlene and Gail, but a close friendship had developed among the three during a period while they occupied adjoining quarters in a house run as a professional woman's club. The club had gone on the rocks but during that jolly winter the three had shared small treats, exchanged books and used each other's electric irons, and the fellowship thus established had remained.

Arlene West who was only twenty-three did fashion drawings for an exclusive dressmaker who submitted the drawings to patrons willing to pay stupendous prices for original costumes. Arlene evolved the designs with wary attention to the probable next jump of Paris style-makers and had the acumen to indicate in her drawings only the most costly fabrics. One or another of these sketches was always propped on the easel in Arlene's studio; — attenuated ladies, all at least nine heads tall and with long-lidded eyes and an expression of most horrible sophistication combined with perfect inanity. Their supple bodies writhed in garments that, while conveying an idea of drapery, had none of the stodgy reticence of actual covering. They made the eyes of willowy patrons gleam and the eyes of pudgy patrons dream. And the young artist who couldn't have kept a roof over her head with the really excellent landscapes she was able to turn out, received a hundred and fifty a week for these sartorial atrocities.

Arlene possessed parents somewhere in Ohio. Occasionally the maternal parent descended upon the metropolis and when she left, the studio evidenced a good old-home cleaning and Arlene had plumped out under a sustaining diet. Miss Braithwaite and Miss Ormsbee always came for a meal during these maternal sojourns and Mrs. West departed for Ohio shaking her head over the dangerous emancipation of daughters nowadays, but somewhat reassured by the safe-appearing pals with whom her child consorted. Arlene who was now relaxing after one of these motherly invasions, lit her fourteenth cigarette that evening from the end of the one burning out and blew smoke rings at the narcissus.

"If you absolutely can't control your yearning for the wide open spaces, Gail Ormsbee, why squander five thousand, acquiring a lodge in yon wilderness? Why not get it the natural, orderly way?" Arlene added in a mincing tone: "In the real womanly way, dearest. Why not marry that widower of yours? He's got the lovely garden — or space for it I daresay. And the little house out in God's country. Even lilacs, probably."

"And other things," darkly reminded Miss Ormsbee.

"Two dear little kiddies," responded Arlene sentimentally. "Playing in their blue rompers amid the golden poppies. If it were me, I could paint 'em —"

"You'd do more than paint 'em," Gail retorted. "You'd wash 'em and wipe their noses. And hold their heads when they had whooping-cough. And gently and judiciously and with infinite pains form their little characters. Not for me, thank you — I want to write."

"It seems a pity," said Hilda Braithwaite. She poured the last drop from the percolator into her coffee cup. "I've known John Ingram, man and boy, for sixteen years. I knew him before he came out of college and went into Warren Atchison's office. I knew him before his wife died — even before he got married. And any women he honors with his affection — any woman he takes care of and makes a home for — well, she will be a lucky woman, that's all I have to say."

Gail frowned. "Let's leave John Ingram out of it," she said. "I don't want to be taken care of, as you so touchingly put it, Hilda. I am quite capable of taking care of myself. I don't want anybody else's home, or any ready-made family. I want my own background that I make myself. It's the thing I've wanted all my life: a place all my own where I can plan my time and have nobody else's rules or hours to consider. I've worked in an office almost ten years — ever since I was seventeen. And I want to be somebody — in a community. Somebody that counts; not just a commercial drudge, trailing back and forth between an office and a boarding-house." She threw up her chin, a resolute, obstinate little chin. "And I want to do it myself — not have to be eternally considering somebody who has given it to me."

There was silence for a moment because Gail's voice had been so very earnest. Then Arlene lit another cigarette. "Well, even so, you could do it without burying yourself in the wilds. You could have a set-back apartment and one of those roof gardens

— plus theaters and art shows and decent music. And you could have your own pals in, peppy live people —"

"'The intelligentsia, the sophisticati, the cognocenti and the illuminati,'" quoted Gail. "I don't want that sort of thing. You don't understand, Arlene."

"I do." Hilda turned unexpected champion. "Gail's got a husky domestic complex warring with the writer's instinct. A lot of writers suffer from it — but very few artists, Arlene, my love! You rarely catch artists hemming dish towels, but many writers do it. Of course Gail is madly extravagant, expressing her domestic complex to the tune of five thousand dollars, yet I don't know but I admire her for it. At least —" cryptically — "she'll learn her lesson."

"What do you mean by that?" demanded Miss Ormsbee.

"I mean you can't swing it, Gail, that's all. Not the way you are planning to. You can't run with the hare and hunt with the hounds. Either you are a hard-headed, self-supporting business woman with friends of the same sort and speaking the same language; or you are a sheltered female protected by an income or a husband (and believe me, the income's usually a lot more protection!) and possessed of all the diplomacies, obliquities and polite reservations necessary for conducting life according to best social regulations. You'd far better stick to your own tribe. If you do manage to edge into that other clan, that much edge will come off you. You'll grow socially tactful and insincere; those women can't stand downright opinions straight from the shoulder. You'll get to worrying about what people think and suspecting hidden digs under affectionate protestations. You'll take on feminine tricks — you'll have to, or you won't be warmly regarded by the clan —"

"And yet," interrupted Miss Ormsbee who, being no smoker, was fiddling with her coffee cup, "you urge me to get married."

"As a married woman," said Hilda, "you'd enter such a community on a different footing. You'd be inside, looking out. The way you are so optimistically planning it, you'll be outside, looking in. And they won't let you in till you conform to their pattern. Moreover," continued Hilda, "you are too young. Don't ever attempt to be a lady-in-a-garden sans husband or authentic chaperone, short of your fifties. Hedges are all right after fifty; before that they invite suspicion."

Gail was gathering up the dishes. She was always the first to do this; the messy plates cluttering Arlene's couch bothered her. She stopped, on her way to the door. "Do you remember that day we went to the golf match out at Shadow Hills?"

Arlene was examining paper napkins to see if they would do, with a pressing out, for another occasion. "You mean the time your John dined us at his country club?"

"Not my John, if you please, Arlene."

"Well, your Mr. Ingram then. I'm sure I make no claim on him. Yep, I remember. Nice country out that way. Real suburban gathering —"

"There was a girl there," said Gail. "She came tramping in from the golf links. You liked her hair, Arlene, with her green golf coat."

"Um — tawny hair. Tall girl. Lanky. Had a dog with her. Everybody hailed her with glee. What about her?"

"Her name is Jule Vernon. John Ingram told me about her. She lives all by herself. After her parents died she kept on the house and the servants. She goes everywhere. And people drop in to see her. You saw how popular she was and how everybody welcomed her. She is not any older than I am and nobody chaperones her."

"You overlook the main point," said Hilda. "She grew up there. They take her for granted. Her background was there, ready for her. That's quite different from making one — as you'll find out."

"Well," said Gail, "I'm going to try. Not there, of course, but somewhere. I can see my way now to do it, and I'm going to have a little house and a garden and a maid to get the meals. And I shall write a novel."

"All right." Hilda was removing pins from her improvised apron preparatory to using it as a dishtowel. "And when you corral that paragon of a maid you seem to think you have only to pick from an assortment of winners, see that she's middle-aged and heavily respectable. That'll help the background a whole lot. Between paragons, Arlene and I will come out and stand by."

"Not on your life," said the artist. "We'd ruin the picture. Gail's got it all planned pretty and bourgeois. Casements and hollyhocks. Nice friendly neighbors, real salt-of-the-earth sort, to exchange dahlia bulbs with, over those hedges. She'll probably have them in for bridge. Just-for-the-pleasure-of

-the-game bridge — nothing up, of course. And for real diversion there'll be lectures at the Woman's Club — mind you think of that, Miss Ormsbee, before you consider sinking yourself in those deeps of rural serenity. Cottages with casements! Lilacs — help!"

CHAPTER III

What Price Solitude?

THE boarding-house had a black and white tiled hall with a strip of green carpet at the foot of the stairs. On the marble-topped table where you looked for your mail was a Boston fern and when you opened the front door the hall light, screened with green glass, made flickering shadows of the fern on the tiles, so that you seemed to enter into a weird undersea effect: dim and green and with shadows of moving seaweed on an ocean floor at your feet. This marine flavor was slightly discounted by the inevitable boarding-house smell: tonight's dinner subtly backgrounded by reminder of past and gone things fried in some substitute for butter.

Green plush curtains of tremendous length, because doorways in the old brownstone mansion were so high, hung at the left. Gail tiptoed up the stairs. She knew exactly what it looked like, behind those curtains. Old Mrs. Okker would be crocheting washcloths and her companion would be reading close by, one eye alert for a dropped ball of yarn or a mislaid handkerchief. The two little Misses Van Velt, in dressy silks and with eyeglasses balanced on thin, aristocratic noses, would be playing double patience, their veined hands hovering a little like claws over the outspread cards. Miss Plummer, the high school principal, would be digesting *The New Republic*. And fat Mrs. Minton whose daughter had gone out with one of her eternal young men, would be yawning on the sofa, her feet up, but ready to be instantly lowered if a gentleman came in.

All the gentlemen, of course — Mrs. Minton's baldheaded husband and Mrs. Okker's stout, middle-aged son, and little Mr. Murtrie, the bank teller who had the fourth floor hall room — were, in accordance with that curious boarding-house custom of segregating the sexes, in a back room whence clouds of tobacco smoke drifted into the hall. Probably the custom had started, Gail reflected, in the days before females had the vote and male boarders had to be provided with a place sacred to discussion of affairs of the nation. But lived there yet, in the length and breadth of the land, a landlady who didn't put unattached menfolk sociably together in her dining-room, herding ditto females in pairs to entertain each other?

Having achieved sanctuary of her own room, Miss Ormsbee switched on the lights and locked the door. Her own atmosphere here! Her own ecru net curtains blowing in the breeze which after the storm had turned chill. Freshness, here, and quiet. The nicest room in the house; second floor rear, overlooking a double row of tidy back yards. No asphalt. No honking motor cars. Little grass plots. Even a tree — only a spindly acanthus, but in summer it threw leafy shadows on the window sill.

Most of the furnishings were her own. Three warm-toned Oriental rugs. Two softly shaded lamps. A huge cosy overstuffed chair (for acquisition of which she had gone without a new winter coat). Pleasant little tables; on one books, on another her small sewing basket, on a third a gray jug holding pink hyacinths. A few framed etchings on the walls and a colorful sketch signed by Arlene West: boats reflected in water, painted up at the Maine island where Hilda had her shack. In a corner the special treasure: an ancient claw-footed desk that had been bought at an auction for thirty dollars and then rubbed and oiled and polished until its surfaces yielded mellow reflections.

Miss Ormsbee's glance went complacently around her little domain. So much, had she achieved. But with the arrival of that five thousand perspectives had widened.

"Green and white check scrim in the bathroom window," she planned, while tidily whisk-brushing coat and hat before hanging them in the closet. "And a green rug — soft. Not one of those skimpy washable abominations. And a green bath-mat hanging on the tub. White towels — lots of them — good size and with white initials." She visualized it all.

Joy — to be done with skulking down a hall mornings, both hands encumbered with soap, sponge, towels, toothbrush, toothpaste and other essentials of an adequate grooming.

Joy — to eat breakfast in leisurely solitude at a little table set where you could look out at your own garden. Strawberries and cream — and crocuses coming up! Batter-cakes with syrup — and snow swirling outside! And when you had skimmed the morning paper, your desk quietly waiting. No more faring forth in all weathers. No more necessity of appearing alert and busy every minute, no matter how you felt. "Two thousand words at once, please, Miss Ormsbee, for that Chicago fashion supplement. Oh, about anything! They want it mailed Special tonight." So easy, to dash off two thousand words "about anything" at four o'clock in the afternoon, when you had a splitting headache after a rushed day!

No more of that. A gentlewoman, head of your own household, backgrounded by things expressing your own personality. Busy in your study and your garden. Or, when the mood struck you, whisking about in a delightful kitchen that looked out on an apple tree.

Pleasant neighbors, substantial, worth while people. (Like the people who came into town for the Flower Show. People who had gardens!) Friendly, sincere people among whom you would have a recognized place. "The author, Miss Gail Ormsbee, lives in that little house down the road. Yes, I know her well. She has a lovely garden and serves tea in the most ravishing old blue cups that were her great-grandmother's."

Gail glanced at the blue china — genuine Josiah Wedgwood — arranged on a rack against the wall. How lucky that her sister Rosamund had preferred great-grandmother Curtis's rose point collar and let her have those cups!

During these felicitous musings the prospective householder had been getting out of tailored frock and sturdy street pumps, and now in dressing gown and slippers, curled herself in the big chair with a copy of House and Garden purchased on the way home. The new April number: full of entrancing illustrations with spring backgrounds. Even the advertising pages had alluring pictures of garden gates, sundials, bird baths and roses that would bloom in no time at all if you planted them at once.

Cuddled in the big chair, with cropped fair head bent over the magazine and one hand grasping the ankle of the foot tucked under her, the prospective householder looked less the efficient business person who had an office cubicle to herself; and rather pathetically young and optimistic, to be embarking on such an adventure in independence.

Someone knocked.

Reaching hastily for a pad and pencil, ready-to-hand on the table, Miss Ormsbee began to scribble industriously.

"Are you in, Miss Ormsbee?"

"Yes, Mrs. Fox... I'm writing."

"I don't want to interrupt, but I thought I smelled something scorching and I was afraid you might have stepped out and that electric heater you bought might be —"

"No. I'm here, Mrs. Fox. Everything's all right."

A board creaked. The landlady had moved on. Joy — to have a place with your own front door with a bell or a knocker that you could ignore if you felt like it. Joy — to escape constant supervision and snooping.

Then Gail threw down the scribbled pad, walked to the door and opened it; made some inconsequent remark that brought the landlady back to the doorway where a glance might assure her that no inimical contraption was using up expensive electricity.

Immediately, after the way of landladies, Mrs. Fox veered from suspicion to solicitude. Was Miss Ormsbee perfectly comfortable? It had been so warm today she had let the furnace go out. Of course it was a little cooler now —

On the tip of Gail's tongue was the logical retort that one soft March afternoon scarcely presaged summer, but she did not say it. Hilda Braithwaite insisted that Gail was a truly sweet-tempered person because, though she always thought of the trenchant retort, she rarely made it. The landlady departed in happier mood and Miss Ormsbee, after locking the door again, returned to her chair. This time she took up the scribble pad and fell to figuring.

Figures are attractive when they come out right — that is, on your side. And tonight they were coming out right. They even suggested margins. It was all perfectly safe. Five hundred in the bank — that took care of possible illness and emergency. The five thousand would make a substantial payment on a little house and take care of the mortgage and the coal for at least two years. (By that time book royalties would be coming in. If they didn't — if she were a failure as an author — the house could be sold and she would just give up and go back to office work. But anyway she would have had the glorious adventure.) Meanwhile she could count on two hundred a month from the newspaper copy. It was good of Joe Bussing, at the Buyer and Retailer office, to allow her to keep on with that fashion copy and mail it in. And the other syndicate had grabbed at her offer of a weekly household page. The two hundred would run the house and pay a maid. And for clothes and incidentals there was the tiny income she shared with her sister Rosamund.

How fortunate that her mother had left the Brooklyn house to Rosamund and herself! But for that, papa would certainly have gotten rid of it and there wouldn't have been a cent left. Rosamund needed her half, Gail knew... Rosamund, widowed and taking in roomers down in Atlanta. And with five children on her hands. Gail thought she would still be able to send Rosamund something each month. She must! But for that regular contribution to the Atlanta menage Gail might have had her two-and-bath like Hilda, or a studio like Arlene. For Gail had been earning a good salary. You don't occupy second floor quarters in a brownstone front within a stone's throw of Fifth Avenue in the East Thirties for any song. And only those who board in pairs may, with economy, enjoy space enough to walk about in; being a "single" and occupying a "double" you pay well for it.

Rosamund would be envious about the five thousand. No kindly godmother had remembered *her*. But Rosamund had been named for one of mamma's book heroines. It had just happened that before Gail made her entry, rich old Miss Abagail Trent had taken a fancy to mamma at a summer resort and the acquaintance had been kept up, after the return to Brooklyn; partly, Gail surmised, because Miss Abagail had her own coupé and coachman and mamma was so fond of driving in Prospect Park. So the new baby had been named Abagail and the pleased godmother had stood up at its christening. Gail remembered the silver mug and the interesting dolls: gifts from an unknown godmother who lived abroad. She remembered dutiful little letters that mamma had made her write, and having her photograph taken in the frilly bridesmaid frock, made for Rosamund's wedding. "It is for your dear godmother, Gail darling; don't scowl so, try to look pretty and sweet."

And now, out of the blue, had arrived this amazing token of her godmother's affection. Well, it had been worth staggering under the burden of the name Abagail for twenty-six years: to have the hated name bring, now, this prime good fortune!

Gail remembered Rosamund's wedding. At a church on Gates Avenue. The line of carriages had stretched clear down below Classon. The front parlor of the St. James Place house had been banked with palms and smilax. Rosamund had been such a pretty girl and her veil had trailed from a pompadour done over a "rat." But she was not, papa had insisted, as lovely a bride as mamma who had been a belle of the eighties and had worn a wedding dress billowing over a curious contraption called "reeds." It had been Gail's belated arrival, ten years after Rosamund, that had made mamma an invalid. "But for you, darling," she had often said, plaintively, to Gail, "I'd be running around strong and well like other little girls' mothers." It had invariably reduced Gail, no matter how stubbornly her little will had been bracing itself against parental coercion, to instant and unquestioning obedience.

Gail's memories of her mother were backgrounded chiefly by the St. James Place parlor that had a tall mirror between windows hung with long lace curtains and tasseled lambrequins. A moquette carpet, soft, with garlands of flowers. A marble-topped table with a framed photograph of papa, handsome and slim-waisted in his uniform of the 23rd Regiment, taken while he served five years in the National Guard. Mamma, drooping on the piano stool, singing "Every morn I bring thee violets," and when she was particularly gay, "A bicycle built for two." Mamma, in a trailing teagown, making sweet effort to entertain callers; — or dressing up, with heartrending effort that racked the whole family, to attend concerts of the Apollo Club in which papa sang tenor.

These early memories of Gail's were of easy comfort — even luxury. Maggie in the kitchen and Nellie opening the front door when one came home from private school. Birthday parties over which mamma presided, looking exhausted but self-immolating. An atmosphere of homelikeness shadowed always by an intangible anxiety which never quite came out into the open. About papa. Because he had to be away so much from dinner. And often came home so late, walking queerly up the stairs (if one peeped down from the third storey to see what the noise was, in the middle of the night).

Distressing arguments in mamma's room, with mamma crying and papa seeming to be blamed for something, and afterward mamma having one of her sick headaches. Whisperings between mamma and Rosamund that ceased abruptly when Gail came in because, being ten years younger, she was not admitted to grown-up confidences. But Gail had derived the idea, as children do, that papa was mainly to blame for mamma's continually exhausted nerves.

Papa had been handsome and merry. He slipped

quarters into Gail's hand and winked at her roguishly after one of the disturbing conferences, running down the stairs and clapping on his hat — a little toward one side. He had a jaunty walk and Gail remembered his cane with the ivory dog-head making a handle. Maggie and Nellie whispered together; sometimes Gail heard snatches, "Sure, 'tis hard on a man with an invalid wife when he's good-lookin' and likes his fun . . ." But he had cried when mamma died — cried so, at the funeral, that he had to go out of the room while the minister was talking. Gail had thought it so pathetic, but Rosamund had looked stony. After that, the St. James Place house had been rented to a lady who took in boarders and papa and Gail had boarded with her and Gail had continued at the private school. The lady had been unfortunate; her husband had deserted her. She was rather sweet and Gail felt ashamed, not being fond of her — but there was something . . . Papa and Gail were the star boarders. They had rooms on the second floor and sat up near the head of the table; and little extras came their way: real cream for papa's coffee and the tenderloin part of steak, plentiful helpings of butter.

Gail had hated the boarders — strange people using mamma's room and her beautiful parlor as though it were theirs. Sometimes the landlady came and tucked Gail in at night — papa never thought of that. Even though one did not like Mrs. Crosby much, it made one feel less desolate, to be tucked in. Mamma had never been able to climb the stairs, but there had been Nellie to tuck one in and turn out the light. Nellie and Maggie were gone, but even Mrs.

Crosby who smelled too much of perfumery was
better than nobody.

One night Gail, tortured by toothache, had crept
down through the darkened house to the back parlor
room of Mrs. Crosby. And through the half-open
door glimpsed not only the cosily glowing grate
fire and little table set out with a tempting midnight
lunch, but also her parent, in Mrs. Crosby's most
comfortable chair — with Mrs. Crosby cuddled on
his lap.

Twelve-year old Gail went back to her room, got
into her clothes and, being without pocket money,
walked all the way to Flatbush where her sister
Rosamund was living.

After that, five years with Rosamund. Public
school in Flatbush and then in Mount Vernon. Then
back to Brooklyn, down on Congress street. Tom
Lovelace, Rosamund's husband, always changing
jobs with long rests between. The apartment
always cluttered with toys and drying baby essentials
and small, noisy children with buttons off their
shoes and noses moist and snuffly. Somehow
Rosamund could not manage — even with so much
brought in from the delicatessen. Gail helped after
school, making beds at three o'clock in the afternoon,
washing out small garments, running to the grocer's
on last minute errands — always with Rosamund's
tired voice calling after her: "Mind taking the go-
cart, darling? Baby does need his airing and I
haven't had a minute all day." Gail was fourteen
and lanky. Then she was sixteen, sitting up till
midnight, to make her graduating dress. Rosamund
had been generous: not minding about having her

white crepe cut up. And they got the spots out with gasoline. "If only we knew where your godmother is, Gail, she'd give you a white georgette to graduate in."

But the godmother had slipped out of Gail's life like so many other things. The St. James Place house had been rented to new people and papa sent irregular sums to Rosamund from Buffalo where it was understood he had a new position of some sort and whither (the information acquired from a long-distance telephone call when Rosamund badly needed a delayed remittance) his old friend, Mrs. Crosby, had gone to open another boarding-house.

Then the terrible year of the war. Tom Lovelace gone. His slim pay and papa's uncertain remittances from Buffalo all they had to depend on. Gail never forgot that winter. The dingy flat. Insufficient heat. The children ailing half the time. Her work at the canteen;—she had been young enough to get fun and excitement out of that, for all the gloom and privation at home. And that year had marked her first love affair, a brief and futile little romance stimulated by the hysteria of the time. Gail hated the memory of that episode.

Then Tom Lovelace invalided home and moving his family down to Georgia where his parents would give shelter until he could find work again. It was here that Gail made her break for independence. She was almost eighteen and through high school. She pressed her shabby suit and went out and sought an office job. And when the Lovelace family departed southward she established herself in a fourth floor hall bedroom, worked days, and studied shorthand

WHAT PRICE SOLITUDE? 49

at night. And that had been the beginning of a business and boarding career.

Nine years of steady climbing. Sturdy traits of her mother's New England ancestry and artistic qualities inherited from her father had combined in her as efficiency, grit and a talent for turning phrases. Now she wrote endless "copy" with speed and ease and had acquired a facility of expression that made her believe she could do a novel — if she had the chance.

And at last the chance was hers! Five thousand all her own. A dependable earning capacity. And the tiny assured income to eke out, since the St. James Place house had been sold on her coming of age and her father, with the two thousand dollars forwarded to him on his assurance that it was to set him up in a nice little business of his own out in Omaha, would not be likely to trouble them again. The West had swallowed him up — probably he had married again.

"When I am all settled and have a guest room," planned Gail, studying the figures that came so admirably right, "I'll have Rosamund's oldest girl up for a good visit. Lucy Lovelace must be sixteen now — almost grown up. I'll give little Lucy some happy times. Rosamund was good to me. . ."

Gail's face, gentle because of her sister's kindness and the hard luck poor Rosamund had experienced, froze when a knock sounded on the door. She reached for her pencil.

"Who is it, please? I'm writing."

"Oh, Miss Ormsbee, we didn't know you were in. Couldn't you come down? Mrs. Okker does hate to go to bed without her rubber of bridge — she's been watching for you all evening." Plump Mrs. Minton outside the door.

"Sorry," said Gail in an inflexible tone. "I'm writing."

Mrs. Minton went away. Gail frowned. Then she flung down the pencil.

"Selfish. Disgustingly selfish," she remarked to Miss Gail Ormsbee. "Why is your precious evening so much more important than theirs?" Running to the door, she called to Mrs. Minton who was clumping down the stairs on her foolish high heels. "I'll play a while, Mrs. Minton. Be right down — just have to slip on my dress."

At the foot of the stairs she was stopped by the landlady. "Telephone for you, Miss Ormsbee."

It was John Ingram, speaking from his neck of the woods.

"You never told me the big news —"

"Just thought of it, have you?"

"Don't be catty, little one. Atchison put it out of my mind. You hadn't got round to it —"

"Well, you didn't register passionate concern, did you? Since it was not going to threaten your personal routine. I believe those were your words —"

"You know very well I am interested, Gail. What is it? Tell me now."

"Oh, it'll keep," she answered. "They are waiting for me to play bridge, John. See you tomorrow."

John Ingram would just have to find out she could manage her life very competently by herself.

CHAPTER IV

April Indecisions

HILDA BRAITHWAITE had an idea that Gail's homemaking impulse was not so much independent determination of the New Woman to express herself according to her own inclinations, as a rather pathetic reversion to type.

Victorian traditions and ideals had surrounded her plastic years. She had come into the world at a particularly unfortunate time; — just at the turn of a century. Product of the nineteenth, yet constrained to cope with conditions of the twentieth! After twelve years, hedged in by Victorian inhibitions, and then an unsettling adolescence passed during the abnormal excitement of a war era, she had been thrown at seventeen on a world full of bewildering new conditions for which her training, mental and spiritual, had not fitted her.

She could not, like Hilda Braithwaite who was forty, ignore the new conditions, contentedly abiding by the old. Nor could she, like Arlene West who had grown up since the war, blithely pursue new paths unhampered by old signposts.

In the year 1900 when Gail had come into the world, it was still considered deplorable for a female to have to labor for a daily wage. Impoverished gentlewomen did fine needle-work or took in boarders; spinsters still burdened sisters-in-law, and grandmothers knitted in armchairs and did not have permanent waves and preside as club presidents. For a lady, the sheltered life was the admirable life; "sheltered" meaning a husband, as well-to-do as possible as soon as possible after an elaborate coming out party had launched a girl on the matrimonial market. Between the last day of "finishing school" and the beginning of the trousseau, she "just had a good time." Which meant as many American Beauty roses and boxes of Huylers and dance programs stuck around her mirror as her popularity was able to achieve. And at dances arranged by carefully pruned invitations nothing occurred in deportment to annoy the row of chaperones along the wall.

At the century's beginning only girls who had "serious aims" went to college. The vote for women was being talked about, but few women bothered to read newspaper editorials. There were women who smoked, but they were called "fast." And there were women who made addresses from platforms, but they were called "strong-minded." No really nice woman (that was, socially successful woman) did these things. Home and shelter was the ideal lot for a female — and the gentlemen had all the fun!

Into this atmosphere Gail Ormsbee had made her entry and for the first twelve years of her life she had breathed it in. For she had been born — of all places — in Brooklyn where Victorian ideals held on as long as there was a fringe of raveled Victorian traditions to hang to. It is said that in Brooklyn they are hanging on to that fringe yet.

What Gail secretly coveted now, Hilda Braithwaite opined, was that sense of shelter — of protection — represented by stability of background.

The wage-earning woman had no opportunity to establish roots. Getting on in a career meant incessant adjustment to the next move. And one must be ready to move both ways: advancement meant expansion and pleasanter living conditions; hard times, cheerful curtailing of expenditure. Not until years of saving and economizing had put something substantial to the wage-earner's credit, either in the bank or in canny investments, might she hope to establish herself against a background that had something of permanence. And so feminine urge toward domesticity took itself out in rented rooms with one-burner gas plates, chafing dishes and such pitiful makeshifts.

And unless the urge was very strong it speedily atrophied, for the business woman was as well taken care of as the unattached man. Unlimited tearooms supplied good dinners with no dishwashing afterward. There were comfortable hotels with maid service (when one was making enough) where the busy wage-earner did not even have to pick up her nightgown mornings, before faring forth to her job, much less bother to make her own bed. Beauty shops attended to her grooming and valets did her mending and pressing. If she desired to entertain informally there was always the telephone; sandwiches, salads, sherbets would be sent round at any hour on fifteen minutes' notice.

When a business woman had an overpowering home-and-hearth urge she usually gave up wage-earning and got married. But here was Gail Ormsbee at six-and-twenty, and all woman in spite of her obstinate conviction that she was patterned of the stern stuff requisite for a bleak and solitary mental existence, planning to placate her homemaking instinct with a spinsterish establishment that would amuse her perhaps for two years and leave her stranded and lonely in her thirties.

What a pity, thought Hilda, that Gail's subconscious desire for anchorage did not drift her toward that safe harbor so conveniently at hand ... But if Gail were not in love with John Ingram there was nothing anybody could do about it —

Or was there?

No woman of Hilda Braithwaite's calibre — no straight-thinking, independent-spirited woman, herself earning a livelihood and contemptuous of feminine compromises — could urge another woman to make the fatal mistake of marrying "for a home." But did Gail Ormsbee really know her own mind? Did she fully realize, in her own self-concentration, what she was throwing away? Or how bitterly she might come to repent — in those lonely years she was so blithely planning for herself?

It was unfortunate, of course, that she had so set herself against those youngsters of John's. Yet Hilda knew about the years when Gail had slaved and chafed, little more than a servant in her sister Rosamund's home. "From the time I was twelve," Gail had once said passionately to Hilda, "I always had a baby on my hip, dusting and doing housework with the other arm. It's a wonder I didn't grow up lop-sided. I had enough of it. No children are going to tie me down again, thank you — not if I know it!"

It was, however, children in the aggregate as general pests and hamperers that Gail objected to, Hilda decided. Nobody who took so much interest in small, cheeky, apple-munching office boys could really hate children. And only last winter, Hilda had seen Gail walk the floor for hours with a screaming earache-tortured baby whose parents, a young vaudeville pair, were absent from the boardinghouse. Gail had been tender with that baby — she had had a way with it.

Then there had been that little lost, sobbing child at the railroad station. Gail had told it stories and it had been sitting contentedly on her lap when the distracted mother turned up.

What Gail Ormsbee needed, right now, before she tied up her chance of happiness with this preposterous scheme of hers, was a husband to furnish the background she coveted and a few children to take the self-centeredness out of her ridiculous plans for her future.

This lady-in-a-hedged-garden idea was nonsensical. The more Hilda Braithwaite reflected upon it the more nonsensical it grew. On an April morning she called up John Ingram at his office.

"No, John, it's not about that book on suspension bridges that you're advertising for us. This is just a friendly confab. Seen Gail lately?"

"Had dinner with her last night."

(Hilda knew this very well.) "She told you the news? About her plan to buy a house —"

Something that sounded like "confounded foolishness" came over the wire.

"Of course," said Hilda, "a woman has a perfect right to express herself in her own way."

"I suppose," he retorted suspiciously, "you have encouraged her in this priceless idea."

Hilda chuckled. Evidently Gail had not reported to Mr. Ingram all of Miss Braithwaite's earnest advisements. "You might call it encouragement — and again you mightn't —"

"She said you understood her, if I didn't."

"I do ... Far better than you do, you poor male." Miss Braithwaite appended the last phrase inaudibly. "Gail is one girl in a thousand," she assured him.

"My patience, Hilda! Who said she wasn't?" John Ingram blazed back. (Why was everybody trying to convince him what a wonderful girl was Gail Ormsbee — as though he had offered argument to the contrary?) Hilda, at the other end of the wire could see him glance impatiently at a cluttered desk.

She continued imperturbably, "I'm for her, whatever she elects to do. But that wasn't what I called up about. I have an inspira — I mean, an idea. Want to submit it to you —"

"Oh!" Mr. Ingram returned with alacrity to business matters. "About that new publication you're planning to advertise in scientific magazines?"

Miss Braithwaite was non-committal. "Suppose I drop around. Could I see you about twelve-thirty?"

"No — I go out for lunch from twelve to one . . . Wait — Why not have lunch with me and talk it over then?"

"Fine," agreed the assistant publicity manager of Dimmleton Doland Company. "Nice of you. I'll meet you — where?"

"Say Chapitan's. Twelve-forty-five sharp?"

"Right."

Miss Braithwaite put down the receiver with a bland expression.

"And to think," she reflected, "that only a few nights ago I was talking about the obliquities of females of the social clan."

CHAPTER V

Won't You Walk Into My Garden?

GAIL knew the house the moment she set eye on it. A little house by a brook that tumbled through a ravine.

On one side a slope down into the woodsy glen; on the other, well-kept grounds of a considerable estate. Beyond the ravine, visible through still leafless trees, another modest house. Neighbors not too far away, yet not close enough to press upon one.

Across the road a clump of woods. And beyond the woods undulating stretches of golf meadow. A perfect place to write. And in summer that ravine and the brook would be heavenly.

It had been terrifically hard to find. Hilda Braithwaite had been a trump: sifting out enticing real estate offerings in the Sunday papers and trekking about with the home-hunter on Saturday afternoons in suburban busses and trollies. Arlene, while admitting herself ready to lend advice later about the trappings, said she must positively refuse to have anything to do with selecting the tomb. It would, she averred, depress her too deeply.

Westchester was canvassed. And Long Island. And Queens. Even Staten Island. But most houses offered at prices that Gail could consider were new and ugly and close together in cheap little rows — and peramublators and roller skates abounded in these districts. Homelike, maybe, for gregarious matrons, but impossible for one possessed of literary aspiration. About more picturesquely located domiciles, enjoying decent privacy in ample acreage, there was invariably (if the price proved tempting) something radically wrong: insufficient plumbing, lack of electric light, or obviously inadequate heating apparatus. Hilda called attention to these drawbacks which frequently the home-hunter, concerned with garden space and views from windows, would have overlooked.

"Gail," protested Hilda to John Ingram one noonday when they were all lunching together, "will walk straight through any room to see what the view is, from the window — without so much as a glance to make sure said room has a radiator. She liked one place so much she almost took it, until I convinced her there wasn't a spot for an icebox except down cellar and not a pantry in sight."

"It was such a lovely kitchen," sighed Gail. "It looked out on an apple tree."

"You haven't tried my neck of the woods," reminded Mr. Ingram.

"No," said Miss Ormsbee. Finality in that single syllable!

Westchester had to be given up. Graciousness of outlook and dignified privacy, in Westchester, were unprocurable unless your yearly income ran well over the five thousand mark. It was charm you paid for, in a house, not size; Gail speedily learned that. Long Island had its beauty spots but they were for householders who could afford lawns and glimpses of sea. Gail hated the enterprising little "developments" with rows of small houses precisely alike; and the ugly little shops with casual, uncivil tradesmen. And never in her life, Hilda declared, had she seen so many fat women as on the north shore of Long Island; it was a healthy place no doubt, but one couldn't say there was much artistic atmosphere about it.

After all, it was John Ingram who found the house. There had been some likely propositions in the old towns out Hempstead and Roslyn way, but as Hilda mentioned: "What's the use of rooting yourself in the soil of an island if you can't turn your face to the sea?" And added, "You wouldn't know a soul, out here." To Gail, staring speculatively at a little brown house behind a picket fence and envisioning hollyhocks along the fence, had come sudden, rather sickening premonition of lonesomeness. Many of the almost-attainable houses, she now recollected, had conveyed that hinterlandish suggestion. It might really be better to start somewhere, knowing at least one name on the local telephone exchange. Not necessarily next door. . . .

So when Warren Atchison asked, one noonday when he and John Ingram stepped into the elevator at the fifth floor, "Why don't you look around, out our way, Miss Ormsbee?" the home-hunter regarded him without the expression of impatient disapproval which hitherto had met all suggestions about that particular locality. John Ingram had sense enough to refrain from mentioning that he had offered suggestion of the sort himself.

"Nice country out there," pursued the editor. "Fifty minutes' ride, of course, but you wouldn't be coming into town every day, and fifty minutes will get you out beyond the commuting crowd who use the locals. We haven't much asphalt yet — not even pavements except right in the village. Mail delivery though, and taxi service from the station. Or you could have a little car to run about in."

"But I couldn't afford cars — and gardeners." Gail had been driven past the Atchison place on that memorable day of the golf match, the preceding autumn. "I couldn't run a place like yours."

"Not till the novel royalties begin to come in, eh?" The editor grinned genially. "Plenty of little houses, though, down nearer the village. Some of them for sale too. Why not drive her around, John, and let her have a look?"

"I've offered to," contributed Mr. Ingram.

"Nice little country club too," said the older man. "Glad to put you up. Mrs. A. will run over when you get settled."

Gail didn't specially care for Mrs. Atchison who was, she had commented to Hilda and Arlene, one of those bovine women without an ambition in her soul beyond her house and family. But it was kind of Mr. Atchison . . . Somebody you would know . . . Not like the house behind the picket fence, suggestive of aloneness in the world. Of course there would be John Ingram too. Within telephone call, but not dropping-in distance. She could make sure of that.

"How about it?" Mr. Ingram asked, as the elevator arrived at the ground floor. Anxiety, if any, was not apparent in his eye — only the familiar, friendly twinkle.

"Well," conceded Miss Ormsbee, "I might take a look this Saturday, if you won't be too busy."

There was a friendly twinkle also in Miss Braithwaite's eye (unnoticed by the home-hunter) when she learned that John Ingram was to display the advantages out Shadow Hills way that week-end. Hilda remarked, not too enthusiastically, "Prettier country, to my taste, than Westchester. And prices probably lower. Now, mind you watch out about furnaces and plumbing and cellar floors. Wish I could go with you, but I'll be busy."

The roads were winding. Gail approved that. No rigidly laid out avenues with cross-streets at accurate intervals. The winding roads were confusing to a stranger but that was as it should be. Why should a stranger expect to rush into any community and find his way immediately about? Homes should be placed for privacy and not to afford easy intrusion of the horde.

John Ingram pointed out his dwelling. Five minutes' walk from the station. A pleasant street in summer, no doubt; young April leaves now casting gauzy shadows over pavements laid between borders of springing grass. Houses far back and well apart, with shrubbery and neat lawns. Forsythia showering its gold everywhere and back of every house white drift of pear or cherry blossoms. Gail regarded, without undue display of interest, the Ingram abode. A yellow kiddie-cart leaned against the porch steps and a red train of cars dangled from the porch rail. Her glance flicked over these.

"Comfortable house. Good furnace," the owner

remarked briefly and in another moment they were swinging around one of the endless curves of the highway. It had been just that felicitous opportunity for making acquaintance with the children that John had always seemed so keen about, and Gail rather wondered that he hadn't suggested stopping; but it almost seemed that he was in a hurry to get by. Gail felt relieved.

After that they drove up and down the winding roads. Several nice little houses for sale. One seemed rather near a cemetery; and another too far from the village. "I have to be within walking distance of the post office," Gail reminded. "I couldn't live way out here."

"Only a half mile from the station. These roads confuse you."

"Well, I wouldn't consider this one anyhow," said Miss Ormsbee. "It has a bay window. All it needs is a begonia to be a perfect Old Maid's Retreat."

Another place had too much front lawn. "Three dollars a week at least, to keep that cut," objected the home-hunter. "I'm looking for a garden, not acres of grass with weeping willows on it. Aren't there any places with hedges?"

Still another small house Mr. Ingram seemed to feel it his duty to enthuse about. The terms of sale were easy and there was good garden space at one side. But he conscientiously pointed out a large buff brick structure just beyond. "The school. Of course kids would be likely to swarm over your front lawn, rounding this corner —"

"That's enough," said Miss Ormsbee crisply. "I don't want it."

"There's a little place up this road—" Her guide swung the car around a curve and across a stone bridge over a tumbling brook. The brook followed the road on one side and on the other golf meadows stretched away toward purple hills.

"Oh, lovely!" said Gail, looking off at misty April distances where dogwood drifted in white patches amid leafing birch and maple trees.

Another turn, and a dip into a little glen. John gestured with a gloved hand as the car moved up the slope.

"Hedges?"

"Oh, stop a minute!" Gail was leaning forward. She saw something else. Lilacs — almost out. "I've got to have a look at this place."

He ran the car alongside the hedge. There was no driveway, just a walk of stepping-stones sunk in grass. A little house. Two shallow steps before a door with small-paned side-lights.

"Cosy!" exclaimed Miss Ormsbee, adoring the house at once.

"Needs paint," commented Mr. Ingram.

Gail was looking at the hedge, a tall hedge that had been growing for many a year; badly in need of trimming, but lending a delectable air of exclusiveness to the tiny place. A little patch of front lawn with those lilac bushes. And crocuses coming up beside the stepping-stone walk. Back of the house — Gail dashed around to have a look — a generous garden space with a grape arbor at the rear flanked by rows of currant bushes.

In one side of the tall hedge was set a small gate. It opened into the ravine from which came faint murmur of the brook they had crossed further up. Beyond the grape arbor at the back could be glimpsed backs of houses on another road. In summer, Gail reflected, trees would completely shut off view of those houses. And one's garden gate would open picturesquely into a wood — with a tumbling brook!

"I must have it," she decided. "It's perfect."

"You haven't looked inside the house," he reminded.

"I don't care what the inside is like; I've simply got to have this garden." Her eyes were anxious. "Do you suppose the price is frightful?"

"Can't be. It is one of the houses they told me were within your stipulated limit."

"But why? — such a heavenly little place."

"Well, there's no garage — and no place for one, or even for a driveway. That brings down the value of course."

"I suppose its a hopeless distance from the station, too." Her bright look clouded over.

"Not so far as you'd think. This road curves into the turnpike a little way above here, and the turnpike runs across the village main street. About fifteen minutes' walk to the station ... or you could cut across through one of the yards back there —" he indicated the dwellings at the rear — "Save quite a distance, that way."

"No, I'd never do that. Fifteen minutes' walk is nothing. I could get a taxi when I needed one. Of course I'd have a telephone." Her eyes were roaming about the garden, envisioning growing things. "It must be quite a long way from where you live, isn't it?"

"Well," he assured her cheerfully, "I could get here, any time, in a few minutes, with the car."

She nodded. (Of course a car would go a long distance in a few minutes.)

"This is a pretty old house, you know." He seemed conscientious about pointing out disadvantages. "You won't find things smart and modern. Hedges like that don't grow in a few years."

"Who planted them; do you know?"

"Two old ladies lived here for forty years. I remember them when I first came out here to live. They were eighty, then. Twin sisters. They never went anywhere and hated visitors. Did all their own work. Three winters ago they died, within a few weeks of each other."

"They must have loved this garden," said Gail dreamily. She could see the little old ladies, in worsted shawls, pottering among their rose bushes within their kindly hedges. She intended to buy this place and live in it forever!

"Who owns it now?" she asked.

"Some nephews — married — out west. They had the house fixed up some, to rent it. Bathroom and electric lights — things like that. But it has been standing idle for over a year and they want to sell."

"H'm —" Gail contemplated the little house which had a withdrawn, secretive aspect behind its closed green shutters. There was a kitchen ell, alongside which ran a small porch that overlooked the garden. Casement windows would be expensive to put in. But the house would have to be pretty impossible, to persuade her away from that garden with a gate opening into the wood.

She elected not to drive back to the village for the key. So Mr. Ingram dashed off by himself and, returning, found her pacing off distances in the garden.

"John! There are lilies of the valley in this shady spot under the hedge." She seized his arm. "Look. Aren't those lilies of the valley?"

He stepped gingerly over the moist earth. "Seem to be. Look at your shoes! You ought to have brought rubbers, if you intended to poke about in April mud."

She was beyond consideration of footgear. Her eyes were shining.

"And, John — look! What are these little red things?" She was down on one knee in the grass, blue eyes gazing eagerly up at him.

Here was a person who bore not the slightest resemblance to staid Miss Ormsbee of the office. He caught her elbow and hauled her to her feet.

"Look at your skirt." He stooped and brushed it off with his gloves. "Didn't you ever see peonies coming up before, you little goose?"

"Peonies!" breathed Gail. "And roses — I know rose bushes when I see 'em. What are you grinning about so secretively, John Ingram? You look like a Cheshire cat."

"I'm not grinning — it's quite a different expression." There was, indeed, an element of the pathetic in this intense wistfulness about a few growing things in spring. "I didn't know you loved a garden that way," he said.

The shine was still in Gail's eyes. They were very blue, gazing about at scraggly rose bushes, at crimson peony shoots in the dark soil, at the little gate opening into a wood. "It is what I have wanted most on earth — and I have found it!"

It was apparent that he, and his concerns, had, in this materialized dream of hers, no place at all.

"I've found out something too," he told her. They had come to the front of the house now and the modest two steps leading up to a door with narrow glass side-lights.

"Found out what?" Gail asked inattentively. She was envisioning a brass knocker on that door and a wreath of Christmas holly hanging on the knocker.

"The little girl in you." Aggravatingly slow he was, with the key he had produced from a pocket. "That little girl I've always known was there, but you would only let me catch glimpses of. I know where she is, now."

"Oh, for goodness sake," retorted the home-hunter whose train of thought he was interrupting, "don't be ridiculous. Open that door and let's have a look inside the house."

"Well," inquired Hilda Braithwaite when Gail called her up that evening, "did you see the famous children?"

"No, and I'm not likely to; they are a safe distance off, by automobile. Listen, Hilda! I've got my house. Perfect peach of a place: tall, stately old hedges. Lilac bushes. Roses. And guess what: a gate opening into a wood. With a BROOK! And the cutest front door for a knocker —"

"Wait a minute," interrupted Miss Braithwaite. "Did you notice whether there was a furnace?"

"Oh —" the home-hunter's voice fell. But it rose again, cheerily. "John must have seen there was one."

"He picked out the house did he?"

"No indeed! He showed me a lot of places that were for sale, but I pounced on this one the minute I saw it. I am going to make the initial payment, Monday. Wait till you see it, Hilda!"

"I knew," responded Miss Braithwaite comfortably, "we could depend on John."

CHAPTER VI

Apple Blossoms From Kitchen Windows

ON A day in May, Arlene West, laden with packages, descended from a station taxi in Brook Road and walked up the stepping-stone path that curved between borders of blue iris. The taxi man followed with her suitcase and set it on the step. Before lifting the brand new brass knocker which she contemplated with grudging approval, Miss West turned and gazed off, beyond lilac bushes bending under weight of purple bloom and feathery green of young birches across the road, into hazy distances bounded by violet-shadowed hills.

"Not bad," pronounced the artist-eye of Miss West . . . "But ten thousand miles from anywhere," appended her cosmopolitan soul. She lifted the knocker.

Gail opened the door. She had on, over her linen house frock, a good thick sweater. "You won't mind if it's a little coolish," she apologized, lifting the suitcase into the hall. "Of course it does seem absurd to start a furnace in May. But I have an oil stove in the guest room and there's a nice range fire in the kitchen."

Miss West voted for sitting in the kitchen. "I'll keep on my fur coat, if you don't mind. Hilda couldn't come — some new advertising account to attend to. I've brought that stuff for your curtains."

"It was jolly of you, to come instead. And you'll really stay over night?"

"Until Number Three arrives," assured Arlene. "Or Number Four, is it? What happened this time? You didn't tell Hilda over the phone."

The homemaker sighed. "Too far from the village — and no motion picture place when you get there. Another one is coming tomorrow. I'll keep at it until I find The One — or she finds me. There's always The One, on her way to you if you just keep expecting and believing in her —"

"Pollyanna!" moaned Miss West. "Well, let's hope she turns up soon. Much as Hilda and I dote on country weekends, of course this is a busy season for all of us."

"Nonsense," said Miss Ormsbee cheerfully, "you know you are having the time of your lives: waking up and smelling lilacs under your window and eating waffles for breakfast. And bossing my furniture and draperies about. And reminding me you told me so! You wouldn't miss it for worlds."

"Well, maybe," allowed Miss West, drawing a little nearer the good warm range. "Are those waffles you're making now? Yum! We are going to have lunch out here, aren't we? We can see those apple trees from the window."

She regarded Gail searchingly. "You have lost some weight. Still think a house in the country is ecstasy's complete dream?"

"Of course I do," retorted Gail who was scraping out the waffle-iron because the first batch had stuck. She gestured with a fork. "You saw those lilacs, didn't you, and you ask me that? And in the ravine down there, pink laurel still in bloom. And wild violets, my child. Naturally it takes work to get a house started — and a garden. And turn off also a couple of thousand words a day of newspaper copy. I'll be all right when things get running, if the right maid takes hold —"

"When ... And If," echoed Arlene. "Too bad John Ingram had to chase off to Chicago just as you were settling in. He might have helped a lot."

Gail was setting a jug of golden syrup on the little table drawn up in a window where, as the artist had suggested, one could look down the length of the hedge-enclosed garden space to pink flush of apple blossoms in a yard at the rear. "I'm just as well pleased not to have him hanging around, making suggestions. It's my house; not his."

After lunch, Arlene had to view all the improvements since her last visit: the green-painted furniture in Gail's room and the black-painted furniture with little stenciled roses that was so smart with a mulberry rug in the guest room. Buying the furniture second-hand and painting it had been an inspiration. The homemaker regarded her achievement with satisfaction. "Don't the mirrors look stunning, Arlene, unhitched from the bureaus and hung that way with cords? We'll get at the living-room this afternoon. Didn't I cover that old sofa nicely?"

"I told you to glue the gimp on, not tack it." Arlene was running a finger along the upholstery. "It is a ducky old sofa for only twenty-five dollars. Of course he didn't know what good lines it had — not many of 'em left as innocent as that. We got it on Third Avenue, didn't we?"

Both girls laughed reminiscently over the fun of prowling and picking up bargains in second-hand shops. Arlene, canny artist, had instructed Gail in the proper procedure. "Never go into one of those places, my dear, togged up in your fur coat and with kid gloves on. Wear your shabbiest duds and have one finger sticking out of a cotton glove; and act poor and anxious. If you sail in and say: 'Show me something in hall tables,' — you'll pay for a hall table! What you want to say is: 'Do you suppose you have a little stand strong enough to hold a washbowl and pitcher in my fourth floor hall room. I need it for one of my lodgers. I don't want to pay much — just to get something that won't break down on me.' Then keep your eyes peeled and maybe you'll pick up a bulging-front Sheraton imitation for six dollars."

The mentor had further instructed: "Never look directly at anything you particularly fancy. Walk toward something else and en route give the thing you do want a vicious shake and mention disparagingly, 'This might do — if it were in good order.' And whatever he asks, offer him less. Remember, every gleam of interest you evince boosts the price."

Adhering to these tactics, Gail had picked up congenial pieces that when oiled and polished or treated to a coat of paint grouped together in gracious amity. Rugs, draperies, beds and two upholstered chairs for the living-room she had purchased new. And further following the advice of the artist, she had confided to all the second-hand dealers that it would be more convenient if she might pay in weekly installments (a method with which they are familiar on Third Avenue) and had thus managed to assemble all her purchases for a moving van to pick up on the same day.

Her little house was taking on a settled and home-like aspect and Gail was rapidly acquiring the passionate love of her own that is the instinct of the born homemaker. She felt deep affection for every derelict stick of furniture retrieved by laborious scraping and painting. She loved her living-room where the old claw-footed desk had found just the right nook; loved her little workroom that had glass doors opening on the porch and in which were established her flat-topped writing table, her typewriter and a shining new set of files; loved her tidy kitchen, big enough to whisk about in and enlivened by green checked floor covering and curtains of glazed chintz.

"I have one of those patent ice-making contraptions in my kitchenette — so convenient," Hilda had commented, the way best friends do. But what were two steps down and two steps up, every time you carried things to an icebox — when the pantry window faced east? Hilda would not see the sun come up through bare apple-tree branches next winter.

Arlene had to be shown the garden. With that praiseworthy patience of the visitor in May, she gazed at patches of grubby soil and thought of whatever guests do think about while an ardent gardenmaker depicts in detail the coming glory.

"Poppies here, red and yellow. And that bed all blue cornflowers with tall blue larkspur at the back. And sweet alyssum in front, here. Over there — you are not looking, Arlene — sweet william and lovely old garden pinks. And candytuft of course. And down this path —"

"Oh yes — path." The visitor could see that, at any rate.

"Along there, snapdragon and canterbury bells. I shall have salvia and cosmos ready to blossom later. Those roses are going to be gorgeous by June. (Next year when I know the neighbors I'll have tea out here in rose time.) By August there will be marigolds and zinnias. Of course I may not have luck this summer with the asters —"

"For Pete's sake!" Arlene lifted a slippered foot out of the damp turf and warmed it by holding it back of the other knee. "Where'd you learn all this?"

"Garden books — from the library. And I've kept things, clipped out of magazines, for years." Gail surveyed lovingly the squares and oblongs of newly spaded soil. To her they were not uninteresting dirt, but Vision. "I have longed so for a garden!" she whispered. Lost in the Vision, she forgot her guest who had wandered across the garden to the hedge. A familiar smell brought the garden-maker out of her dream.

"Arlene! Please don't smoke out here."

"Why on earth not?" Miss West regarded with some resentment the snatched cigarette her hostess was stamping out in the grass.

"Don't you see the second storey windows of that house across the ravine?"

"What of it?"

"A woman up there watches everything over here with a spyglass."

"Cheek!" Arlene turned and stared up at the windows.

"I was furious myself at first. But the poor soul is an invalid. They wheel her out on that porch. The iceman told me she has been shut up in those rooms for fifteen years — some accident that injured her spine. I suppose a newcomer is an exciting diversion in her dull life."

"Well, if it diverts the dame to see me smoke a cigarette, why deny her?"

"Arlene, you know how people are, in a place like this."

"I do indeed, my dear." Arlene's expression turned impish. "Here, I'll puff smoke toward her old window. The moment you yield to such people you're a goner. They have the upper hand. If they are looking for a shock give 'em a real one. Knock 'em for a finish right at the start. They have more respect for you."

"No you don't — " Gail laughingly stayed Arlene's hand that had reached for her cigarette case. "Be sensible, old thing. I'm not setting out to educate these people, but to make friends with them. They got here first. I'm a lone female, trying to establish myself among them — pleasantly, let's hope. That invalid has a lot of visitors. They all know probably that I'm a writer; and as such —" Gail's smile showed the dimple — "I have to prove that I'm also a lady — according to their standards. It won't do me any good to have them gossiping about my wild Greenwich Village friends who puff cigarettes all over the place. The whole inside of the house is at your disposal, sweet child."

Arlene switched away from the gate. "You make me sick. Getting the silly social attitude already! 'What'll the neighbors say?' ... You're going bourgeois. I can see you sliding."

"All right," said Gail good humoredly, "but don't you give me a bad bump on my way. That woman has a daughter — stunning girl. Red hair — I've seen her going in and out. Very likely she smokes cigarettes. But I can't afford to. Not till I establish myself. It's just part of the game, Arlene; be a sport and realize it."

"Let's go in, then. I don't care for your garden." Arlene, chilled hands stuffed in sweater pockets, strode across the grass. She stopped and pointed: "What's that gap in the hedge — at the back?"

Miss Ormsbee frowned at the aperture. "Children have been playing in here while the house stood vacant. They probably liked the high hedges — children would. They won't come any more." The homemaker's chin had grim resolution.

"Who lives back there?"

"Oh — families. On that other road. When the leaves come out I shall not see the houses; and all that shrubbery and those garages form a barrier. I need never think of them. With that big estate on one side and the ravine and brook on the other I've all the spaciousness I want."

Gail looked around her domain with serene content.

It was at this bland moment that serenity was violently disrupted. A veritable cyclone of disturbance swept through the gap in the hedge. First emerged a small girl howling at the top of her lungs and evidently fleeing for dear life. Her little red sweater was torn. One stocking was down. Cropped yellow hair stood out backward in the breeze of her coming. Behind her trailed a frayed length of rope whose end was tied about her fat middle. Hard on the heels of this quarry pelted a small boy, equally dishevelled, and equally enraged. Pursued and pursuer ploughed through neatly raked and seeded garden beds and the small girl, evidently envisioning sanctuary, flung herself at Gail and wrapped desperate arms about her knees. The boy, brought up short, stood crimson-faced and defiant.

The feminine invader, finding herself, instead of caught up and comforted, seized by the scruff of the neck (or by her sweater collar which was the nearest thing to it) and set forcibly on her feet, stared in stunned silence at this unsympathetic grown-up, a grubby finger in quivering mouth.

"Now then," demanded Miss Ormsbee with impartial sternness, "what do you two mean, tearing through my hedge like that?"

"He — He — He —" Resentful sobs shook the tiny girl. Dirty as she was, she was an engaging tot with her mop of yellow hair and her chubby softness buttoned tight in the torn sweater. Her brown eyes brimmed over with big tears.

Arlene, highly diverted, approached and waved a friendly cigarette. (Under shelter of the grape arbor she had ventured to light one.) "You're too sharp with her, Gail. She is only a baby... What's the matter, chicken? Did he hurt you? Don't cry, you're all safe now."

"What did you do to her?" Miss Ormsbee fixed the male invader with an accusing blue eye.

He shuffled his feet. "Nothin'. She's a 'fraid-cat. I'd have untied her in time if she hadn't cut and run."

"You tied her up? What for?"

APPLE BLOSSOMS 79

"She's Jonah Vark. I had to tie her to the stake."

"Well, you and Joan of Arc go play somewhere else. You are not to come into this garden again. Understand that."

"Won't be burned up!" screamed the small girl. She implored piteously: "You take 'em away from him. Take 'em away."

"What have you there?" Miss Ormsbee demanded, seeing the male culprit hastily thrust one hand behind him. He opened a grimy paw and displayed a box of safety matches.

"She's no nerve at all," he said disgustedly. "The minute she saw 'em she howled. I was stampin' out the fire before it got to her —"

Gail dashed for the gap in the hedge. There had been no rain for a week and the May sun had dried the underbrush. "Where is this stake? Show me at once!"

She was almost toppled over by a stout Irish woman who came panting through the gap.

"'Tis here they are, is it? And me eyes not off thim tin minutes whilst I run up to change me dhress ... And himself puttin' th' fear o' God into me, not to lave th' two av thim pester ye whilst he do be gone. 'Katie O'Hara, whativver ye do,' the last words out av his mout' and his bag in his hand, 'don't be lettin' thim childhern ann'y the young lady as has bought Lilac Cottage —'"

Miss Ormsbee stood rooted to the soil of her petunia bed. "What's your name?" she shot at the small boy.

"None o' your business," he retorted, resentful of the rape of his matches which had been procured with difficulty and only by strategic maneuver.

The feminine culprit, sensing sympathy on her side was more ready to produce the amenities. "He'th Fifke Ingwam and I'm Fweddy Ingwam. I'm four and he'th thix."

Fiske ... and Fredricka. Too familiar nomenclatures, that had tarnished the brightness of many an otherwise pleasant dinner! Gail glanced at the Irish woman, a capable-looking person in starched print.

"Where do these children live?"

"Joost behint here, Miss. Our yards do be j'ining. But I'll see these limbs o' Satan don't bother ye no more. I'll trounce th' two av thim good for comin' in here afther me orders to thim. Not that most people —" she flung over a shoulder, herding her charges through the gap — "would take it so irritated-like, whin a coupla innercent childhern run into their back yard."

"Wait a minute." Gail ran after her. Gail — to whom justice was a fetish. "The boy is the only one to be punished. The little girl was frightened; and anybody, frightened, will run for the nearest safety. You have no business at all to punish her."

The duenna turned and set hands on her hips. "I know me business. And it's me and no other that is gardeen o' these younguns whin himself is away. It's no advice I'm needin'."

She extended a protective hand to each of her charges and the three vanished in the shrubbery, the small boy turning at the last moment to make a face in the general direction of Lilac Cottage.

Arlene, on the living-room sofa, kicked slim silk-stockinged legs in convulsive agony of mirth.

"It's too priceless. 'Quite a distance by automobile' ... Of course it is — round by the road! I take off my hat to John Ingram for a fast worker. What an opportunity for you to learn to love the cunning little things. Nothing like propinquity — and really getting to know children's endearing ways. Wait till I tell Hilda!"

"Oh, do shut up."

Gail's blue eyes had sparks in them. She heaved a log on the fire with unnecessary violence.

Arlene sat up and wiped her eyes. "Don't be too hard on him, darling. All's fair in love and widowerhood. Didn't he beg you to get acquainted with his precious infants? And you wouldn't. I'll say he has accomplished his end very neatly."

"His 'end' — whatever he thinks it is — is a good long way from being accomplished," stated Miss Ormsbee succinctly. She went and stood in the window to hide furious tears. "For two cents I'd sell this house tomorrow."

Through blur of tears she saw her lilac bushes, drooping under weight of purple richness. And beyond, fainter purple of hills against an amethyst sky. A man and a maid were strolling down a far slope of the golf meadow. Up the road, a car turned in at the gates of the adjoining estate and was lost to view behind clumps of shrubbery. Space. Dignity. Beauty. And her little gem of a place within its exclusive hedges. Gail suddenly realized how she loved it. How it was part of her and she of it.

"No, I wouldn't." She swung round on Arlene. "I wouldn't move away from this place for a million dollars. The entire Ingram tribe cannot disturb me a particle. They'll find it out."

With an expression that boded no good to Machiavellian schemers now in Chicago, Illinois, the homemaker set about preparations for tea.

CHAPTER VII

Considering Valley Lilies

THE lilies of the valley were up: fairy bells, chiming a noiseless carillon of springtime. Gail was picking a great handful to send to Hilda. The afternoon sun, slanting through tree branches, made golden splashes on her garden smock and on her hands, delving among cool green leaves of the lily bed.

Everything had been going serenely. Arlene had departed and the perfect maid had "taken hold." At least, Gail felt certain this was the awaited treasure at last. They had found each other. The interview had been brief and congenial. Epitomized, it might be set down thus:

"You see I am an author and have to be busy at my desk. The housework will be your job and the writing, mine. Go ahead your own way and I am sure everything will be all right."

"Yes'm. We likes to work for ladies who does writings or musics. We manage. They not trouble."

This mutual viewpoint had produced an amiable atmosphere. The house took on a shining specklessness. The homemaker divided her time happily between desk and garden and ten minutes' interview after breakfast settled marketing problems of the day. There had been only one occasion of friction. Gail had decided to spend her morning making curtains. Glancing up from a cutting-table strewn with lengths of chintz, she beheld a determined intruder armed with brooms and dust-cloths.

"Oh, Regina — I was going to sew this morning. Did you want to clean, in here?"

Inflexibly, she was informed: "This Wednesday. Tuesdays we cleans downstairs. Wednesdays, upstairs. Fridays, halls and silver."

Gail gathered up her sewing, tucked it away and sought the garden. Fairness was fairness: if you gave a person responsibility you couldn't hamper her later with niggling objections.

The Perfect Treasure was a very black and very tall West Indian woman. With a voice so gentle it was almost comical in a body of such stature and sturdiness. Gone, intriguing dream of cute little maid in cute little apron — this majestic person could not be insulted with suggestion of a cap.

But she had had the benefit of English training on her Barbadoes island and was any homemaker's ideal of respectable dignity in her plain frocks and spotless aprons. Gail had been touched by a tray of tea and toast, presented at her workroom door on the third afternoon. "You write many hours without resting. Better have this," the Perfect Treasure had urged. And next day there had been sheets and pillowcases on the line. "Not enough to send to laundry. We does our own wash; just as well do all. You very good to give whole Sunday each month to visit cousins in Newark."

Thus were amicable and even affectionate relations established. "I can't see," Gail wrote to Hilda, "why housewives have so much trouble with servants. It's simple enough if you are square with them."

But Hilda thought that Gail had dumb luck.

Dinner was a daily treat. Candles. Amber goblets. Darwin tulips in a low bowl. And a little tender porterhouse on the shining "pine tree" platter. No cluttering bird-baths of watery boarding-house vegetables; no eternal passing of salt-shakers. No querulous sotto-voice complaints ... "At this time of year you'd think, Miss Ormsbee, she might give us something beside canned peas." Many a time had Gail run away to a restaurant to dine in peace.

She recalled those places also with pitying superiority. Tiny tables with paper doilies on the bare wood, instead of this gracious damask cloth. A paper napkin, sliding off your lap. Never quite enough butter to finish your roll. She revelled now in the daintiness of her own dinner table. Regina stepping softly about, passing things. And through the open window, scent of lilac and syringa coming in. (When she knew people in the neighborhood she would give some little dinners. Regina would be able to manage six or eight beautifully.)

But just now she basked in the undisturbed peace of it all and in her sense of ownership of all this heavenly luxury. Gail, who had lived continually among people and amid more or less disturbing clamor — in her sister Rosamund's crowded flat, in a business office, in boarding-houses — felt no loneliness in her aloof existence. Not yet at any rate. One of the fortunate people, called by less resourceful persons, self-sufficient, she was never bored by her own company if there were books or a pencil at hand, or a bit of needlework to be completed.

After dinner, she slipped into a loose coat and took her evening stroll. Down the road as far as the bridge. She liked to listen to the brook tumbling over stones in the dusk and to sound of birds twittering in the woodland.

Then back to her cosy living-room with garden books to look over until bedtime. Of course by and by people would be dropping in. That pretty girl across the ravine perhaps. She looked nice. And the pleasant boy who lived on the other side, in the big house set back in wide lawns. Gail had seen him talking to the girl, evenings. They sat on a rock by the brook in the ravine. The trees were so thick now, that woman with the spy glass could not look across any more — nor down into the ravine, probably, where her daughter was sitting with the boy. Gail wondered why he did not go up to the girl's house to have his twilight chats. Or why they did not go for drives in his speedy little roadster.

Several cars, besides that roadster, over at the big place. A smart yellow station wagon and a huge limousine which went every evening to meet an older man who walked with a cane and who must have been good looking in his younger days before he got rheumatism or whatever it was. His wife was a plump person, bustling and busy and rather overbearing, Gail thought, with the gardener. But the lady had nodded in a friendly way one afternoon when Gail had been passing the gates as the limousine purred out.

Pleasant looking neighbors here in Brook Road. Especially the nice elderly gentleman in that house across the ravine. The girl's father of course. A little stoop-shouldered — like a student — but such a charming smile. Poor man — with a wife who had been an invalid for fifteen years! He had lifted that old black felt hat with an air when he spied Gail behind her hedge, shaking dew-wet clusters of lilacs and piling them in her basket.

"Fine morning, young lady. I see you are enjoying the springtime."

Gail had been unaware that she herself looked like springtime, under the leafing birch tree, her arms heaped with wet lilacs, her linen frock fluttering in a May breeze and a happy May morning smile showing her dimple.

It was fun to be a householder in a pleasant community . . . as for instance, this Saturday afternoon: out in one's own garden, picking one's own lilies of the valley to send to a city-imprisoned friend. Gail, full of contentment, her hands buried in the wet coolness of the lily bed, glanced up and beheld Mr. John Ingram loitering in the gap of the hedge. Pipe in mouth, excellent legs encased in wool hose and baggy knickers, he was the complete picture of the country gentleman. His expression of eye was half quizzical, half anxious.

He said ingratiatingly, "Howdy?"

"Oh — so you are home again!" Miss Ormsbee sat back on her heels and regarded him stonily.

"Two hours ago. Had my lunch and came right over."

"I don't know whether to speak to you or not."

"Don't think twice about it, then. Say it quick and get it over with." He advanced with comical suggestion of the naughty small boy who knows he deserves rebuke but counts on leniency because he meant so well. In truth, Mr. Ingram had worried considerably during the past three weeks. He stood, smiling down at her, legs in the good-looking knickers braced well apart and hands in the pockets of his loose coat. "You see I knew it was exactly the sort of little place you wanted and if I had told you it bordered on my land you wouldn't have taken it ... Would you?"

"No," said Miss Ormsbee, tugging at lily-of-the-valley stems, "I certainly wouldn't have."

He dropped down on his heels beside her, culling lilies in an engaging effect of helpfulness and looking sideways at her unsmiling countenance.

"It is a nice little place though, isn't it?"

"So nice," she agreed, one corner of her mouth tilting up and almost revealing the dimple, "that only that and nothing more prevented my moving out instantly." After all her furious resentment, which she had tried to keep fanned to fever heat, it was disconcerting, now, to find herself so glad to see John that wrathful resolution to squelch him for undertaking to manage her affairs seemed to have evaporated.

There was something — it secretly worried Gail — that invariably caused her, however hardly she thought of John Ingram when he was not with her, to feel in his presence the impulse to give in — to subordinate her will to his. A silly softness that made her combat him — or this disquieting quality in him — all the more strenuously when they were together. After all, she thought now, wasn't it rather pleasant,

CONSIDERING VALLEY LILIES 89

if you looked at it that way, to have a dependable friend right on the other side of a hedge?

John had not missed the almost-appearance of the dimple.

"Am I forgiven?"

This time her blue eyes laughed at him. "Oh, I suppose so — though you played a trick on me, don't forget that!" She added, with her unfailing instinct of fairness. "Wherever I had seen this place I'd have been likely to grab it — even away up in Westchester."

She rose to her feet and so did he — with a distinctly relieved expression.

"But there is one thing, John —" her face was serious again —"I can't have those children running into this garden."

"Of course not." Hastily.

"I have my book to write and I can't be disturbed."

"Most certainly not." The vast seriousness of her tone was matched by his. "How's the great work coming on?"

"Well — I have been getting settled. Curtains to hem and things like that. And this garden. And there is my regular copy to do every day. But I expect to get down to work on the book soon —"

She had paused and was glancing toward the hedge from behind which came sounds. Canine yelps. Infantile squeals. Excited shouts of a small boy. Mr. Ingram stepped briskly to the gap in the hedge.

"Come here, both of you!"

The clamor outside continued.

"Come here, I say, Fiske. D'ye hear me?"

A juvenile voice piped shrilly, "Can't. He's chasin' a squirr'l."

Clamor faded into distance. Mr. Ingram strode through the gap, followed by pricking comment from the garden: "How well they mind!"

Presently there appeared in the gap; Mr. Ingram again, somewhat disheveled from hard running; a pair of small blue-clad figures; and a snow-white bull terrier dragged by a leash. John herded his charges carefully round the sprouting delphinium bed.

"We've brought you something."

At sight of the delightful dog, Gail had fallen on her knees in the grass with arms outstretched and lips puckered in a coaxing whistle. A truly delightful dog she saw: sleek lined and snow white, his sharp ears pink lined, his slim tail switching with ardent friendliness. One moment he held back, sniffing tentatively, then he dashed toward the kneeling girl and was clasped in adoring arms. Any dog would have recognized those arms as dog-haven and that heart against which was pressed his head as heart that found no flaw in him.

"He ith a pwethent," Miss Fredricka Ingram announced cordially. "For you."

"We thought you ought to have a protector," John appended. "Hilda Braithwaite told me about your staying here two nights all alone. Won't do! This fellow will look after you in any emergencies of that sort."

"But, John —" she was stroking the long head of the dog that lay against her breast. His pink-rimmed honest eyes gazed up at her ecstatically — "this is no dog you have picked up. He's a thoroughbred. You must have spent an awful lot for him. I can't —"

"Yes, you can. It would worry the life out of me to have you sleeping in this house by yourself. Don't fuss; he has a pedigree all right, but I got him — well, for a song — from a friend of mine who owns a kennel."

"His name is Bill," vouchsafed Fiske. "He's a norful squirr'l chaser."

The pathetic forgiveness of children! All but shoved off the place the other day, now they were ready to share in her pleasure over her gift. Gail got hastily to her feet.

"I'm certain Bill wants a drink. And I think there is some chocolate cake. Won't you all come in?"

The children trotted ahead and Gail, holding Bill's leash, told John about the Perfect Treasure. It was going to be rather nice to have John near by, to tell things to.

Established in a big chair, with a cup of tea and a huge wedge of chocolate cake, Mr. Ingram had the immediate appearance of one delightfully at home. He might have been taking tea in that chair for years. The two children, on their very best behaviour, shared the sofa and a small table loaded with cake and lemonade. The day was too warm for a fire, but Gail's living-room was charming, with the new curtains fluttering at open windows and everywhere vases of lilac and lily of the valley. The hostess felt pride in the deftness with which the Perfect Treasure produced and served refreshment for unexpected guests. A happy and auspicious occasion. Fun — to be a lady dispensing hospitality in your own home.

"Had any callers?" John asked.

"Several. Three in a group yesterday and two this morning. From the Baptist and Congregational churches. Delegates or something. They told me how attractive their minister was and what nice times they had and how much was done for the young people." Gail chuckled. "Made me feel like a college freshman being rushed by fraternities."

"Let me recommend the Methodists," John advised. "They give the best church-suppers. But of course our rural congregations have to get right after a new prospect in town who looks as likely as you. Their intentions are the best."

"Don't I know it? They were all nice women — dears. Homey and jolly. We talked cake recipes and transplanting time for salvia seedlings. Only one of them displayed interest in my literary achievements — no, that was one of the Episcopal delegates."

"Ah ha — my church. The intelligentsia attend there."

"She said, 'So you write! Poetry, may I ask?'"

"Good grief, one thing you don't resemble is a lady poetess. What'd you say?"

"I said I was doing a novel," Gail informed him with dignity. "You know I am — at least I shall be when I get at it. No need to tell the whole town I do syndicate fashion copy and pay my grocer's bill that way."

"No need at all." Mr. Ingram's visage was entirely serious. He could get the lady-in-her-own-garden idea as well as anybody. "Not that they'll care what you write so long as you have other qualifications."

Gail dimpled. "Oh yes, they assured themselves about that! The Presbyterian lady said casually, 'And you have never married?' . . . You see I might not be plain Miss, but back-from-Reno Miss. They had to make sure. I must tell Arlene about that. She'll adore it."

"Well, we have to be careful in our village," agreed Mr. Ingram. "Of course all you need to do is to tell them you are a close friend of mine —"

"Is that so?" Gail's blue eyes sparkled with rekindled resentment. "A little too close, maybe. Unknown young woman you bring out here and establish handily across your back fence. The less said about 'close friends' the better, Mr. John Ingram, until I get acquainted in this town on my own."

John sat up straight. "Why, I never thought of that!"

"No — you wouldn't!"

He looked properly abashed.

"Oh, I like it a lot, here," she told him amiably. "But you let me establish myself my own way." The dimple appeared again. "Salvia seedlings are a safer recommendation than masculine sponsors. Ask Hilda."

"Why Hilda?" he inquired rather anxiously. "What's she got to do with it —"

John's daughter pressed against his knee. "I wanna go home. It'th no fun, here."

"When I have finished my pipe, Freddy."

Fiske added his plea. "I got a good look at her now. I seen all I want."

"Saw," corrected John. Then, attentively, "What'd you mean by that, son?"

"Yes," inserted Miss Ormsbee interestedly, "I'd like to know what he means by that, too."

Fiske regarded her without embarrassment. "I asked father why he was giving Bill to a strange woman and he said, 'Take a good look at her, son, and you'll see.'"

"Oh, indeed. And what do you think, Fiske, now you've seen me?"

The two stared at each other; Gail Ormsbee and John's son. And Gail, meeting that straight little-boy gaze, felt more of secret qualm than she would have before tribunal of maturer judgment. At least the grown-up would not venture on uncompromising frankness. Fiske produced his verdict:

"Not so bad."

What Fiske was thinking, but was unable to put into graceful phrase, was that though complete judgment must be reserved, he rather approved of this young woman. She wouldn't be one you could get around, but on the other hand she wasn't mushy, wanting to maul you and set your tie straight. And she looked at you without a laugh at the back of her eyes as though you were funny; or (still more heinous crime) without glancing at the nearest grown-up with suggestion of a shared joke. And she was a just person; he had learned that. She had pronounced against him, the other day, and in favor of Freddy, but it had been himself who was naughty ... And gee, but her cook could make chocolate cake!

"Pretty fair, I guess," he supplemented magnanimously.

Small Freddy contributed her opinion. "I don' like her much. She'th cwoth." John looked pained.

CONSIDERING VALLEY LILIES 95

"Your constituents," Miss Ormsbee submitted, "do not seem over-enthusiastic about me."

Freddy tugged at the parental hand. "I wanna go home."

John did not believe in giving in to children; they must learn to wait on the pleasure of their elders. He instructed his offspring to "go play with Bill" until he had finished his pipe. And in the agreeable quiet that ensued he enjoyed being shown Gail's little workroom with its glass doors set open to the garden and her table-desk graced by a jug of lilacs.

"You'll do great stuff here," he encouraged. "Tidy. And quiet." He looked about, enviously (Nobody put lilacs on the writing table of his disheveled den.) "Remember if you need a husky arm any time in the garden or around the house I'm right within call —"

"Thank you, John."

"Kind of nice to be neighbors," he said, "isn't it?"

He met that swift, bright glance of blue eyes under upsweeping lashes. Gail's friendly glance.

"Kind of —!" she admitted.

"You're not sorry you're here?"

She opened her mouth to answer him — kindly. But the moment was spoiled —

Frightful clamor, outside in the hall. Sharp smash of glass just above. (A sound exactly like that new jar of green bath salts splintering in the porcelain tub).

Fiske was descending the stair, two steps at a time, immediately preceded by Bill who had taken the whole flight in three leaps. Fredricka, howling dismally, clumped after, one hand clutching a small object. The linen costumes of both children were soaked, and roar of water from a turned on faucet came from the bathroom.

Bill took refuge between John's legs and Gail fixed an eye on the object in Fredricka's fist. "What were you doing with my toothbrush?"

Fredricka stopped howling and pouted. Fiske explained:

"We didn't mean to break the big bottle. I was just reaching for the toot' paste. We were brushing Bill's teeth. We'd have put the toot'brush back."

"Well, thank heaven you didn't!" remarked the owner of the toothbrush.

Mr. Ingram evidently deemed the moment propitious for departure. Herding his damp constituents through the front door, he mumbled apology to his hostess. "They're only kids, you know. Of course what they need is a mother's hand —"

"It'd have to be a good strong hand," retorted Miss Ormsbee. She ran upstairs to shut off water and discover what damage had been done to her beautiful new bathroom. Descending, she found the Perfect Treasure with the first sullen look her visage had registered, digging crumbs out of the rug.

"Childrens make much bother," asserted Regina. "We not like to live in house with those two, all time."

Her mistress nodded. Her own sentiments, precisely.

She put on her hat. Just time before dinner to take Hilda's lilies of the valley to the post office — and to stop at the drugstore for a new toothbrush. Bill was in the hall, one eye wistfully upon her, an ear pricked to keep track of what was happening elsewhere in the house. As long as she had Bill that would be his attitude: her immediate movement his passionate interest; her safeguarding his first concern. Her dog!

John Ingram was rather a dear — there was no getting around it.

Later, that evening, the druggist's boy leaned his bicycle against the hedge and handed in a parcel. It contained a five-pound box of choice candy and a dozen toothbrushes in sealed paper jackets. There was also a card with two lines in Mr. Ingram's neat script: "Please forgive us. We mean well."

CHAPTER VIII

Lilacs In The Rain

TO ONE intent on literary accomplishment nothing is more congenial than rain — unless it be snow. Your author, waking on a morning of torrential downpour, has that exultant and vigorous feeling common to lay persons when gorgeous sunshine promises ideal condition for the day's pursuits. Here, reflects your author, gazing out contentedly at dripping eaves and writhing tree branches (or better still, at a raging blizzard), is a day for getting something done! Without prick of conscience about faring forth for necessary exercise, or visiting that friend at the hospital, or attending to this or that. No fear of callers; or of entreaties over the telephone to join in diversions urged as beneficial to the worker though undoubtedly bad for the work. Even the postman likely to be late with probably disturbing mail. Blessed rain, paraphrases your literary laborer, that leaves the world to silence and to him.

So, during the "blossom storm" that pelted for three consecutive days and an ensuing week of those bleak winds and drab skies that make a modern May so far from poetic conception of Maytime, Gail worked busily and happily at her desk. The Perfect Treasure looked after the house and there was nothing to be done in the garden. Rivulets flooded the paths and the borders were sticky mud. Luckily the baby seedlings had not yet been set out. There would be plenty to do later, but no use worrying now. With that power of intense concentration on the thing in hand that was one of Gail's endowments for successful mental accomplishment (precious gift for an author, but not a fortunate quality in the woman who must find happiness in diversified occupations of a domestic career) she drove ahead, during this auspicious period, on her novel, putting all else out of mind.

She revelled in her little writing-room — her "study" she magnificently called it — with the big flat-topped table desk and typewriter within reach. Bill snoozed on the floor and outside the closed glass doors sheets of rain swept by. And, mingled with the rain, petals of cherry blossoms that gave the effect of flurries of snow.

She turned off reams of copy, attacking this drudgery task early each morning to get it out of the way before settling down to real work on the book. There were the eternal "fillers," six of which must be provided to tuck into corners of each newspaper page. For lengthy fashion articles she was provided with photographs which came in huge manilla envelopes and stirred the heart of the village postmistress to compassion because the good soul imagined they were rejected manuscripts faring home to the new author established at Lilac Cottage. These long fashion chats, built around definite style-information, were not half as troublesome to do as the hundred-word "fillers" which could be about anything at all — except religion or politics, barred on a Woman's Page. If only, thought Gail, all the people who burned to write could know how avid were Woman's Page editors for "fillers." Wherever women were gathered together, chatting about this and that, one picked up something for a "filler."

Time had been when Gail had to haunt the shops, collecting material for her copy. Now, familiar with the formula, and supplied with printed reports of Paris style movements, she could have done her weekly copy very nicely on a South Sea island, given time for mailing it out. She did not hate the fashion copy. She put into it zest and sparkle because that was the way she worked; — putting her whole self into whatever she tackled and getting enjoyment out of it. And because of this she was paid good money for the work. But her soul yearned to be at her novel. Real literary production. Concrete achievement to stand in her name; not endless phrases poured into the newspaper maw; unsigned; bringing no recognition.

"Think of the columns of my stuff lining garbage pails all over these United States on Monday mornings," she had once said to Hilda Braithwaite. "And think of your book — in bookshop windows!"

Whereupon Miss Braithwaite told her tartly that if she cherished dream of beholding book of hers adorning bookshop windows in this era of cruel competition, she'd better stick to syndicate copy and garbage pails. "Anyhow, some woman might glimpse your copy through the potato peelings and know you are alive!" was the arrived author's gloomy pronouncement. But the fact that Hilda had a published work to her credit filled Gail with secret envy. She too was going to be an arrived author as soon as ever she could accomplish it!

She got her novel well under way that fortnight of the "blossom storm." And mornings, while dressing, looked out at her lilacs in the rain. Their wet purple glisten was an inspiration for the day. What was there about lilacs in the rain that made you so intensely, contentedly happy in ownership of the place where they grew?

She loved also the dogwood in the grove across the road — Japanesey flat surfaces, mistily white through gray-green tones of the spring woodland. And underneath, coppery gleam of wet, last year's leaves on the ground. Regina had carried the typewriter upstairs when the study became too damp for comfort. After a day of numbed hands and sweater huddled around her ears, the author decided that upstairs was a safer place to pursue literary avocation — until the weather changed. John Ingram, responding to a telephone summons, sloshed over one evening in raincoat and rubber boots and tinkered with the furnace, Gail holding a candle for him because there was no electric light in the cellar. But the furnace, it was discovered, needed several things done to it and the owner of Lilac Cottage decided September was the season for such repairs. They had good fun, however, tinkering over the furnace. You did a lot of things in the country that would never have occurred to you as diverting, in town.

Hilda and Arlene put off their weekend visit. Keen as they were, Hilda wrote, to witness wonders performed by the Perfect Treasure, city landlords were mercifully supplying steam heat and the same was now sizzling in her radiators. Gail could picture the pleasant warmth if she would.

Arlene wrote that she really preferred rural life in haying season. Raptures about spring always made her feel shivery, Arlene protested, and "With Verdure Clad," sung in church at Easter season, invariably gave her the sniffly sensation of a cold coming on.

So Gail worked all day without interruption and every evening donned raincoat and galoshes and took Bill for a run. They went as far as the bridge — until it was discovered that John also took his after-dinner tramp as far as the bridge, coming round from the other direction. After two meetings when John implied that the way he liked a girl best was in wet weather togs with wisps of hair blowing over cheeks rosy from the rain, the thing savored too much of a tryst. So Bill was tramped the other way, up to the turnpike. But either way, along one side of Brook Road stretched undulating meadows of the golf course. Real country; no make-believe. Gail adored it, even in the rain.

Sometimes she saw the boy and girl who lived on either side, sitting on their rock in the ravine, one umbrella sheltering them both and their feet in last year's sodden leaves. They waved to Gail now, acquaintance having been established through Bill. Nobody could resist Bill's friendly overtures and genially wagging tail. Hilda had once asserted that if a lone woman wanted to make friends in a new community or at a summer hotel, she must have with her a dog or a child. Whereas it might require weeks of best behaviour with desolating loneliness ere a lone female could edge her way into the clan, given the dog or the child, within three days every woman in the place would have made friendly advances.

"My mother is an invalid," the girl said to Gail, "but dad and I are coming over to call some evening." The boy said his mother also was coming to call. "But don't mention that you saw us," they warned her, laughing.

"Certainly not!" Gail laughed too, as befitted youth sympathizing with youth. And the two went back to their damp rock and their joint umbrella.

Some sort of family feud here. She must ask John about it. She had made up her mind to discourage John at first indication of a dropping-in habit — since dropping-in could be so easily accomplished by stroll through adjoining back yards. But rather to her surprise there hadn't been anything to discourage. John had called only once at Lilac Cottage (not counting the candle-lit session with the furnace) and on the occasion of his call had arrived in his car which he had driven around by the road. A long week of rain had made her — oh, not lonesome, of course! — but a bit fed up with being indoors all day and then having nothing to do but read until bedtime. She had been glad to see John. There had been a fire in the living-room and he had told her all the office news.

She wondered what John did with his evenings. It had never occurred to her to be curious about it when they met in the city. He had mentioned strumming a lot on his piano, once, during one of their little dinners together in town. Rather jolly those weekly dinners. Tables with shaded lights, violins playing soft "dinner music" and waiters slithering about with trays. And then a theater afterward . . . Well, when you lived fifty minutes out, town junketings could be only occasional happenings.

Probably John read, evenings. Sort of forlorn, for a man: strumming on a piano or just reading. Though of course John was fond of books and bought a good many. Well, at any rate he wasn't running over all the time, taking advantage of that gap in the hedge.

Which was perhaps just what Mr. Ingram hoped would be her conclusion. John had possessed one wife; he knew a thing or two about women. On several evenings he had strolled down to the gap, from whence could be seen cosy lights of Lilac Cottage. (Regina's light in the kitchen, and in her maidenly bedroom above, to be exact). But each time, after whistling a bit under his breath in a speculative way, he had turned and walked back to his domicile.

He told Hilda Braithwaite who was having lunch with him that Gail was far too busy to bother with him.

"John, she doesn't hold any grudge about what you did —?"

"What I did!"

Hilda looked at him anxiously. "I hope you have had sense enough not to let her know I had any —"

He interrupted with a chuckle, "Be at rest about my sense — I have a little. Anyhow, all you did was to make a suggestion that was a heaven-sent inspiration. I take all the blame."

"Well, see you do," warned Miss Braithwaite. "If she should happen to hold any grudge —"

John smiled at her. "Gail couldn't hold a grudge. She'd be capable of breaking off a friendship if indignation convinced her judgment it was the thing to do.

Otherwise she'd put the matter behind her and forget it. She would never harbor a grudge about it."

Hilda nodded. "Gail's a girl in a thousand, John —"

"Don't I know it?"

"— only she needs to have those executive talents of hers directed into channels —"

"Where they are most needed," Mr. Ingram inserted.

"Where they will make her happiest." Hilda smiled across the table at him. "She doesn't know it, but I want her to find it out —"

"Me too," John agreed.

"She's so young," Hilda said wistfully. "And so terribly efficient. I'd hate to have her wake up, fifteen years from now, to the knowledge that a few empty laurels are all she has to grow old with; and that her life has never been lived. Yet you can't convince Gail by talking to her. She has to feel things, not be argued into them. I know Gail."

"But not better than I do," said John. "You leave it to me, Hilda."

She looked at him kindly. "I'd leave my daughter to you, if I had one, John Ingram, and know that I couldn't have done anything better for her."

After days of lowering clouds and intermittent showers, there came a change in the weather. The wind veered to the north and a yellow sky at sunset made an eerie light in Brook Road where the trees, now thickly leaved, made arches overhead. Gail, tramping homeward with Bill, sprang off the roadway at clatter of horses' feet behind her. A gay cavalcade swept by: half a dozen young men and girls, hatless, all astride and aglow with vigorous exercise. They glanced down at Gail; and mud from puddles through which the horses splashed spattered Gail's coat and struck her cheek. Standing aside, waiting for them to get by, she had that inferiority-feeling of the plodding pedestrian who gazes up at privileged beings who ride.

One horse came to a clattering stop and a girl's voice called crisply, "If here isn't my Bill!"

The white bull terrier bounded forward and showed by every token of dog delight that here was someone he knew and liked well. Gail, scrubbing mud off her visage and making a bad smear of it, stared up at the rider. She was the tall girl who had strolled with her dog into the country club, that day of the golf match last fall, and had instantly become the life of the party. The girl who had income and complete independence, who lived alone and had the established background and effect of belonging that Gail, desiring these things, had so envied. She sat now astride her horse, booted feet resting easily in the stirrups, riding breeches splashed with mud, the saffron sunset light on her blown, sandy hair. And a friendly grin on her face.

"You're making it worse," she admonished Gail, down in the road, desperately mopping a mud-smudged cheek. "We shouldn't have come so fast through this back road. It's too wet for riding, but we couldn't wait another minute to get out. Why bother with that? Water'll take it off."

She stooped to the dog. "And so here's my Bill. How do you like him?"

One of the young men had reined in his horse and returned to range himself beside the girl. He stared amiably at Gail, down at the roadside with her smudged cheek. For some reason which she would have found difficult to explain, Gail felt an antagonism toward them both. Sitting up there on their horses and looking so gay and casual. Here was the girl whom she had set up in her own mind as a sort of pattern; picturing herself also strolling across golf meadows, dog at heel, and being genially greeted by a friendly crowd that accepted her as one of them. Now this person splashed mud on her. And she claimed Bill! Miss Ormsbee's manner took on dignity — the dignity that had discouraged cheeky salesmen invading her office.

"You know my dog?"

"Well, I raised him. I've a kennel you know. John bought him of me. Told me you ought to have a dog because you live all alone. I hoped you'd like Bill. You do, don't you?"

"Oh, I do!" Gail was pleased that Bill, after tempestuous greeting of a former mistress, now returned to her side and sat down. She stooped and fondled his ears.

The girl grinned again. "I'm glad. I have a dozen dogs around all the time, but Bill knows when he's found his own mistress. That's what they always want: to be the only one. This is Mr. Beecroft, Miss — You'll have to tell me your name, I've forgotten ... Oh, Ormsbee? Yes ... Bob, make a bow to the lady."

Mr. Beecroft nodded cordially — from his saddle. The girl continued in her brisk, assured way: "My name's Jule Vernon. Everybody calls me Jule, around here. I'm an institution. Coming to see you sometime — John asked me to."

"Very nice of you," Gail murmured. Dignity was only slightly impaired by necessity of holding handkerchief to smudged cheek.

"John's a lamb, isn't he? Special pal of mine. We team up at the bridge tournament, Tuesday nights. He's so lonesome, poor Johnny, but nobody will take him on because of those precious tykes of his. We all try to keep him occupied so he won't get into mischief... Don't we, Bob?"

"Sure do," answered Mr. Beecroft, obligingly polite, but obviously chafing to get on and join the others.

Miss Vernon gathered up her bridle rein. She smiled the wide, frank smile that Gail had decided (last fall) made her such a general favorite. "We'll have to get you into the country club, Miss Ormsbee. After you know everybody you'll like it out here."

"I like it very well now." Gail hated herself for meeting cordiality with stiffness. "And I am afraid I haven't much time for golf." (She who had wistfully contemplated rolling greens and envisioned herself swinging over them with a bag of clubs!) "You see I'm rather busy." She didn't know why she added: "I'm doing a novel."

Miss Vernon was unimpressed. "Yes, so John told me. Wish you luck. I'll drop round sometime and talk about Bill. Don't feed him any sweets."

She and her cavalier clattered away.

Round a bend of the road she remarked to the attendant Beecroft, "Bit upstage."

"Nice blue eyes," commented Mr. Beecroft. He had noticed them.

"Pity to ruin 'em, doing books. She'll be wearing glasses in five years. Well, there must be something to her; Johnny quite raved about her. Gave himself away, rather."

"Seems a stern sort of a dame," Mr. Beecroft said doubtfully. "Not exactly the winning kind."

"You never can tell," averred Miss Vernon. "She's a business woman, you'd know that. They always act that way; — sort of on the defensive, in a social encounter. But if John fancies her we'll have to round her out somehow; she would never fit, in this community, with that no-time-for-frivolity attitude. Who wants an author nosing around, spying out all your secret motives and probably jotting them down? That won't get her anywhere."

"Maybe she doesn't want to get anywhere. She seems to like those hedges of hers pretty well."

"You can't hide inside hedges and get anything out of life," said Miss Vernon oracularly. "And anybody with eyelashes like that is silly to do it." She had a flip way of talking, but she was a good-hearted girl. She concluded: "Anyhow if John Ingram likes her she is worth knowing. And I mean to know her. Let's trot, shall we? It's almost dark."

CHAPTER IX

A Dreamer In The Dusk

MISS ORMSBEE, resentfully scrubbing a smudged cheek, plodded homeward. Far off, she could hear horses' feet striking the hard surface of the turnpike. She was glad Bill hadn't made any effort to run after that pair. He was her dog now and he knew it. Good old Bill! She stooped and stroked Bill's long head and he leaped up and tried to lick her face. You couldn't be lonesome if you had a dog.

Not that she was lonesome, of course. So John played in a bridge tournament, Tuesday nights. Youngish, personable widowers who played bridge would naturally be in demand in a rural community. He probably played bridge many nights; that girl needn't have talked as though she owned his bridge talents... A lamb... Special pal of hers... And he'd told her all about poor solitary, as yet unacquainted Miss Ormsbee — begged his good pal to take the forlorn newcomer under her socially assured wing.

Leagues and leagues of difference between that girl and Gail Ormsbee... Gail Ormsbee, who hadn't had time to play; who had been drudging in offices all the years while this Jule Vernon was riding and playing golf and dancing at country clubs. Gail Ormsbee, who had learned to be watchful (instead of smilingly expansive) because only by battling and by holding her own could a woman climb steadily in a business environment. How could such a one have dreamed she could fit into any suave social circle whose chief business was play? Devotion to work wasn't going to get one anywhere in this community, that was certain. "I'm an author —" said with such asinine complacence... And that girl's airy dismissal of the fact as unimportant.

Most of all rankled that belittling disposal of the great undertaking. Arlene had said "You can't go bourgeois and succeed in a career" — something like that. Well, she had her work to do. And she had her garden, all hedged around. And she had Bill. And the Perfect Treasure. She could stay inside her hedges and do her work. She didn't need anything else.

Coming up the stepping-stone walk she saw the last of her lilacs, two clusters high up. She reached for them and sniffed their wet purple sweetness in the dusk. Within the house, soft radiance of lamplight and her big chair drawn up by the table that was piled with garden magazines. Regina had gone to Vesper service; she was a devout Episcopalian and her well-thumbed prayerbook always lay on her bureau beside her comb and brush.

Gail went to the kitchen and set the lilacs in a white lustre vase which she carried to the living-room. She stood, idly flipping pages of the garden magazines. Then she took the vase of lilacs to her study where she snapped on the table-lamp. It threw a mellow light on her green blotter and on the pile of buff manuscript paper all ready for commencement of chapter six. The lustre vase reflected the green of the blotter and the purple of the lilacs. The room was heavenly quiet. Perfect environment for a cosy evening of work by any earnest-minded author.

That gang who had clattered by on horseback were probably at the country club now, chattering and laughing. Luxuriously tired after their good exercise. Not one of them had a serious thought or any worth-while ambition. No — it was unfair to say that! Just because they had been lighthearted: getting out after the long rain. A week of rain made anybody feel that way . . . Restless.

The author, glancing not enthusiastically at admirable preparation for labor, opened the glass doors and stepped out on the porch. Bill cocked an anxious eye from the rug where he had just turned round four or five times and settled down for pleasant repose of a dog who has returned from quite adequate evening exercise.

Out on the porch the air had a wet freshness. There was smell of damp earth and — yes, faint fragrance of honeysuckle. It must be blossoming; she would look, first thing in the morning. How little she had dreamed, a year ago this time, of ever possessing a porch with honeysuckle growing over it! She sniffed the sweetness and listened to wind moving treetops of the wood. Up above the branches a blue gleam — Vega, climbing out of vanishing storm clouds and reminding that summer was almost here. A few weeks more and the roses would be gorgeous in the garden. . . .

Afar off, someone was playing on a piano. Tschaikowsky's *Lonely Heart*, just audible above the murmur of the rising wind. On still, summer nights very likely that piano would be annoying, though not as bad as a radio. But no piano or radio was actually near enough to be disturbing. An ideal place for an author to work. A nip in this wind, better to get inside and be at the novel. Why was it that in moments perfectly fitted for concentration you never seemed to feel like it? Passionate urge to write always seemed to come when you were in the subway, or walking the street or when the clock was striking midnight.

The author, on the point of slipping inside the glass doors of her study, suddenly became rigidly still, gaze on a black pool of shadow at the rear of the garden. Something was moving back there! Someone — on all-fours apparently — was creeping through the gap in the hedge. Not John Ingram, who would walk erect and come forward, not lurk that way, back amid the shrubbery. The queer, bulky shape was humping along now under the grape arbor. Gail, with a thrill of thankfulness, recalled Bill, just inside the glass doors. She could see him, inside, ears pricked, listening.

The humping shape had cleared the grape arbor now and emerged into less dense shadow by the delphinium bed. And revealed itself as a huge umbrella seemingly propelled by feet attached to four short white-clad legs. Some sort of maneuver was taking place behind the umbrella, now tented on the ground in such strategic position that nefarious operations would be screened from any prying eye in Lilac Cottage.

In less time than it takes to tell it, Miss Ormsbee was across the garden and around that defensive umbrella.

"What are you children doing, this time of night? In my garden!"

"Nothin'." Fiske, squatting on his heels in the delphinium bed and busily wielding a kitchen stove-shovel, produced the disarming password that always gave momentary reprieve from pounce of Nemesis. Behind him, Fredricka stood guard over a basket of evidently precious content. Both children were in their white cotton flannel bed suits. Fiske had buttoned around his middle a wool sweater, but the legs of his pajamas were soaked to the knees. Fredricka trailed a crib blanket, attached around her neck by a safety pin. She had tumbled down and was mud from chin to ankle. One little foot had shed its slipper and sank deep in the wet grass. She began to whimper, for she was cold and damp and a little frightened. The night was darker than when she had set forth and descent of Nemesis had been so very abrupt.

"Where's your father?" Nemesis demanded.

"Stwummin'."

"What?"

"Strummin' on the piano." Fiske diligently pursued his digging, making time while he could. This was a most interfering person. He wished she had never come to Lilac Cottage.

Gail recalled John's vague allusion to evening occupation. She had just heard music — but it hadn't sounded like her idea of casual strumming. She could hear more plainly now, at the rear of the garden. Whoever was playing that Chopin polonaise was doing it pretty well! "Do you mean to say that is your father, playing now?"

"Um." Fiske had quite a deep hole by this time. Miss Ormsbee stooped and grabbed away the shovel. (Her delphiniums, just coming up!)

"Where is Katie?"

"Out. She's gone to the movies over at Millington. She takes the bus."

"Didn't anybody put you two in bed?"

"Favver did. We thaid our prayerth," Fredricka assured virtuously.

"Then how did you get out here?"

"Back stairs." Fiske was sulky. He had changed his mind about this lady whom his father seemed to admire. She assumed that children were always wrong. He explained truculently: "We had to bury Sleekie's kittens. Katie wouldn't tell us where they were but we found 'em in the cellar. Somebody drownded 'em. But Freddy'n I hid 'em so the garbage man couldn't take 'em away like he did Sleekie's last ones. Freddy'n I was goin' to give 'em proper bur-yal. We had 'em hid all day in father's patent leather shoes 't he wears with his dress suit. Freddy's pallenbearer."

Fredricka here produced from the basket a limp object and held it up for inspection. "They wath awful cunnin' kittenth."

"I guess four little baby kittens deserves proper bur-yal well as anybody," asserted Fiske belligerently.

"But not in my garden," objected Nemesis, though more gently. She took the limp kitten from Freddy's clutching hand and put it back in the basket. "We'll have to find some other place —"

"But this is our reg'lar cem'tary!" protested Fiske.

"Lots o' things is buried in this corner by the grape arbor. Two squirr'ls and some toads. And birds —"

Miss Ormsbee recalled an unpleasant object which she had mentally accused the innocent Bill of depositing in her delphinium bed.

"Well, you are not to do it again, do you hear? You children are to keep out of this garden. If your father can't make you, I will; understand that! I'm writing a book and I can't —"

Fredricka sneezed.

The author swooped upon her, lifted her, trailing blanket and all, and with command to the male culprit to follow with spade and basket, made for the gap in the hedge.

Fiske, padding after in soaked felt slippers, persisted: "We got to bury those kittens. That garbage man —"

"All right," promised Gail, a little breathless because Fredricka plus the blanket was no light burden, "I'll ask your father to bury them."

"Tonight?"

She promised, and he trotted along after her, carrying his precious burden. They went up, under the apple trees at the rear of the Ingram yard, and along a path that led to the kitchen door. From two windows of a wing that extended at right angles to the main house mellow lamplight streamed out into the dark. Music also. The *Liebestraum* of Liszt, played with such intense feeling that the player, one knew, must be lost in his music and unconscious of aught else in the world.

And two little forgotten children, soaked and chilled, wandering in the dark! Indignation swelled in Gail's heart. Not so much at John — one couldn't blame John, who could make music like that — but at the situation. At something. She wasn't sure what. Her arms pressed more closely around the bundle in her arms. The little body felt very soft and somehow appealingly helpless. There was instant response to the protective, tightening grasp. Two small arms went up and clung around the bearer's neck.

"That's right, Freddy, Gail can carry you easier that way. Cold?"

"Not vewy."

The music flowed out at them as they approached the house. The draggled procession mounted the back steps and went through the kitchen and along a passage to the front. It was the first time Gail had been in John's home. A nice house. Gracious spaces. Pleasant doorways. A wide, shallow-stepped stairway curving to regions above. But a neglected house — a glance told her that. Chairs and tables set at awkward angles. Curtains unevenly hung. Pictures a little askew. If that O'Hara person had any eye at all she would straighten them instantly.

A living-room at one side of the hall; newspapers strewn about in there, no flowers anywhere. A beautiful mahogany console table defaced by fingermarks. These things Gail's eye noted in passing. The procession halted at a curtained doorway; — the slight girl holding the heavy child, the small boy in soaked felt slippers carrying kitchen-shovel and basket of defunct kittens.

The musician, lost in the *Liebestraum*, played with gaze on the open window beyond which was the wet spring night. Where had John learned to play like that? Why had he never said anything about it? He "strummed the piano." He also "pottered at golf." And was "so-so at bridge." How little she really knew about John — except surface things. How little, it came over her in a flash of self-rebuke, she had ever made effort to find out.

The eyes of a portrait over the piano beamed down at the player, lost in his dream. A lovely, golden-haired young creature; — her dress something filmy and white, her bare arms heaped with pale pink roses. The late Mrs. Ingram, of course . . .

The music ended with a crash as the player became aware of the group in the doorway. He sprang to his feet.

"It's a pity," said Miss Ormsbee, depositing Fredricka, blanket enwrapt, on the floor, "that you can't see that your children stay in their beds when you've put them there."

"Where were they?" demanded the dazed parent.

"In my garden — as usual!"

Being further informed of the evening's enterprise — a recital three times interrupted by Fiske's insistent, "She promised to make you bury 'em yourself 'fore Katie sees 'em" — Mr. Ingram faced Miss Ormsbee, a hand of each bedraggled offspring grasped in his.

There was something helpless and pathetic about the three of them.

"What'll I do with 'em, Gail?"

"That's your business, not mine." The author waived all responsibility.

"Shall I spank them?" He looked despairingly from one offender to the other. "You decide. They are beyond me."

"I should. Then maybe they'll remember to stay in their beds when they are put there."

Freddy, from beneath tangled curls, peeped at this unexpected female. Any other, having cuddled you in warmly protective arms (and the arms had cuddled; who was better able to judge about cuddling than herself?) would now be pleading for clemency. "Won't be 'panked!" she said decisively — and sneezed.

Gail caught up a folded steamer rug from a sofa and wrapped it around the tiny girl. "Get them warm, for heaven's sake, John. And spank them afterward — or talk to them, if you think that will do any good." She moved toward the door.

John followed her. "What's the matter with your face?"

Her hand flew up and recollection occurred that she had never gone upstairs to wash off mud cast on her by irresponsible riders.

"You fell down," said John accusingly, "carrying that heavy child!"

"I did not. Do you think I'm incapable of carrying a four-year-old baby a hundred yards? I've done it often enough when I wasn't as big as I am now. That's the trouble," she inserted irately, "I got too much of it once and it's no treat to me now. If you want to know what happened to my face, I met your dear friend, Miss Vernon; and her horse splashed mud on me."

For one reason or another Gail felt waspish tonight.

John beamed. "You met Jule? I suppose she recognized Bill. Did you speak with her?"

"She spoke to Bill. She's coming to see me, she says."

"You don't like her," said the mere man regretfully. "I thought she was the one you especially wanted to meet. She could do a lot for you in this place, you know. Corking girl, Jule."

"Why should anyone do a lot for me? I'm perfectly satisfied — and quite contented." Gail moved down the hall. "If you could keep those constituents of yours from interrupting me when I'm working."

He followed her to the back door, switching on a light in the kitchen as they went through it. She forbade his walking home with her. The children must be got to bed at once, and given some warm milk. And he wasn't to forget: those kittens had to be buried tonight. She had promised the children; and promises to children must be kept.

She refused pressing invitation to come upstairs and help put the tykes to bed. "That's your job," she retorted, the dimple appearing unexpectedly through the mud-smudge. And she appended, as she ran down the back steps, "Not mine, thanks be!"

Her own job was waiting for her, quiet and absorbing and congenial. Through the glass doors, as she crossed the garden, she could see the lamplight in her study and the lustre vase of lilacs on her writing-table. Bill's nose was glued against the inside of the door. That was the nice thing about dogs: they looked reproachful only when you left them, registering joy exclusively, on your return. They never blamed you for anything — or made you feel self-rebuked.

She worked with fierce concentration and accomplished chapter six. Regina came in and tiptoed up the back stairs. The concentration had to be fierce — and determined — because there kept recurring intrusive memory of poor John, easing the loneliness of his silent house by losing himself in music. With the pictured eyes of the dead, golden-haired woman gazing down at him from the wall, and two small children prowling out of doors in their nightclothes on a raw spring night.

Some female with ordinary intelligence ought to be looking after that family. Of course not anybody engaged in important work of her own — but somebody. That Vernon girl had intelligence but probably she preferred that dog kennel of hers to taking care of helpless little children. (There was curious subconscious satisfaction in this, despite derogatory opinion of one evading a plain duty).

Later, from the bathroom window, the author glimpsed a moving light in the Ingram yard. John, burying the kittens! He must have waited until Katie was home and in bed, before attending to the interment. It was to be hoped he had changed into shoes and was not out there in those thin soled slippers.

Nothing on earth made so much trouble as children — for everybody in their vicinity. Well, there were no hampering responsibilities of that sort in the way of her own career. She didn't intend there should be.

CHAPTER X

Brooks and Buttercups

THE peonies were out. They all seemed to come out at once, when the long rain was over, under a warm June sun. Peonies to send in long parcels stiffened with split pasteboard dress boxes to Hilda and Arlene. Peonies for the house: flaming, deep colored ones on the little hall table where they were reflected in the ancient mahogany-framed mirror that had been a lucky find in one of those Third Avenue places; dawn pink peonies in tall vases in the living-room; white ones in a blue jug on the porch. Spicy peony fragrance all through the house. One need not be economical, as in the city where three peonies posed in a single vase were a treat. Gail massed a dozen pale pink ones, short of stem and framed in encircling leaves, in a low bowl for the breakfast table, and feasting her eyes, forgot to eat her cereal.

She carried an armful of peonies over to John's house where Katie O'Hara received them at the kitchen door with an inimical expression.

"What'll I be doin' wit' 'em?"

"What does one usually do with flowers?" retorted Miss Ormsbee who had not fought her way up in a business atmosphere without recognizing antagonism when she encountered it. She was not currying favor at the Ingram domicile by bringing gifts and the O'Hara manner distinctly conveyed that implication. This O'Hara person, Gail opined, disliked the owner of Lilac Cottage because of troublesome injunctions not to let children run wild in convenient back yards. But in spite of strong opinions about rights and wrongs of behaviour, Gail was so constituted that she preferred friends to enemies. Remembering that a soft answer turns away wrath, she showed the dimple.

"I thought you would enjoy some peonies around the house. You haven't any garden —"

"What time have I to be idlin' in gardens? But thank ye kindly, Miss." Katie remembered her manners. She warmed to that smile with the dimple as everybody did. "Himself will appreciate yer attintion, I'm sure. 'Tis only that I git wore out, bein' so busy, wid all th' ladies pilin' flowers on him come spring's beginnin'; an' me havin' to find joogs an' jars an' forever be changin' th' wather. A great boonch av these same p'inies come from the Vernon place this very mornin' an' what I'll be puttin' 'em all in I dunno. But himself'll be thankin' ye, Miss. I daresay he enj'ys 'em."

"Never again!" resolved Miss Ormsbee, returning with Bill through the gap, cheeks flushed and head high. So the Vernon girl sent John flowers! (She also had noted the unhomelikeness of that living-room.) And his faithful housekeeper cherished secret derision for single ladies who showered blossoms on the lonely widower. She would! Everything her own way in that house, and no one to interfere with her — window shades at all heights, pictures askew on the walls and mahogany lusterless and finger-marked. And two children running wild through the neighborhood.

"If I ever have anything to say about it, that woman will be the first thing to be sent flying," reflected Miss Ormsbee.

And then was furious at herself for even imagining such situation.

She seized the garden shears and savagely clipped away lower leaves from the hollyhocks which had to be thinned in June (the garden manual instructed) so that other plants might not be crowded. Next week she must transplant the baby salvias to the place where they were to make an autumn glory. And she must not forget to sow those zinnia seeds by the fifteenth. Such a lot to do in a garden! You couldn't just enjoy it as it was; you had to keep one jump ahead of it all the time. But with a garden to look after, and a novel to get on with, and a thousand words of fashion copy to turn off every day (in order to eat while you did the novel) you had no time at all to worry about either deserving widowers or idle women who dashed about on horseback, patronizing you and assuming ownership of things hitherto imagined exclusively your own.

John — the lamb! Well, if one wouldn't have him for her own lamb, what mattered it whose lamb he was? There was no room for lambs — the author snipped briskly with the garden shears — in her full life at any rate.

The girl next door said something, later that morning, that was bothersome.

Gail was picking pansies. The only trouble with pansies was that you had to keep picking them (to keep the plants healthy, the garden manual said) and though they were such cunning flowers to look at, outdoors, a few of them went a long way, in the house. Gail, picking pansies industriously, was hailed by a blithe voice:

"You're a terrific worker, aren't you?"

The girl next door was leaning on the little gate in the hedge. The sun dappled her white frock and made glorious her red-bronze hair that was cut in a proper bob but crisped all over in little rebellious crinkles and curls. Her bare brown arms rested on the gate and a tennis racket swung from her hands. Gail laughed, sitting back on her heels and shoving aside a loosened lock of hair with a grubby hand.

"It's my first garden, you know. I'm so afraid of neglecting it. Won't you come in?"

Gail liked this girl with the merry brown eyes and saucy, tilted nose. She had come over at last to make friends!

"Couldn't. Sorry. Have to work up steam for the tennis tournament. The prof and I are coming some evening to do the polite. My dad, you know. He's Doctor Holbrook, headmaster of the school — not a real professor of course. Just my pet name for him. I'm Mimi Holbrook."

She was making playful jabs with the racket at Bill who had raced to the gate, friendly tail a-wag. "I'm here now to beg. The old ladies who used to have this garden always sent mother some of the peonies. She's just aching for some of these peonies, can't keep her mind off them —"

"Of course!" Gail sprang to her feet. She ran to the gate and flung it open. "I'm so glad you came."

"I've been dying to. I'm the prize little gate crasher and I was bound to get in, the first excuse."

"Why shouldn't you?" Gail was slashing away with her garden shears and piling long-stemmed blossoms in the other's arms. "I'm so sorry about your mother; I've seen her wheel chair up on that sun porch—"

"Her spy glass too, haven't you? She can't get out, you know, and things do interest her — especially anything new."

"Oh, I didn't mind."

"Didn't you? I'd have been boiling. She can't see across now on account of the trees, but you want to watch out when autumn comes."

"She's welcome." Gail laughed. She felt gay and hospitable, with this pleasant new neighbor, come to call on her.

"You know my mother has a very special interest in this garden — I suppose you have heard all about that. You haven't? Oh well, you will. Everybody does, sooner or later, around here. It's the reason Jimmie Jessup and I meet in the ravine. You won't say anything about that I know —"

"Of course not."

"If my mother found out there'd be a terrific row. And if Mrs. Syd Jessup found out — well, there'd be a cataclysm. In other words, hell would bust loose. But I knew you weren't a tabby, the first time Jimmie and I talked to you. I liked your eyes — they are so blue and sort of straight-ahead looking. I've been wanting to make friends —"

"So have I," confided Gail cordially.

"Well, now we are. That's settled, isn't it? And I'll have you on my side," concluded Miss Holbrook with satisfaction.

"Who's on the other side?" Gail asked, amused.

"Four determined parents — though the male contingent might be brought round, I shouldn't wonder," amended Miss Holbrook, "if it weren't for the females. Adamant is putty compared with them. Not that I am worrying, or Jimmie. Merely biding our time till he is twenty-one. In September."

She looked speculatively at the gap in the hedge. "You and John Ingram are pally, aren't you?"

The manner of Miss Ormsbee became a shade more reserved. "He has been very neighborly."

"But you knew him before you came out here, didn't you?"

"In a — a sort of business way."

"Oh — was that it? Well, J. I. is a peach and if you take my advice you won't let 'em worry you. People always talk, no matter —"

They had come to the gate and Gail, on the point of swinging it open, turned startled blue eyes on her guest. "Why should I be worried? People talk about what?"

"Well, naturally," Mimi's brown eyes laughed, above the nodding peonies, "they can't help being *interested*."

"Interested in what, Miss Holbrook?" The Ormsbee manner now was distinctly dignified.

"Oh, do call me Mimi — everybody does. I sha'n't believe we're friends if you don't. Well — they are interested in you: your coming here without any staid duenna or anything like that. And choosing a place with these high hedges all around —"

Gail stiffened. "I write, you know."

"Yes, I know." Mimi's eyes twinkled. "A wonderful alibi."

She laughed outright at Gail's frozen expression. "Don't mind me. Jimmie says I'm impossible. And don't be mad; I'm not accusing you of anything. I know well enough you write — haven't I heard that typewriter going sixty-to-the-dozen? But you know, my dear, you do look per'lous young to impress folks as having no more ardent pursuit in life than lit-er-a-toor. You'd be surprised," she chatted on in the face of Miss Ormsbee's ominous silence, "if you knew how they are all guessing about your age. The prof was thrilled when he heard a lady author had moved in, next door. Somebody with brains to exchange ideas with at last! Then he saw you picking lilacs and he said, 'Far too young and pretty to be very weighty, intellectually.'"

Gail could not help laughing at that — and feeling a bit pleased too, in spite of underlying indignation.

Mimi continued, "And when Mrs. Syd Jessup was talking about you at the country club last week —"

"At the country club!"

"Sure. You're the newest excitement. You don't know country places very well I guess. Mrs. Jessup insisted you must be around forty, living here alone and all. But Jule Vernon said she didn't think you could be more than thirty-one or two —"

Thirty-one or two! Another count against that Vernon girl. The immediate impulse was to broadcast at once through this lively partisan the plain truth of a mere six-and-twenty... Better not, however. Twenty-six, unchaperoned behind tall hedges, would be infinitely more "interesting" to inquisitive minds than a safe and staid thirty-two. The age of

an author was unimportant anyhow — one should
remember one's main object in life! "What did you
mean," Gail asked, "when you made that remark
about an alibi?"

"Now you really are on your dignity." Miss Holbrook was remorseful. "And I was only trying to
warn you — passing you the high sign, you know.
They say much worse things about me and I don't
give a whoop. One has to —"

"'Worse things'?" — that was as far as Gail had
heard. "Do you mean they are saying really unkind
things about me? What sort of things?"

Mimi saw the warm color in Gail's cheeks. "Now
don't get all fussed up," she admonished. "They
haven't started anything like that. They are just
curious."

"But what about?" Gail looked bewildered. "I
wanted a little house in the country; and I —"

Mimi's nod expressed full and satisfactory understanding of youth's prerogative of independence.

"To write my book in," insisted the author.

Mimi nodded again. "But don't work the writing
gag too hard — not in a place like this. Look here,
Miss Ormsbee, we're friends, aren't we?"

Gail's blue eyes, troubled and irritated, met the
brown eyes that smiled at her over the peonies. Her
own frown faded and the dimple reappeared. "Of
course. But I can't see why you said a thing like
that — 'alibi'."

"Well, it's this way:" Mimi hesitated, evidently
considering the advisability of careful steering. "I'm
no tabby either, you'll find that out if you know me
long enough. And I like you, lady. I liked you the

minute I set eyes on you. And I'd like you anyhow because John Ingram does. Anybody he picks out has recommendation enough for me —"

"Picks out!"

"My goodness, you are prickly about your boy friends — I suppose it's being an author, and temperamental." From the other side of the gate Mimi grinned impishly at her neighbor within the garden. "Be that as it may; and it's your business, no one else's, my advice to you — if you don't contemplate sooner or later announcing any engagement — is to produce that work of literature in reasonably snappy time."

And with racket gripped under one arm and the peonies nodding over the other, she raced down the slope, hopped across the brook on some stones, and dashing up the further slope, waved the tennis racket before she disappeared.

All of which was the reason Miss Ormsbee had an unsatisfactory afternoon in spite of conditions ideal for literary production. The house was heavenly still. No juvenile voices were audible even outside the hedge. June shadows lay softly on the grass and peonies in wealth of bloom made charming objective for wandering eye during mental pursuit of illusive phrase. But the novel went poorly. Finally the author abandoned her desk and went out to weed the garden. Weeding is a vicious business; it gives you a chance to yank at something.

Alibi! . . . amusing. The good honest work that had kept a roof over her head and food in her mouth for almost ten years. She wished people who talked so easily of alibis could try doing a thousand words of copy a day for three hundred days in a year and see how they liked it. Alibi indeed! No, it was not amusing; it was infuriating. In this day and generation a woman of brains and ability could live where she liked, sufficiently protected by the dignity of her work. No modern, independent-spirited woman would let her poise be affected by 'curiosity' or 'interest' of idle gossips. It was mid-Victorian to care about what anybody thought. If she were Arlene she would snap her fingers... But she was not Arlene; she knew she cared very much for other people's liking and approval. She was over-sensitive about it — that was the trouble.

Hedges were all right, after fifty, Hilda had declared; before that, they invited suspicion.

Nonsense. It wasn't the hedges that had made these women "interested." It was John Ingram on the other side of the hedge. If she had taken that house with the picket fence out on Long Island nobody would have said anything about alibis. The whole thing was John's fault — establishing her here at his back door...

But if John hadn't, she would never have had this adorable house and garden. So much more desirable than that picket fence place. She looked at the June shadows lengthening on the grass; at the cool darkness of the ravine with the afternoon sun now dropped behind the trees. Tinkle of the brook came through the still air. Butterflies hovered over her peonies. She veered away from John's culpability.

No use calling on Hilda and Arlene for sympathy. They would merely utter cynical "I told you so's" and further inane remarks about the futility of trying to go bourgeois and pursue a career at the same time. And if she poured out her exasperation in a letter to Rosamund, Rosamund would ignore the point of the whole matter and prick up her ears about John Ingram. Rosamund had a fundamental feminine fixation about marriage and nothing else being the end and aim of feminine ambition — in spite of that shiftless Tom Lovelace. Give Rosamund a chance and she would state what, in her opinion, Gail Ormsbee should do with her life. Notwithstanding the very substantial assistance Gail's successful business enterprises had brought her way.

Besides ... Rosamund might take it into her head to come north for a visit. And before any visiting relatives invaded Lilac Cottage, the possessor of that idyllic retreat proposed to get full benefit herself of its quietude and its opportunity for concentration on work. You could not impart perplexities to relations, anyway. They always knew how much better you would have fared had you managed the way they would.

She would talk to nobody. She would simply pursue her own dignified way and rise above gossip and curiosity of people who had no worth while ambition in life and no absorbing work of their own. And meanwhile, the less she and John Ingram — for the present — saw of each other, the better. She would convey that idea to him, tactfully, but with uncompromising firmness.

Therefore when she encountered Mr. Ingram during her stroll with Bill that evening, her greeting — for a lady who had that morning carried floral offering to a gentleman — was reserved.

BROOKS AND BUTTERCUPS 133

It was a beautiful evening. Overhead a June breeze stirred the treetops and a little sickle moon was dropping down behind the hills. Between the Holbrook place and the turn toward the stone bridge a narrow footpath wound between fairy hedges of buttercups, the golden blossoms on feathery stems, waist-high as one walked between them. Gail lingered in the buttercup path, listening to the brook whose murmur was always loveliest at twilight. From far away came the long whistle of a train with that agreeably remote suggestion the sound has in the country: something that emphasizes our own aloofness from a world's crude clamor. After a truly upsetting day the author felt soothed and quieted. Then, rounding the turn, she beheld on the bridge the cause of all her troubles. Lounging idly, pipe in mouth, Mr. Ingram looked comfortably at peace with the world and the evening.

Bill, tail a-wag, dashed forward in friendly greeting. Bill was no one-man dog. He gave of genial affection to all who enjoyed his mistress's favor. (And he had been led to believe this nice fellow was one of these.)

Miss Ormsbee's greeting, as has been mentioned, was restrained. Polite — yes, certainly, but in no wise warm.

"What's up?" inquired John anxiously. (He could not recall any unfavorable report about juvenile pursuits of the day.)

"Up? Nothing."

"Then why the frosty eye? What have I done?"

"Nothing. I didn't expect to meet you, that's all."

"My mistake," acknowledged Mr. Ingram meekly.

"But I suppose I have a right to stroll out and see the moon rise — I mean, set. Look behind you — no, over the other shoulder! It's a new one, you know."

"I saw it." Miss Ormsbee dismissed foolish superstitions. "What are you doing, way down here by the bridge?"

"Just thinking," said Mr. Ingram. "You overlook the fact that this has been my favorite spot for twilight contemplation for years. As a matter of fact" — he gently took her elbow and, facing her round in a homing direction, stepped along beside her — "I was on my way to visit you. I've got a new contraption for you."

From a pocket of his loose country coat he produced the contraption: the latest marvel in weeding-hooks. A nifty looking contrivance; the gardener perceived at once its possibilities. Her enthusiasm rose.

John demonstrated its excellence, attacking some weeds by the roadside. "Fellow said it fairly spirited them out of the ground, with no effort at all. I was bringing it around to you."

Gail laughed. Any heart concerned with gardening projects would have melted over that weeding-hook. "I'll say you took a lot of trouble — walking half a mile with it. Why didn't you come through the hedge?"

"We-ell," Mr. Ingram hesitated. Then he produced resourcefully: "I sit a good deal during the day; exercise is good for me."

So John also had been advised of "interest" in doings of lady authors with no sturdier protection than hedges.

Protection — ridiculous archaic term expressive of the very spirit of the Victorian creed. The petty suspiciousness of these protected women! Gail felt all the antagonism of the self-supporting woman who competently conducts her own affairs, toward these others who sought to judge emancipated souls by their own hampered standards; who tried to make the enviable free woman pattern her life to fit their little concepts of propriety. These women who had always been taken care of and whose first preoccupation was and always would be to make sure — no matter what calamity befell the rest of the universe — that responsibility for their own maintenance should not devolve upon themselves.

And here she had been, at first hint of their disapproval, afraid of them. Afraid to be herself with her good friend, John.

What if they were "interested"? Whose business, as that clever little Mimi had pointed out, was it, but her own and John's?

Suddenly upswelled within Gail a fierce instinct of protectiveness of her own — though not at all would she have so labeled it or admitted that it proved her sister to all these others for whom she experienced such fine contempt. Nobody was going to interfere between John and herself, or be allowed to spoil their friendship.

He strolled beside her, hatless, through the June dusk. Birds called sleepily in the wood that bordered the road and there was splash of water where the brook, under the bridge, tumbled over a great stone. John looked so nice in these country clothes — the freshly ironed white knickers and dark coat — and with hair sleekly brushed, still wet from a before-dinner shower. Good old John, the best friend she had!

She questioned him interestedly about affairs at the office, and listened to his relation of matters concerned with publication of a trade journal. And told him she was going into town soon to interview her chief at the Buyer and Retailer about the Fall Styles Supplement copy that must be tackled by July first. It was all as jolly and pally as strolling across from the office to her boarding-house in the East Thirties. And they arranged a little dinner and a theater for the evening of her day in town.

In the buttercup path they had to walk closer together and John slipped fingers under her elbow — as one does, pushing with a friend through a narrow space. The young moon was hanging now just above the dark line of the hills. Dusk was merging into soft June night. High over their heads the treetops rustled and near at hand was the tinkle of the brook. Bill plodded behind, satisfyingly tired after his good run. Gail was telling John about the bird bath she planned to get for that grassy space among the rosebushes. The moonlight on it would be lovely. "Don't you think so, John?"

"Swell!" he enthused with the occasional lapse into outrageous slang that he maintained was so restful to an editorial laborer. "I'll come around and help plant it."

"You'll come across, through the gap," she directed briskly. "I guess you can step into my back yard now and then without the whole neighborhood getting excited."

"There's one way, of course —" John stood still in the buttercup path and since her elbow was gripped she had to stop too. He bent down and looked into her eyes. "You know what I mean, Gail."

Her blue eyes met his. They could just see each other in the dusk. For once, she didn't bound away, physically and spiritually, at such suggestion.

His arm stole round her. "Couldn't you, Gail?"

Leaves whispered above their heads. The brook's ripple was intensely clear. No other sound except the far off honk of a taxi on the turnpike. Gail had sudden, inexplicable impulse to yield to that arm, so closely and strongly holding her. To let John shoulder all responsibility. Something — the sweetness of the June night, the whisper of the leaves, the murmur of the brook — made her want to yield to John ...

John felt the slight relaxing of her body to his clasp. He whispered huskily. "We need you so, Gail — Fiske and Freddy and I —"

That was unfortunate. In a second she was three feet ahead of him, brushing buttercups aside with her swift movement. Bill, who had sat down patiently, got up and dashed ahead.

John was a patient chap. He looked at the uncompromising back moving along ahead of him. She had relaxed — yielded — for an instant. No mistake about that. Well, he could wait ... but it was a pity: a summer night like this, and the years flying so fast ...

They were down in the hollow by the ravine and he was about to start further argument when Miss Ormsbee turned and clutched him by the arm.

"John! What's that?"

"Where?"

"Up the hill — in front of my hedge. It looks like a station taxi. Who is getting out?"

Gail raced up the slope. It was a station taxi and the driver was assisting out of it an elderly lady and countless bundles.

"Is that you, Abagail? I'd never have recognized you. I'm your cousin Prunella Poppe — your dear mother's second cousin twice removed. Your sister Rosamund wrote me about how smart you were and how you had a place of your own now. 'Tisn't fitting for a girl young as you are to be living by herself. I've come to stay with you a spell."

CHAPTER XI

On Bird Baths And Home Truths

GONE, security of an author's isolation within encircling hedges. Gone, soothing comfort of well-ordered routine. No more pleasant breakfast trays on the porch followed by leisurely perusal of the morning paper. Or hours of dreaming peace within a garden.

Miss Prunella Poppe pervaded the place. And she never stopped chatting. She was up at six, long before Regina (which caused immediate dissatisfaction) and her tongue did not rest until her bedroom door was shut at night. She even begged to have bedroom doors left open, but on this Gail was adamant and immediately cultivated the habit of reading and scribbling in bed till all hours, safe behind a bolted door.

For Miss Poppe loved to chat. She had begun the moment of her arrival when she sat down with a definite air in Gail's living-room while John fetched in odds and ends of packages. The packages were done up in brown wrapping paper with patent handles for convenient carrying thrust through the string. Four or five packages could be carried in one hand — far less expensive than expressing a trunk! Gail recalled that cousin Prunella Poppe had arrived with just such packages at the St. James Place house in Brooklyn. Relatives had always been arriving for extended visits. Papa had been bored, but then he was out so much. Gail remembered how Cousin Prunella Poppe had fluttered and bridled when papa teased her, and had doted on having him stay home of an evening and sing. Gail could see again the St. James Place parlor: with mamma languid and pretty on the sofa, a worsted "throw" over her feet, and papa by the piano singing *Punchinello* while Miss Poppe struggled with the accompaniment, a rapt expression on her visage and bony hands stabbing at the keys. She had always cried when papa's touching tenor came to "One winter's morn they told him sweet Columbine was dead . . ."

Cousin Prunella Poppe looked much the same; spare and angular with thin ash-brown hair (gone rather gray now) crimped the same way in front. And she had the same band of black velvet around a lean throat above a jabot of pleated net that modestly filled in the V of her bodice. Gail wondered if she had gone on making those jabots for almost twenty years, always the same way. Miss Poppe's nose was pointed at the tip, suggesting, Gail was sure, a ferrety instinct; and her pale blue eyes had a way of half closing when she listened to you, as though she suspected you were not telling quite all the truth. Later, Gail discovered this was because she needed glasses which she was unwilling to adopt. She wore skirts to her shoe tops and the shoes — wherever she had procured them — were the neat button kind of before-the-war. Gail heard her remark one day that she was proud to say she had never worn a silk stocking, or a silk *anything* next her skin. It made a woman feel creepy, she averred, and have not quite nice thoughts.

She was the kind of old-fashioned spinster who adhered to the Victorian code of keeping-things-pleasant, even if one had to pretend a little to do it, and whose idea of excellence in behaviour was the supremely genteel. "Such a lady, my dear!" was the highest praise she could extend, in speaking of another female. And she put no faith in any man (except, of course, ministers of the Gospel,) though the presence of a gentleman in the room robbed her of poise and made her self-conscious and arch. But until she was convinced of the safe intention of a male, he was "that man." On the evening of her arrival, when Gail returned from bidding John goodnight at the porch door Cousin Prunella Poppe inquired suspiciously:

"Who was that man?"

"A neighbor, Cousin Prunella. Would you like to go up to your room now?"

"Is he married or single?"

"Well — a widower."

"I see. Where had you been with him: coming up out of those woods?"

"There were no woods. That road goes down through a ravine. I was exercising my dog and I met Mr. Ingram." Gail, furious with herself for offering explanations, picked up five or six of the packages and stood aside for Cousin Prunella to precede her up the stairs.

"I see. Well, seems to me it was high time some of the family came here to stay with you. Living in this unprotected way is bad enough for a single woman, your age, without traipsing round after dark with widowers. I felt all the time Rosamund didn't approve or she wouldn't have written plain directions how to get here."

All of which, said with an effect of sprightly gaiety, moved her hostess to controlled fury... Because Mr. Ingram, slipping through the porch door, had just whispered humorously, "At least now I can stroll over frequently — and through the gap. Instead of hiking half a mile to your front door. A chaperone was just what we needed."

Miss Poppe settled down with every evidence of making herself cosily at home. The contents of the paper bundles amply filled bureau drawers of the guest-room. She had even brought her hymn book and her Daily Thoughts calendar, with something bright and encouraging to start every day of the year when you tore off the leaves. She approved Abagail's thrifty efforts at furnishing though she had never cared herself, she said, for daubing up honest walnut with sea green paint, nor for making beds look foolish with ruffled coverlets you had to remove at night — instead of using good white marseilles spreads that gave some weight over you. But it was a real comfort, she averred, when somebody in a family set up a nice home where a body could come for a visit and feel welcome.

"Boarding's no life for a home-loving female," declared Miss Poppe. "But what with everybody moving into apartments with no spare rooms, a single woman is likely never to get out of a boarding-house, once she's in." And visiting round, Miss Poppe admitted, did save room-rent.

Gail looked anxious. "You haven't given up your

room in Elmira, have you, Cousin Prunella?"

"No. There's my own carpet on the floor. And some of pa's and ma's furniture. But a woman with two children was glad to find a nice room with kitchen privileges and a door to the side porch. She's taking care of my bird."

Thank goodness for one blessing, reflected Miss Ormsbee; the bird hadn't come too. An author and a cheeping canary in the same house —!

"I sub-rented," announced Miss Poppe, "till September."

September. And this was only the beginning of June!

The Perfect Treasure waited on the breakfast table, the morning after the guest's arrival, with an expression of austere disapproval. And when Gail went to the kitchen later to discuss luncheon (the gay little tray of sandwiches and glass of milk, amply sufficing an author who liked to pick up her mid-day snack when she came to a place where she could stop, must now be abandoned of course) there was muttered objection to elderly ladies who came poking and prying into icebox and pantry.

"We not care for relatives making visits," said the Perfect Treasure. "We engage service with one in family and weekend guests."

Gail's blue eyes filled with tears. She was feeling very low this morning. Why couldn't you run a house like a business office? Anybody upsetting to office morale could be fired at once. But what were you going to do with relatives who planted themselves on you with a lot of bundles and took your hospitality for granted?

"Oh, Regina," she implored, "stick it out with me! We'll get rid of her somehow."

Compromise was effected by slight raise of wage scale during periods when guests remained more than three days under the roof. And by firm assurance that kitchen domains should be sacred from intrusion.

An author's study might be considered equally sacred, but as many an author has discovered, it is so difficult to impress upon members of a family the delicate balance of creative imagination. Three times during the morning Cousin Prunella presented a deprecatory face in the chink of the study door protesting that she wouldn't interrupt for more than a minute. But (the first time) what was the name of the minister at the Methodist church? It might be he'd preached up at Elmira. (And the second time) If Abagail had any number eighty spool cotton she might as well be hemming those new table napkins she'd just found in the linen closet. (And the third time) Would it bother Abagail any if she sat on the porch? 'Twas pleasant to look at a garden while you sewed and of course she wouldn't speak a word. But every six minutes she dropped her scissors. And each time they clattered to the floor the author's concentration fled to the four winds of heaven. Finally, when Miss Poppe tiptoed with elaborate caution through the study, (having left her handkerchief upstairs) the typewriter stopped with a crash and the author gave vent to an exasperated sigh.

"Now, now, don't pay any attention to me, any more'n 's if I weren't here," enjoined Miss Poppe cheerily.

"I'm afraid you'll have to sit somewhere else, Cousin Prunella. The porch is really part of this room when the glass doors are open. You see I am doing literary work —"

"Certainly. Certainly." Miss Poppe looked at the typewriter with slight awe. On it this smart young woman made enough to run a house. "I wouldn't think of interfering, Abagail, when genius is burning... What you writing now — a love scene?"

The author hastily whipped paper out of machine. What she was writing was a letter to Rosamund and it contained a Piece Of Her Mind.

"Oh, well," Miss Poppe nodded with benevolent understanding of authorish sensibilities, "likely you wouldn't want to show anything to anybody unless it was in print. Same's a cooked chicken looks more inviting than a raw one. I'm sure I wouldn't want to intrude. By and by when we get settled in a regular rut we'll know each other's ways better. And, speaking of cooking, there's no earthly use now, having that girl cluttering up the place. Wasteful she is — don't tell me! Ordering lamb chops over the telephone, with a good steak tailend in the icebox for a tasty hash. You let her go and I'll attend to the cooking. 'Twon't be any job with just two women, eating light. And you can put that girl's wages into the bank."

"I couldn't let Regina go, Cousin Prunella. You see when your visit is over —"

"You don't have to worry about that," assured Miss Poppe. "I could plan to stay right along. You and I being, as you might say, two lone spinsters in the family, seem's though we might join forces.

There's a Methodist church here. I could settle down real comfortably. And I certainly feel I'm needed."

But under too much strain even the most controlled forbearance must snap. Gail came in from her after-dinner tramp with Bill, cheerfulness somewhat restored by the serene loveliness of the evening and by a pleasant chat at the Holbrook's gate with Mimi and her father. Doctor Holbrook walked home with her. A really delightful person, Doctor Holbrook, witty and whimsical and with old school courtliness of manner. Miss Poppe had been sitting in a front window.

"Who was that man?"

"A neighbor, Cousin Prunella."

"Why didn't he come in?"

"I didn't ask him. He merely walked up the road with me."

"Seems's though you do a lot of walking up that road evenings with neighbors." Miss Poppe was arch again. "This one a widower too?"

"No." Her hostess answered rather shortly from the hall where she was hanging up Bill's leash.

"Where's his wife?"

"She is an invalid."

"Hp-hm," Miss Poppe cleared her throat with that annoying, significant sound with which Gail was becoming familiar. "Your father was quite a one to gallivant. Maybe you take after him."

This was exasperating, but Gail held her peace. She loved peace too passionately to shatter it for doubtful satisfaction of resentful retort. But her mouth was set in a straight line as she went up the stairs. No dimple was imaginable in conjunction with that stern line. Changing to slippers in her bedroom, she was summoned by a sibilant whisper from the stairfoot:

"Abagail! What's that man doing in the back yard? He never got in the front way; I've been right here in the window. The girl's out and we're all alone in the house."

Miss Ormsbee stepped to a rear casement and threw it wide.

"Hello," called up John Ingram, who appeared to be measuring off paces in the grass, "I was going to surprise you — saw you go out with Bill. I've got the bird bath. Come on down."

Miss Poppe, fluttering out to the garden, took great interest in the bird bath. And in Mr. Ingram whom she found to be a very pleasant gentleman — once you knew he was all right. She liked pleasant gentlemen. She thought Abagail might be more gracious about the attractive ornament he had so kindly brought for their garden. She made quite a little fuss about the bird bath herself, to make up. She regretted when heavy dew forced her indoors and departed, cautioning Abagail about thin slippers in wet grass.

"John — what can I do?"

"Don't look so downhearted, my dear. Why do anything? She seems a harmless little person. You expect people to come and visit you, don't you?"

"But I didn't want anybody — for a long while."

"You have plenty of room and a competent maid." He was tamping down the turf around the little bird bath. "I think it is a mighty good thing she has come — for some reasons."

"You don't understand how she'll bother me," said Gail irritably. She felt irritable tonight — and imposed upon. John might be more sympathetic.

He was carefully pressing down the turf, close to the bird bath, with his foot. "The trouble with you, Gail, is that you hate too much to be disturbed."

Her head went up. "Why shouldn't I?"

"You are going to be almighty sorry someday if you let that habit get ingrown. You know what Emerson said once: 'Be careful what you set your heart on, for it will surely be yours.'"

She knew of course that what John had at the back of his mind, talking about "disturbance," was that pair of tiresome children. Her blue eyes were cold, matching her dignified manner. "I have my work to do. Fairly important work, to *me*." She stressed that. "Haven't I struggled for years in an office against constant 'disturbance'? Now that I can afford peace, why shouldn't I have it? Haven't I earned it?" She was angry because she couldn't keep a quiver out of her voice.

John had brought a bucket of water and now carefully poured the water into the bird bath.

"You can fill it with the garden hose, nights," he instructed in parenthesis. "You are still pretty young, you know. Only in your twenties. Most people don't feel they deserve immunity from turmoil — their quiet backwater of peace — until they are at least in their fifties . . .

"After all," he went on, gathering up trowel and bucket, "what have you given — to life — yet, Gail, that life should grant you immunity from all bothersome disturbance?"

She was coldly furious.

"I think you are beastly," she said, "to take that tone with me. You haven't the least right to do it. I wish you'd carry your old bird bath away — I never want to look at it again!" And she flew into the house, Bill racing after her and only just slithering through before she slammed the porch door.

She would telephone Hilda and Arlene. At least they, earnest pursuers of careers of their own, would understand. And appreciate her predicament. It was provoking that she had to wait until Miss Poppe was in bed, and then sneak noiselessly downstairs and close the study door — before she could use her own telephone to call up her own pals.

Arlene's voice came over Hilda's wire. Hilda was giving a party and was in the middle of a rarebit. Arlene appreciated instantly the impossibility of an author's being pestered with chatty relatives in that ticklish period of creative effort that produces the first draft of a novel.

"We'll come and smoke her out," Arlene promised. "Just leave it to us."

But she couldn't refrain from an I told you so. "If you'd taken a one-and-bath in town it wouldn't have happened. Your loving kinfolk don't stay long when they have to bunk on the parlor sofa and dress by the bathroom mirror. Or when you take 'em out to restaurants for dinner. They never feel pained about your extra expense if you feed 'em at home, but somehow it puts 'em in the wrong, not to offer to go Dutch on restaurant eats."

"But she insists on sharing food-expenses." Gail's voice was depressed.

"She does? Must be a decent old duck. Though that kind is hardest to get rid of. Determined to stick. Well, here's hoping we'll be too many for her."

Hilda came to the phone for a word. "We'll be out next week. Too late now for this weekend. Expect us in our warpaint and armed with our hatchets."

"It's good of you, Hilda; I know how you hate rooming with anybody."

"You might tell auntie — or cousin, is it? — what a hardship it is to have tother guest room occupied ... But seriously, Gail, don't get too upset about it all. The situation has its points. You don't absolutely have to get that book done this summer, but you do have to establish yourself solidly in that community within the first six months — if the place is ever going to be any satisfaction to you. Why not an elderly, beyond-reproach relative for a few weeks, even if she is trying. I'd say myself it was a good idea."

"You don't have to stand her," said Gail.

"I don't," admitted Hilda, "but you and I are different propositions. Well, I can see your side of it. I'll do my best."

But Gail felt that even Hilda had failed her. Hilda — who had been such an inspiration with her successful independence and her accomplished work — offering instead of whole-hearted sympathy Mrs. Grundyish suggestion about advisability of chaperones! Hilda was as bad as John Ingram.

At any rate, thought Gail grimly, tiptoeing back past cousin Prunella's door, with *that* in the house there would be no further occasion for remarks about "alibis."

CHAPTER XII

Church Bells In The Village

TO YOUR peace-lover, who consistently avoids altercation, brief outburst of temper is far more devastating than a whole day of tidy rows to the irritable individual in whom wrath is no more than escape of a safety valve. Though Gail's indignation remained at white heat for twenty-four hours — because of Mr. John Ingram's presumption in undertaking to tell her what, in his opinion, was the matter with her character, deploring the self-centeredness of one who did not profess enthusiastic delight about sharing her home and her time with elderly maiden ladies who came and camped on her to save room rent — though she steeled her soul against the offender, effort to keep it steeled made a wreck of her. For two days she felt limp — and a little ill. Unable to enjoy meals at any rate. Quite unable to concentrate on work. And Miss Poppe, perceiving her hostess's inertia, outdid herself to be chatty and companionable.

It rained, so escape to the garden was impossible. And anyway, the bird bath was out there. Through the slanting rain and protruding from the drenched grass, it had the melancholy look of a little tombstone, suggestive of something buried and lost. It looked even more tombstonish at night when the light from the bathroom window picked it out with a spotlight ray in the dark. Just as well one didn't see the garden much at night.

That had been another outrageous count against Miss Prunella Poppe; — depriving the homemaker of back bedroom windows. It had been such joy, these soft June nights, to linger in the open casement, scent of honeysuckle coming up through the friendly dark and the young moon making leaf shadows on the room wall opposite the casement. The still, full content of that late hour shared with her garden had been one of the precious things the new home had brought.

Why should she not resent the shattering of that content? Why should she be willing to share immediately what she had so long labored to achieve? John was unjust!... Asking what she had done to deserve peace! Hadn't she supported herself since she was seventeen, instead of being a burden on anybody? Hadn't she sent regular sums to her sister Rosamund at sacrifice of comforts for herself? Wasn't she at work on a book that might (how could John Ingram say to the contrary?) be inspiration to countless souls? Wasn't ambition for work like that worthy of being safeguarded?

Men safeguarded their work all right. Imagine Mr. John Ingram suffering a chatty old lady for one hour in that editorial office of his, merely because she happened to be a second cousin of his mother. Imagine any man doing it. But a woman's work and ambition were nothing, of course. Men measured worth in a woman by the yardstick of their individual needs. If you looked to them like a potential good wife and mother (what they thought they needed at the moment being a good wife and mother in their home) you were an estimable, even a noble person. If you concentrated on a career that threatened to interfere with their own plans, then you were selfish and self-centered. And they didn't mind telling you so.

A man's friendship meant nothing at all. He was incapable of looking at your affairs in the abstract — comprehending your need — as another woman would. What you were, in yourself, meant nothing to him; what you might be to him was what counted. All his pretense of interest and pleasant little gifts (like bird baths and patent weeders) and his little festivities in your honor (like restaurant dinners and theaters) had an ulterior motive. Couldn't you, Gail ... Meaning: "My children are neglected and my house is a mess; what's success with a book or two compared with that?"

It was always what they wanted. Long ago, during that first foolish little love affair of hers, she had found that out. Back in 1917. She hadn't been a poised and sophisticated business woman then. Only midway through her teens, a young thing carried away as everybody else had been with war excitement and fervor and hysteria. Drudgery and discontent at Rosamund's. So many children to tend. So many dishes to wash. Disorder and slackness that never got caught up with because Rosamund was that kind. Evenings, jollifications to cheer up the boys before they sailed away to France. Laughter to forget tears. Feverish gaiety because of Fear — Fear, always looming just ahead. And Gail Ormsbee, an emotional little schoolgirl, caught up by it, whirled along by it. Slipping out at night from the untidy apartment and Rosamund's complaints to dance and to be irresponsibly young: what she had thought of, in the moment's jargon, as "doing her bit."

A brief and tempestuous love affair — pitiful, looking back on it now. Joyous, because they had both been so young. Full of laughter because parting and tears were so imminent. Insistent, because all the world's values were awry. Only today left. Only tonight. Only this one hour... "Won't you, Gail? Won't you? Won't you?"... And so nearly she had; for nothing had seemed to matter then but surrender of self. Glorious giving...

If she had... Her whole life might have been spent regretting it. He had turned on her at the last; flung away from her in anger. "You've a hard streak in you, Gail. Too many brains and too little heart, that's what's the matter with you. Self-concerned you are. If you weren't, you'd think of me, not yourself — me, going off to be cannon fodder!" Sorry for himself, he had been, for all his jaunty bravado of the young soldier. In 1919 someone had told her of his marriage to a girl he had met at a canteen in France. But that had been after the long months of watching for letters that never came, the reading, sick-hearted, of lists of wounded, the sleepless nights and wet pillows. And then concentration on work and, with discovery of her own ability, awakening of ambition.

Now she was twenty-six and had too much sense to let a man's demanding whisper (*Couldn't you, Gail? Couldn't you?*) and some urge of physical nearness, some trickery of Junetime, stir her to impulse — oh, only impulse, but frightening! — to yield. To forget the career mapped out for herself. To harken to the possessive summons: Give up your life to me. Give up your will to mine.

If you wanted to own your own future, you had to keep free of men.

And stay in a working environment — she said that to herself sardonically. Stay where other people were working and domesticity was discounted; where hearthstones and cookstoves and gardens made no appeal to submerged homemaking instincts. Where you could meet men briskly (with a pencil behind your ear, so to speak) in an office, or pal with them — good fellows together — and juggle smart cynicisms over a restaurant table... not in buttercup paths beside murmuring brooks.

Well, if you had real character and authentic ambition, you could have domesticity (your own kind, not somebody else's kind with a string tied to it) and a career too. And you could prove it to Hilda Braithwaite. And to John Ingram. And to all who were "interested."

But wrath cannot be kept forever at boiling point, nor even righteous indignation. The sun came out and so did some of the roses, adorable little amber colored ones on a tall bush. And the bird bath no longer looked tombstonish, but rather jolly, a gay addition to the garden with little feathered things splashing and spattering in it — so quickly had they discovered and made use of it! And on Sunday Cousin Prunella Poppe went to church. The Methodist edifice was at the far end of the village — a good half hour's walk each way. Gail spent a blissful morning transplanting salvia seedlings.

Busily and happily digging little holes (with an orangewood manicure stick as the garden manual instructed) and pouring in water before inserting tender rootlets, the contented gardener wondered what on earth she had been feeling so cross about. It had really been awfully good of John to lug that bird bath out from town, probably driving his car all the way in, to do it. Of course John Ingram mustn't be allowed to think he could buy her with presents. But there was no sense in being churlish...

And after all, since people were so "interested," perhaps it wasn't a bad idea to have Cousin Prunella here now, instead of later. She'd have been certain to turn up some time. A sort of chaperone on the premises wouldn't do any harm until one was accepted without speculation.

Carefully setting inverted strawberry baskets over the transplanted seedlings, (as the garden manual advised: to keep off full force of the sun until they took hold) Gail hummed happily "I know a lovely garden..." and abandoned further wearing effort to steel herself in wrath against anything or anybody. It was too nice a morning to bother.

Church bells in the country had a lovely sound — mellower than church bells in town. A fretful tempo to city church bells, a dictatorial note, as though they were, a little irritably, trying to detain attention above din of automobile horns. Ding...! Across these wide spaces: reminding you what day it was. Dong...! A whole minute later: solemn and compelling. Not another sound except twitter of birds and ripple of the brook in the ravine. Peaceful.

Mr. Ingram appeared in the gap in the hedge. He carried a golf bag and grinned amiably at the line of inverted strawberry boxes. (If he had been worrying about anything for two days he didn't betray it, unless by exceptionally enthusiastic response to Bill's cordial greeting.)

"Mind if I step through your diggin's? Car's out of order and cutting across to the links this way saves a long stretch."

"Step along," said the busy gardener hospitably. And when he had stepped three steps and leaned the golf bag against the arbor, to rest it, she added: "Where are your constituents this morning?"

"At least you miss 'em; that's comforting. They've gone to Sunday school."

Gail smiled approvingly. "I see you have a proper conception of parental duty."

John did not smile. "I do the best I can. When I was a kid I had to go, and my kids will go. Maybe Fiske'll play golf Sunday mornings when he's a tired business man, but at least he'll have something underneath his golf complex — for times when golf can't suffice. If you get what I mean."

"I do, John. I'm glad they go. Who takes them — Katie?"

"Jule Vernon stops for them on her way down; and picks them up when she goes back for old Mrs. Duryea. The old lady's eyesight has failed and she can't get to church alone. Jule takes her every Sunday."

"How very nice of her!" Miss Ormsbee straightened a strawberry box.

"Jule's one of the best," Mr. Ingram agreed.

"She gets in her nine holes while my youngsters are at Sunday School."

"And can spend the whole afternoon on the links," Gail murmured.

Mr. Ingram always stood up for his friends. "Well, at least she goes to church, Sunday morning." He grinned at the long bivouac of strawberry boxes.

Gail laughed. "Shadow Hills doesn't quite approve of garden labor on the Sabbath, does it? But of course golf is different! That's the beauty of these tall hedges: nobody knows how sinfully industrious I am. People who live by conventions never do appreciate that a writer has to get things done when she can. These church-going ladies don't have to run a house and plant a garden with one hand while the other hand earns their living. I'm willing to let those who do half my job and therefore have twice my time, take care of the proprieties."

"Very well put," conceded John. "Though if you are referring to Jule Vernon, she runs a pretty thriving business with that kennel —"

Gail flushed. "Oh, I wasn't referring to her. I'd forgotten her." She glanced rebukingly at his golf knickers. "I gather you are not attending Divine service yourself this morning."

"But look at the morning!"

He was not looking at the morning, however, but at her. She had bound a wide ribbon around her head to keep her hair from tumbling forward while she stooped over the garden bed. The ribbon was deep blue, matching a crisp linen smock, and both were exactly the shade of her eyes. The coat of tan she was rapidly acquiring gave her skin a golden glint and through the becoming tan warm color showed. She sat back on her heels before the flower border — a position that only supple and vigorous youth could retain.

No trace of office pallor now, or of that tense little line between nervously knitted eyebrows. Here was a face, possessing as he had always known, a fine intelligence. With potentialities of tenderness, or there was no believing the curve of lips (when they were not set too firmly together). And of gay companionship (when that dimple showed itself). But this morning, a face downright pretty. Mr. Ingram studied it.

"I remarked —" Miss Ormsbee dug industriously with the manicure stick — "If you stay away from church yourself, why should it concern you what other people do?"

"Well, you know," Mr. Ingram admitted ingenuously, "I'd like to feel that the mother of my children would be there."

"And that's exactly where you'll be likely to find her." Miss Ormsbee pressed in the root of a seedling. "In view of all the other admirable qualities the applicant will have to possess."

"You betcher," responded Mr. Ingram.

He bent down and picked up something from the brick walk under the grape arbor. "Nice jack-knife. Not mine. Who's your other gentleman friend?"

"It might be the milkman's; he comes through this way sometimes."

Mr. Ingram laid the knife on the rim of the bird bath. "Better take it in the house. Bad thing for the children to pick up."

"They won't pick up anything that will hurt them if they keep out of this garden," reminded Miss Ormsbee with perfect good humor.

"None of us would!" said Mr. Ingram. He lifted his bag of golf clubs and with a word of cheerful farewell, went his way, around the house to the road.

Gail looked after him. Maybe he had meant to sting, with that last. She had really felt so friendly toward John, too, this morning. It was always hard to tell, behind that quizzical way of his, whether he was just being funny — or meant something more.

Miss Mimi Holbrook's auburn head popped round the hedge, over by the gate.

"I didn't like to interrupt. But I'm dying to see the bird bath John Ingram brought you."

"How did you know he brought it?"

"Mrs. Heddon who lives back of us — and of course next door to the Ingram place — saw him toting it down through his back yard to that gap in your hedge. She's a pal of mother's; runs over every day."

"And now I suppose," said Miss Ormsbee, "all Shadow Hills has learned I had a present of a bird bath."

"Well, what of it? You don't mind, do you? It's a peach of a bird bath." Mimi drew nearer to admire the new garden ornament — pounced on the jackknife. "Jimmie Jessup's knife! He's been looking everywhere for it."

"How on earth did it get in my garden?"

Mimi hesitated. "Where was it?"

"Under the grape arbor. John Ingram picked it up."

Mimi regarded the knife thoughtfully. She slipped it in the pocket of her sport frock. "Well, anyway it's found. Miss Ormsbee — tell me: I'm so thrilled and I won't breathe it to a living soul — are you and John Ingram really en —"

Gail had drawn herself up with dignity, as far, that is, as her kneeling position permitted. "I am not interested in Mr. Ingram — in that way."

Mimi was unabashed. "Aren't you? I don't see how you could help it — seeing so much of him and all. I could be quite mad about him if it weren't for Jimmie. But J. I. wouldn't look at me; thinks I'm a kid because he used to pull my pigtails and call me 'Red Head.' That was when his wife was alive. You never knew her, did you?"

"No."

"She wasn't a bit like you. One of those sort of appealing little things. Golden hair. The purring kind. Always talking about 'my babies.' And having her photograph taken with 'em. Freddy was only six months old when she died but I bet you John Ingram has a couple of dozen photographs of the three of them: Fiske by the chair — sturdy, 'my little son' effect you know, and Freddy in her lap. And her eyes down and her pearls on. She was always saying to people: 'My big man and my babies.' I didn't care for her much. Jule Vernon couldn't abide her."

"I dare say not," thought Miss Ormsbee. But if John Ingram was so partial to madonna types, why on earth —

"Of course," Mimi was placidly fitting three pansies together, back to back, "there is something pathetic about John Ingram — playing that piano all by himself evenings because that O'Hara woman wouldn't stay if she couldn't get out nights and you can't leave children alone in a house. Everybody hopes he'll find someone soon to help him with those children."

Miss Ormsbee diligently planted salvia seedlings.

"But of course," Mimi tossed the pansies away regretfully, "you can't love a man if you can't."

"Love is a subject I am not concerned with," said Miss Ormsbee, hitching her oilcloth kneeling-cushion along. "You see I have my writing."

"I know." Mimi nodded respectfully. "Though Mrs. Jessup says authors have to have had hectic pasts, to put things in books. I guess it's true, though, you haven't much sex consciousness."

Gail laughed. This absurd child! "I don't think about it all the time, at any rate." Then she looked up sharply. "You 'guess it's true' . . . who said anything about it?"

"Jule Vernon did. Maybe she meant it for a compliment. The girls were changing in the club locker room and somebody said something about you — about your eyelashes I think it was — and Jule said you impressed her as a person with a lot of common sense and not much sex consciousness. Hello, there's Jimmie waving, down by the brook! We're going for a spin in his car while his fond parents are safe at church." She was off, the gate swinging madly behind her.

Why one should be so furious it was difficult to explain — when such had been exactly the idea one had been endeavoring to convey: a person of sound common sense and complete lack of sex consciousness. But the curiously annoying speculation presented itself; — was that also Mr. Ingram's opinion?

Once, during one of those friendly, argumentative little restaurant repasts, he had made a remark that recurred now:

"Sex sublimation — that's what you would-be intellectual young women are trying to achieve with your writing and your painting and your self-absorbed solitary existence. What waste!"

Why was it waste? Sex, as everybody knew, who knew anything, was a force that could spend itself, if not in one way, in another. A creative force that was the basis of all achievement. The force that was back of enthusiasm and energy and the will to work. Mind was not enough, you had to possess that force too. If you chose to put that God-given fire into work that should stand in ultimate beauty as expression of your spirit, if you chose to give to posterity that way, why should a John Ingram venture to call it waste?

She was, however, so absent minded at dinner (which on Sunday was served at one o'clock for benefit of Regina) that Miss Poppe babbled on unheard. The Jessups had brought Miss Poppe home in their car. Mr. Jessup was a charming man. A little henpecked maybe. Mrs. Jessup was the one who had the money. She was highly thought of in the Methodist church; head of the entertainment committee — though that might be because she had such a big house. She was coming to call. When you went to church you got acquainted with the best people.

Miss Poppe had met also a Mrs. Heddon. The Ladies Aid would meet at her home this week. "Quite a piece to walk, around by the road, but she said if I went through the Ingram yard it wouldn't be more than a step." Miss Poppe looked arch. "I told her that would only be fair exchange of courtesies and she looked sort of twinkling and said, most likely I'd find a path already well worn. They all asked why you didn't come to church too, Abagail. They seem so interested in you."

Gail went for a long walk with Bill that afternoon. Not anywhere near the golf course. (Sometime since she had decided that, casement windows costing what they had, club membership this season was out of the question.) Anyhow, now, she didn't think she would care about hanging around a country club. A place full of idle women. Gossipy. She went instead out into the meadows beyond the bridge and gathered an enormous armful of daisies for the porch jar.

Bill had a wonderful afternoon.

CHAPTER XIII

June Moonlight

HILDA and Arlene arrived with the roses.
All at once the garden was a glory. Pink roses, like lovely debutantes. Red roses, flaming and passionate. White roses, gleaming in the dusk. Gay rambler roses tumbling over the hedge and making a fairy bower of the kitchen porch. And the great bush of little amber roses that Gail loved best of all; they were so prickly to gather, but so perfect, massed in a bowl of pale green glass on the study table.

Encompassed by roses, the white bird bath basked in the June sunshine and all day long on a branch that overhung the hedge, a song sparrow almost burst his little throat, trying to "let his illumined being o'er run with deluge of summer."

Hilda said Gail's rose garden made her sentimental. Whereupon Arlene protested that Hilda was the most sentimental old thing on earth, in spite of her published book of sardonic humor. "Plump and sentimental," Arlene tagged injury to insult. "Hilda can get teary over a tired shopgirl. She never yet passed a beggar without slipping him a quarter — when he probably had more in the bank than she has. And if you take her violets on her birthday she fairly blubbers.

"Not that I condemn her," Arlene added benevolently. "We artists have to search for truth, but what's an author without sentiment?" "Wring their heartstrings:" good old formula. Any Broadway show that does it, runs a whole season no matter how the critics pick on it. And what woman really enjoys a novel that exercises only her perceptive faculties?

"Let Arlene rave," said Hilda comfortably, deep in one of Gail's wicker porch chairs. "If those passionate petunias she did for a wall panel at the Scribblers and Splashers club were Truth as perceived by the artist, give me the safe emotions of a controlled pen."

Gail laughed. "Remember that evening I dropped in, Hilda, expecting to apologize for disturbing your book-reviewing; and found you eating fudge and listening to Heart Throbs Hour over the radio? . . . She was mopping her eyes, Arlene, and the tenor was trickling honey notes: "Sweetest Story Ever Told." She was just wallowing in slush."

Hilda was unperturbed. "Calms me, after wrestling with highbrow phrases, trying to be more cryptic and caustic than the other reviewers to show the lay mind how brilliant our book-column is. You can't be brilliant, just praising something; it takes satire to reveal wit. If you two suffered nightly bouts with this new reflective fiction in which heroine's neurotic musings reveal everything about her that's safe to print, you'd seek surcease too in moonlight and roses and sweetest stories ever told."

Hilda fixed Gail with a meaning eye. "Isn't there something in it?"

"How should I know?" said Gail. "Ask Regina. She's the one who goes out, evenings."

But Gail flushed and Hilda, noting the flush, smiled contentedly.

Gail laughed more, that weekend, than she had laughed in months. It was good to have these pals of hers about. They spoke her language. Conversational exchange needed no careful reservations for fear somebody might imagine a personal slap. It was like men's talk, forthright, good humoredly challenging. The talk of women who earned their own living. Fearless. Abstract, not personal. No spiteful undertones. One had missed it.

Hilda and Arlene filled the house with laughter and with argument. Simple as children one moment over some brief enthusiasm, deep in sophisticated controversy the next. Miss Poppe watched the pair with anxious eye and bated breath. She never knew what they were going to say next and kept shocked ears pricked. They argued about Foreign Policy relations and birth control with equal zest. And the things that amused them were a mystery to her.

Their clothes appalled her. If any of the Methodist ladies should happen to call, reflected Miss Poppe fearfully, and behold those costumes. Miss Braithwaite's get-up was comfortable and mannish. Tweed skirt and jacket. Beautifully polished oxfords (costing, had Miss Poppe but known, more than the most frivolous buckled slippers). Gray hair, cropped short. Nose glasses on a ribbon. Miss Poppe, watching the frequent exchange of the glasses for horn-rimmed spectacles, inquired, "Why on earth don't you wear bifocals?"

"Impede your step," Miss Braithwaite explained. "No more dashing down subway stairs and leaping off trolley cars. Never put on bifocs unless you are willing to feel fully sixty and act it."

The other one, Miss Poppe decided, looked even more outrageous — from a Ladies Aid standpoint. Her smock blouses of bizarre pattern had strings of beads — magenta and saffron and bold blue — repeating the blouse colors. Her little flat-heeled slippers contrasted oddly with swinging earrings of utter sophistication. And under her fluff of pale gold hair were hazel eyes that had a disconcerting twinkle. It didn't do to bandy words with this one.

Arlene, on the first evening, had with the best intentions in the world halted Miss Poppe who was departing for a chat with Mrs. Jessup next door. (Amazing, how Miss Poppe had made acquaintances all over the neighborhood and had half a dozen places to "run over to" for informal chats.) "Wait a second, Miss Prunella," called Arlene helpfully. "I can see your petticoat."

Now, no lady likes to be reminded that her petticoat is visible — a condition implying slovenliness. One takes it kindly only from a beloved friend. Miss Poppe came back crisply, "And may I mention that I can see your bare knees!"

Arlene, who rolled her stockings, produced that disconcerting twinkle. "But, my dear Miss Prunella, they are not wearing *petticoats*."

The two had come to smoke the spinster out and they were doing their best. Cigarette stubs littered every available receptacle in the house. They smoked and Miss Poppe coughed, delicately, but nobody asked her whether smoke annoyed her. She made one protest but the incorrigible Arlene was too much for her. Discoursing on relative advantages of oil and pastel for floral subjects, Arlene was as usual seeking mislaid matches. Hilda reached in a pocket and flipped her a patent lighter.

"It does seem reasonable," observed Miss Poppe, "if females assume menfolks' privileges: to adopt their pockets too."

Arlene swung round on her with the twinkle. "You consider smoking a masculine privilege? Just because men did it first? They wore ruffles first, and also plumes. The real reason you gentle Victorians are so peeved about feminine cigarettes is because they have robbed you of a prime asset of what you thought charm. You used to dote on telling gentlemen how you just loved the smell of smoke. Now you can't — and be consistent. Admit the truth, Miss Prunella."

Miss Poppe, who had been emptying ashtrays for fear Shadow Hills might call, had just encountered Gail similarly engaged and obviously impelled by the same anxiety. The two had exchanged a humorous grimace that somehow established comradeship between them. Miss Poppe now said tartly, "Abagail doesn't smoke."

Abagail, admitted the artist regretfully, was far from being a free soul; her ambition was lilacs inside of hedges.

"What I hope," Miss Poppe glanced at Hilda, in whom, for all the masculine pockets, she had more confidence, "is that Abagail will get married. This writing business is all foolishness. She ought to have a good man looking after her and a family to do for —"

"I know what you mean," interrupted Arlene with enthusiasm. Swinburne puts it so tenderly:

"... made meek as a mother whose bosom-beats bound
To the bliss-bringing bulk of a balm-breathing baby."
Ever read Swinburne, Miss Prunella?"

"No," said Miss Poppe, "and no lady I knew of ever did!" She flounced out of the room.

"Oh, leave her alone, Arlene," Gail said. "Don't bait her so."

Miss West opened childlike hazel eyes. "But I thought that was what we came for; — to get rid of her."

"I know." Gail frowned. "But after all she's a good sort. She made the most delicious biscuit, Regina's night out, and insisted on doing the dishes — said she just hankered to get in the kitchen. And she has mended everything she can find in the place. She isn't so bad, now I've got used to having her round."

Changing the blouse and beads, which was her method of dressing for dinner, Arlene said gloomily to Hilda:

"Beyond hope."

"What is?"

"Gail Ormsbee. Six months more and she'll be sunk. The perfect pattern of domesticity. Did you notice how hostess-nice she was, never butting in on a guest's conversation, even though she had a bright thought to get in first? Polite restraint — first symptom. And all the time you were telling that excruciating story about the bishop, her attention was on the maid — to make sure the potatoes were passed a second time. She cared more about the way that meal went than what we were talking about. This place is getting her."

Hilda said placidly, "Why not? If she likes it. Did Gail ever really fit in, do you think, with that bunch in town?"

Arlene groaned. "But the woman can write!"

"Well," remarked Hilda, "there are other things women have done."

Hilda and Arlene, Gail admitted, were stimulating — but they were trying, too. More trying than cousin Prunella, in some ways. They cared for only two things: driving work and spasmodic play as relaxation from work. And they had an avid intellectuality that was a little pitiful of life's simpler satisfactions. For instance, agreeable comforts and niceties of a well-run home — details that required infinite thought and planning — were entirely unappreciated by them. They had dutifully admired the green and white breakfast china and then forgotten it, in absorbed discussion of an editorial in the morning paper. And the way their bedroom looked when Regina went in to tidy up was a disgrace.

The little dinner had been perfect, with tall yellow candles and a bowl of yellow roses reflected in cool, bare mahogany; and iced pineapple cup served in the amber glasses. Hilda and Arlene hadn't half appreciated it — or Regina's perfect service. But it fed something in Gail's soul, the order and daintiness, the graceful hospitality she was able to extend.

And now the moonlit garden. Gail leaned back in a long chair, hands clasped behind her head, heart full of rich content. They were lounging on the porch after dinner. Miss Poppe had gone to a strawberry festival at the Methodist church. The garden lay bathed in moonlight and scent of the roses was heavy on the air. The bird bath, touched by the moon's magic to alabaster whiteness, threw an ink black shadow on the clipped grass. So still was the night that ripple of the brook down in the ravine came clearly . . . And also, drifting across the sleeping garden, the B-flat nocturne of Chopin rendered by an unseen player beyond the hedge.

Arlene leaned forward. "Who is that, playing?"

"John Ingram, I suppose," her hostess mentioned. "He strums every evening."

"Some strumming!" observed Arlene. "Don't know as I'd want to listen often to that music . . . and look at this garden," she waved her cigarette in the long holder. "Not if I expected to concentrate on work."

"Keep still, can't you, Arlene?" implored Hilda. "And let us listen."

They listened — for several minutes. The unseen musician had changed his music now. Grieg's *Ich Liebe Dich* was sweeping through the night. Gail stirred restlessly in her chair. The moonlight and the sweetness of the roses — the almost classic loveliness of the white bird bath above its ink black shadow. And that music. As Arlene had insinuated: upsetting . . .

She wished John would stop playing — things like that.

From where she sat she could see, through the glass doors, some buttercups Arlene had arranged with long grasses on her writing table. The light of the desk lamp focused on their feathery gold and gold flecks were reflected in the dark table top. Every chance glimpse of buttercups this week had given her a curious sensation — immediate environment vanishing and, replacing it, vivid recollection of the way an arm had felt about her ... hard, with firm muscles. A safe and dependable feeling about that arm, closing you in and leaving everything else outside. And a tenderness, flowing from its strength into yourself, making you for one mad instant want to yield to it; to forget things like ambition and independence and necessity for untrammeled freedom. Making you want to go all soft and unresisting — as that music John was playing made you feel now ...

Sentimentality! Not to be yielded to.

But Gail was honest enough to acknowledge it had been more than sentimentality, that night in the buttercup path. It had been another side of herself that she must not allow to play her best self false — the strong, sufficient self governed by her mind and her ambition. She sprang up, and going into the study, moved the buttercups out of sight.

"What are you doing?" Hilda called, hearing movement of articles on the writing table. She added that she hoped to heaven Gail was not going to read any of her stuff to them. Gail made appropriate rejoinder and, returning to the porch, was glad to see, coming informally through the garden gateway, Doctor Holbrook and Mimi. John Ingram strolled across later and they had a jolly evening, topped off by an elaborate iced confection concocted by John and Arlene in the pantry.

On the Sunday evening before Hilda and Arlene departed, Gail served supper in the garden. At this time of day the sun, sinking toward the hills at the

"He's a pretty nice dog, isn't he, Fiske?"

"Y-es."

"You like old Bill, don't you?"

"Y-es."

"You wouldn't want to put his eye out, would you?"

"No — I wouldn't."

"Suppose that stone had hit me? Would you want to hurt me?"

Fiske appeared not so positive about this. He temporized. "Aw, a sling-shot couldn't hurt anybody much." He was pulling away. He wanted to go home.

"You think it couldn't. Well, of course a boy who was really brave wouldn't mind having anything done to him that he would do to a lady. Now you stand up there..." She stooped and dug a pebble out of the flower border. "If there's nothing to it, how about my taking a shot at you?"

"Aw, you couldn't hit anything with it," said young Fiske contemptuously. "You're a girl."

"Well, then there's nothing to be afraid of, is there? Stand up now and I'll have a try." She was fitting the pebble into the sling-shot.

Miss Poppe cried out nervously and Hilda warned in a low voice, "Careful, Gail!" Miss Ormsbee favored the group with a glance that plainly said, "You let me manage this!" ... Then, briskly, "Ready, Fiske? You know what I said about a boy who wasn't yellow."

Fiske, looking distinctly sick, stood up valiantly. "All right."

Gail dropped her arm. "Well, I'm not going to —

because I wouldn't take the chance of putting your eye out. You may do that sort of thing, I don't. And I don't believe your father would, do you?" She walked over and put the sling-shot in his hand. "But so long as you don't mind taking a chance of putting people's eyes out, I'll stand here and you hit me."

"No!"

"Why not?"

"Don' wanta."

"Why not? You did it before — you hit Bill. Perhaps you didn't think, then, about putting eyes out —"

"Don't want th'ole sling-shot." Suddenly Fiske's obstinacy was gone. His little face was racked with remorse. Tears coursed down his cheeks.

Gail put her arm around his shoulders and wiped off the tears with her handkerchief. "Look here, Fiske, promise me you'll never again aim that thing at anything alive. Promise me? Then shake hands — hard. I'm not going to say anything to your father; this is just between you and me. A boy doesn't go back on a promise. Not John Ingram's boy! Shake?"

"A'right," said Fiske. The two hands gripped and Gail held the brown eyes with her blue ones. She walked to the gap with Fiske and as he stepped through, patted his shoulder for goodbye.

"Why didn't you give him some of this layer-cake?" Miss Poppe was all for coddling a remorseful penitent.

Gail shook her head. "That wouldn't be my way," she said. "He's got to think it over — not have the edge taken right off it by — cake."

And to think, reflected Hilda Braithwaite, of talent like that being wasted in mere literary production!

But Hilda chuckled, telling John about it later, when they had lunch together in town.

"Indignant at Fiske, you know, but furious with us for interfering. Her job, not ours, was distinctly conveyed. I wish you had seen it."

"If I had, he'd have got the walloping all right," said the fond father.

Hilda shook her head. "Gail was trying to get at him in a surer way, through his sense of justice. She's making friends with him, John. The experiment is working out."

John was moving forks and spoons about on the tablecloth, frowning down at them. "I'm not sure," he said gloomily. "Sometimes I think I'd have got further the way things were . . . Meeting in town just by ourselves."

Hilda didn't agree. "Suppose, that way, you had won her over. She'd have undertaken the children, but with considerable unwillingness underneath. That always spells antagonism. If she takes on the job now, it will be for the children's sake as well as yours — because she sees their need of her. And when Gail Ormsbee undertakes a job she sees it through."

John looked still more gloomy. "It's quite on the cards that having had a good look at the job she'll decide against it."

"Well, in that case," said Hilda, "isn't it better to find it out now than later? You owe something to those children, J. I."

He shoved the forks and spoons aside. "Summer's going — and I'm not an inch nearer than I was when she worked in that office upstairs. Oh, I'm a handy help in time of trouble. She'd call on me if there were a fire. But she doesn't need me a little bit. She's got a garden and a dog and a book to write . . . what more, I ask you, could heart of woman crave?"

Hilda laughed as she rose and gathered up gloves and handbag. "You're in such a hurry, John. You ought to know better, at your age. 'Summer's going' — like a ridiculous college lad. It isn't the only summer. Not to speak of a long, long winter when a garden is no company at all."

He laughed too. "It's that long, long winter I've been thinking about. But you are a good friend, Hilda. Come along, we have both got to get back on the job."

CHAPTER XIV

Afternoon of an Author

THERE is no pleasanter July sound, to your householder, than the sound of coal being put in. Others may not care on a torrid day for rattle of anthracite avalanching down a chute, but to the householder himself it is sweet music. No early settler, gloating over his stacked woodpile, ever felt more complacence than did Gail, hearing the good black coal cascading into her bins. It had cost a lot, but it was in! Everything in a house cost so much more than you anticipated. The fortnightly grass-cutting for instance, overlooked in first enthusiastic estimates ... Like having your hair bobbed for sake of comfort and then discovering the appalling cost of keeping it trimmed. Trips to town for haircuts, because nobody except a little barber in the West Forties could give just the right contour, added considerably to rural expenses. One couldn't go shaggy, running around all day without a hat.

On the town days there were also so many household needs to shop for. Department store bills expanded alarmingly. Yet it was such joy to get back, after the heat and din of the city in July, to serenity of her little house and garden that Gail felt any expense was worth it. Somehow she would manage — and of course when the novel was published there would be royalties coming in.

On one of the town days she met John and they had

dinner and a theater together. But on the late train, returning, there were several Shadow Hills people and Gail supersensitively felt their "interest" in little town jaunts for two. She resolved not to repeat the evening diversion in town.

Summer, as Mr. Ingram had observed, was going. And if summer goes quickly for an impatient lover, it goes even more quickly for the busy author of a book. Especially when there is also a garden demanding incessant attention. "Cut back the daffodils in July" instructed the garden manual. And "Now is the time to spray insecticide on the phlox." Nothing worked you harder than a garden manual.

But a July garden paid for all the planning and work. The phlox was wonderful; it had come up by itself, sturdy and common and cheerful, flaunting rich masses of color all along one side of the hedge. In front of it, sweet william, and in front of the sweet william lovely old-fashioned garden pinks within an edging of alyssum. Pink poppies and blue bachelor buttons in another border, a gorgeous tapestry of color. Calliopsis, rusty and feathery, behind flaming nasturtiums. Larkspur and canterbury bells with candytuft for a border. Little sweet scabiosa, cunning "pincushion flower" for bedroom dressers. Gail loved her annuals. They were alive because she had made them come alive, had planted the seeds, transplanted the seedlings. They were her garden children. If only, she thought, all children were so tractable, so lovable. Always where you left them. And noiseless!

At dusk Gail unwound the hose and watered her garden. John Ingram came over and helped.

"Why don't you bring your constituents?" she said one evening. It had been a good day; the novel had gone well.

John's face brightened. "They'd bother you."

"Not if they kept quiet."

"My dear girl, they couldn't."

"That's the trouble with children," acknowledged Gail regretfully. "You never can forget them when they are around."

He didn't bring the children. But he took heart that she had asked for them. That was something!

"You ought to get out more," he told her one Saturday when he dropped in and found her busy at her desk. "Didn't Jule Vernon come to call on you? She said she would."

"Yes," said Miss Ormsbee. "She favored me — thanks to your concern in the matter."

"Now, Gail, don't talk that way. Jule's a corking girl; she could make it very pleasant for you if you would co-operate a little. Didn't she ask you to tea at the club?"

"Yes — and bridge. I have no time for afternoon bridge."

"You'll have to make it, if you want any social contacts out here. These women do things in the afternoons. If you are going to play with 'em you'll have to adopt their playtime."

"I'm not sure I want to play with them," Miss Ormsbee remarked. "I have my book to do."

Mr. Ingram said something as he went down the porch steps, but only Bill heard. It sounded like "That damn book!"

Miss Poppe was also concerned about Gail's neglect

of social opportunities.

"You ought to come to church with me, Abagail, and get acquainted. You won't make any friends if you shut yourself up in that room all day, writing. Why won't you come in, when people call on me, and be sociable?"

But Miss Poppe's callers were all middle-aged matrons concerned with house and "help" and village affairs, and lean spinsters ardently engaged in church work and jealously competing for notice of the personable minister. The younger set who foregathered at the country club did not seek out a dignified householder who was also reported to be earnestly engaged in literary pursuits. Every day the golf course was dotted with men in knickers and girls in bright sweaters. Gail sometimes looked wistfully across at the links. Next summer, she promised herself, when royalties were coming in from the book, she would join the club and be out there too.

She went to the tennis tournament with the Atchisons who called for her in their car. The courts were sunny and speckless and tanned men and maids in speckless white clothes dashed about on them. From little chairs on the grass well dressed people watched the matches and chatted in low, well bred voices. There was something soporific, lulling, about it all. Still, hot air. Dazzling courts. People moving noiselessly on the grass. Muffled thud of balls on rackets. Droning voice of the referee. How different from the things business women did together on their Saturday half-holidays. This was another world. Gail wished she knew how to play tennis; she thought she would like to dash about those courts and whack at a ball with a good right arm. It would take it out of you, somehow, and be fun. Next summer...

She was introduced that afternoon to many pleasant people. They were cordial but some of them she thought looked at her speculatively after John Ingram attached himself to the Atchison party. Warren Atchison changed chairs so John could sit next to Gail. John mustn't assume such a proprietary air; — she was a little stiff because she was displeased. Presently when Jule Vernon stopped playing, he rose and strolled over and sat with her — for the rest of the afternoon. Then Gail felt deserted and a little indignant. This was foolish of course, John had not come with her. She was growing illogical and unreasonable, she told herself, like women who had no honest work to do and concentrated only on personal concerns. Better to keep away from this sort of thing if one wanted to get anywhere in a career. She was glad to get back to her garden and to Bill who gave her vociferous welcome. Here, within these hedges, was her kingdom and here her worth while work.

But upstairs in her bedroom, changing from flowered georgette back to familiar linen, she told herself that next summer she would join the club and learn to play tennis. What that Jule Vernon could do, she could do.

One morning Miss Poppe said at breakfast:

"Who was that man in the garden last night?"

Gail balanced the coffee percolator that was her special shining joy. "Man —?" she asked vaguely.

"After twelve, it was. I thought I heard thunder and while I was closing the window I saw his white pants and your white dress. I must say I was surprised, Abagail. If 'twas Mr. Ingram, seems to me you might do your courting on the porch before the house is shut up. He wasn't over here all evening —"

"But I was not in the garden at twelve o'clock last night, Cousin Prunella. You must have been dreaming."

"I wasn't dreaming. I know when I see white pants in that grape arbor, midnight or any other time."

The grape arbor! Gail remembered that jackknife. She would have to speak to Mimi Holbrook. Poor children, they had to meet somewhere. But if cousin Prunella had assumed it was Miss Ormsbee, philandering at midnight, somebody else might get the idea too. She could not betray Mimi to one who was now a frequent visitor at the Jessup home, but she convinced Miss Poppe that the white dress had been none of hers.

"It might have been that Katie O'Hara," considered Miss Poppe, "though she's several sizes bigger than you — especially in white. And would a hired girl's followers be likely to wear white pants? In a way, Abagail, I'm kind of sorry t'wasn't you and Mr. Ingram. He's *such* a gentleman. And you'd be marrying so comfortably."

Comfortably! Gail laughed outright — thinking of the terrible tykes. She must tell Hilda that. So admirable when a girl "married comfortably."

"Of course," went on Miss Poppe ingenuously, "I didn't have to. I had the income pa and ma left me."

"I knew that was the reason," Gail politely assured her.

After lunch she went out to the garden with shears and basket and while clipping flowers for the house watched for Mimi who usually started early for the tennis courts and would run across if summoned. Glancing down into the ravine, Gail was surprised to see what a well beaten path there was, up to her garden gate. Mimi frequently leaned over the gate to chat, but there must have been a good deal of meeting in the grape arbor also, to account for that well defined path. Of course young Jimmie, from his side, could easily swing over the fence into the Ingram yard and slip through the gap in the hedge. A convenient meeting place indeed, that grape arbor on neutral ground between two unfriendly houses.

Gail knew about the Jessups and Holbrooks now and why they never visited back and forth and exchanged aloof nods when they met. Once, Syd Jessup and Dan Holbrook had been pals and had ushered at each other's weddings and bought homesites near each other. Syd Jessup, handsome and debonaire and Nell Jessup, plump and domestic. Dan Holbrook, studious and stay-at-home and Sybil Holbrook, pretty and restless, forever craving a good time. And Mimi and Jimmie, playing together from the time they could toddle. Then one night, fifteen years ago, Nell Jessup's husband and the schoolmaster's wife going away together, each leaving a letter. They hadn't gone far. Scarcely outside the village the train had been wrecked and Mr. Syd Jessup and Mrs. Dan Holbrook, among the injured had been promptly carried to their respective homes

... but not before the letters had been read. Sybil Holbrook never left her room again and Syd Jessup, whose leg had been fractured, would walk with a cane to the end of his life.

Nell Jessup was a good Christian woman who did her duty. (She often commented on it herself.) There was no question of taking Syd back. He was back. And she made sure by her forgiveness and magnanimity and his abysmal need of both that he never got away again. After that she had him under her thumb. She had the money and she had built the house; she had her Syd made manager of one of the mills her father had left her. So Syd Jessup slipped back into his place in the community, but Nell Jessup never stopped hating "that woman." Doctor Holbrook she ever referred to as "poor man" and she bowed to him, kindly but aloofly — for further intercourse between the two houses of course there could not be. Naturally, the schoolmaster on his part could scarcely extend friendly greeting to the fellow who had all but run off with his wife; he also bowed — aloofly. He didn't move his family away because he was attached to the home he had at last paid for and which was convenient to his school. And Nell Jessup, having built her home exactly where she wanted it — overlooking the golf links and with a view of the mountains, refused to budge because of adjacency of "that woman." Young Jimmie was sent away to school and when he came back and went into business with his father, he had too much sense, his mother opined, to be more than courteous to "that woman's" daughter.

Nell Jessup had everything she wanted — except

that Jimmie wouldn't go to college. And his private and very personal reason was Mimi Holbrook. Jimmie had to get on in business — fast. And experience in the mills would secure him an opening somewhere else. Meanwhile he could see Mimi — when opportunity afforded. Lilac Cottage garden, within its tall hedges, had evidently provided excellent opportunity. Gail recalled Mimi's remark: "My mother has a very personal interest in this garden." Undoubtedly, in bygone days another pair of lovers had met there — after the old ladies who owned the place were safely abed and asleep. Gail felt that she ought to be stern with Mimi and say warning, older-sisterish things ... but she had a sneaking sympathy for Mimi.

"Midnight isn't late," Mimi protested. "In summer. Of course we won't meet here if you don't want us to — but the ravine is so sort of damp and buggy in the dark. And the arbor has a brick floor and that bench; and I can slip across and be home in no time." Her tone was wistful.

"We-ll," said Gail. "It does seem hard — you poor children. The ravine is certainly no place for you to be meeting at night. Well, all right. But wear dark clothes, Mimi, and ask Jimmie to. And don't stay a moment after eleven. I can't have you meeting there if you do."

Mimi flung warm young arms around her. "You're a peach. We're going to get married, Miss Ormsbee, the minute Jimmie is twenty-one. I guess you know how young people would feel."

Gail looked after the little flying figure that took the stepping stones of the brook in two leaps. Nice

— to be just young and light hearted and in love; to have no aim in life but to be happy. Only six years between Mimi's age and hers, but there might be twenty. "I guess you know how young people would feel." That hurt. Mimi called Jules Vernon, older than Gail, by her first name, as a contemporary. She even called John Ingram "John." But it was always "Miss Ormsbee" — respectfully. Why?

Foolish maybe, at twenty-six, to concentrate so hard on literary achievement and let other things go — things that might never happen one's way again . . .

Gail, leaning on the gate, the garden shears and basket of wilting blossoms behind her on the grass, frowned at the peaceful vista before her. Afternoon shadows lay thick in the ravine and long shafts of sunlight slanting through the trees picked out flashing ripples in the brook. A woodpecker tapped busily at a tree half way down the slope. A squirrel chattered, high on a branch.

"You know how young people would feel."

Well, of course an author even only on the way to success was a Woman. Anybody engaged and just playing about, was a Girl. A girl running in the sunshine. Gay-hearted.

The woodpecker stopped tapping and cocked his head at Gail. Down at the foot of his tree were gold flecks in the grass. Buttercups.

Buttercups on either side of a path . . . Twilight, and a young moon dropping back of the hills . . . An arm, surprisingly hard — not like a woman pal's arm — around you. A possessive arm. And tender.

A husband's arm would feel like that.

Anybody who married John Ingram would be taken care of. She would never have to worry and plan and contrive about next year. She could play tennis instead of hammering out fashion copy on a typewriter. And could do a book too . . .

But, oh heavens, those children! And what were they up to, this minute?

Two small flying figures with guilt written large all over them (or Miss Ormsbee missed her guess) had entered the ravine from the direction of Brook Road and were now making straight for her garden gate — and short cut through the gap, probably, to fastness of their own back yard. Spying Miss Ormsbee at the gate, the two made hasty detour, splashed through the brook, scrambled up a steep bank and squirmed on their stomachs under the barbed wire fence that backed the Heddon's yard.

Only that morning had an aggravated author, with curt syllables, driven those two out of her garden. The hose having been left, unfortunately, attached to the tap, Miss Ormsbee, deep in problems of phrasing at her desk, had suddenly been deluged with showers of spray. They were only washing the porch steps for her, the culprits averred, but incidentally the porch rug and cushions of the swinging seat had been soaked. And fair pages of a precious new manuscript had been spattered.

What had they been up to this time and why were their garments bedaubed with vivid green? They had no business out on Brook Road; that baby, Freddy, might have been run over. Where was the O'Hara person? Somebody had to watch children every minute. (Whoever did it would have small chance to write a book.)

Gail and the attendant Bill went back to the study. Its serenity was inviting. Clean blotter. Flowers. Neat stack of manuscript. Quietude! She wasted no more of a precious afternoon, musing about advantages of irresponsible girlhood running in the sunshine, but attacked with zest fifteen hundred words of copy headed Brimless Hats for Autumn and which would pay the grocer's bill.

Only when the postman rapped and she went out to get the mail did she discover what youthful Ingrams had been up to. An overturned can of green paint lay on the stepping-stone path. And adorning the lower panel of her immaculate front door was an unmistakable portrait:

CHAPTER XV

Misunderstood Husbands

GAIL ought not have minded — knowing so well what might be expected from children. But she thought a little mournfully, calling up the painter: "I did think at least Fiske liked me."

And for one reason or another she did not tell John.

Hilda came out to spend a week of her vacation. She was going on to a writers' colony in the mountains where everybody had a separate shack and did nothing but work from nine to five. Arlene was at Rockport on Cape Ann, painting all day long. Miss Poppe could endure Hilda without "that painter one" as she insisted upon calling Arlene. So could Regina. The week was pleasant. There were discussions of the novel and of the new book Hilda was planning. Gail would have liked to read bits of her own manuscript that she considered good, but she knew Hilda considered this amateurish and betrayal of weak yearning for applause.

Doctor Holbrook strolled over, evenings. He was greatly taken with Hilda. Here, at least, he intimated, was a mature and brilliant mentality that afforded exhilarating stimulus for his own. Mimi came too, but drifted away early, as though — Gail reflected resentfully — she had better things to do than sit around with old folks. Sometimes Jimmie Jessup came — nights when Doctor Holbrook was safely engaged elsewhere. (He was tutoring two or three lads for college entrance examinations.) Once, returning earlier than usual from the village, he dropped in unexpectedly, and Gail saw him nod with curt kindliness to young Jimmie Jessup. A likable lad, Jimmie, slangy and casual after the manner of his generation, but with nice steady gray eyes and a certain engaging earnestness when he was not mauling Bill, ragging Mimi, or teasing Miss Poppe whose special favorite he was.

"Your father doesn't hate Jimmie," Gail said to Mimi who was helping cut cake in the kitchen.

"No. But my mother does. He is 'that woman's son.' How those two do hate each other. Silly, isn't it, to vent it on me and Jimmie? If you could hear my mother go on, sometimes — when she's sorry for herself! It's rotten for my dad." Mimi pressed her lips together and frowned. "I'll tell you something: I have seen dad look sort of wistfully after Syd Jessup and that cane of his. I shouldn't wonder if dad doesn't wish sometimes that Syd Jessup had got away with it!"

John Ingram dropped in also, coming through the gap. And little bald Mr. Heddon, accompanying him one evening because Mrs. Heddon and the girls were at Delaware Water Gap, kept on coming. John brought along on another evening his neighbor on the other side, a Mr. Swain who was a taciturn sort of chap and lived with his mother because his wife was at a sanitarium in the Adirondacks. Gail liked him because he liked books and seemed so pathetically lonely. She tried to cheer him up. Lilac Cottage was an attractive place with its porch overlooking the hedged-in garden. And with two bright, entertaining women dispensing hospitality. An informal atmosphere that was somehow stimulating. And nobody married to anybody else!

"Refreshing," said Mr. Heddon, who confided to Hilda that he was not altogether understood at home.

"These misunderstood husbands!" Hilda chuckled, putting out lights afterward with Gail. "Sooner or later they confide to you that you are the kind they ought to have married. But they never did, you notice, when they had the chance. They picked the fascinatingly illogical feminine kind. Before marriage, logic is the last thing a man admires in a female; and after marriage, lack of it is the thing that makes him the maddest."

Gail was sorry when Hilda left, but she attacked the novel with new zest. As always, Hilda had been an inspiration. The book was really growing. She did not mind when John departed for an annual two weeks at the seashore of which he said the youngsters must not be deprived. He was taking along Katie O'Hara to look after them.

She would get more done, Gail told him, while he wasn't underfoot. She kept the leave-taking gay with laughter. John looked a bit depressed.

"I wish you were going, Gail."

"Going—I? Not much! Sitting on the sand in the broiling sun and watching two infants paddle—? I'd be bored to tears."

"I guess you would," he said without his usual whimsical humor. "I don't look forward to it with hilarious anticipation myself. But when you've kids, you've got to consider 'em."

"It's your job, John." She told him cheerfully.

"But if you were to be along —"

She reminded him: "I have my own work to do. Well, you'll be back in a week or so —"

"Two weeks from tomorrow," said Mr. Ingram. "Get the old book done by then, that's the girl."

Gail laughed him off on his paternal duty.

The next day she felt a bit depressed, herself. The back of the Ingram house looked lonesome, all closed up. And the Heddon house next it. Little Mr. Heddon had gone to spend his vacation at the Delaware Water Gap. Taciturn Mr. Swain was also taking his two weeks holiday in the Adirondacks. Mimi was visiting in Maine and young Jimmie Jessup had been dragged off by a maternal parent on a motor trip through the Berkshires. Even out here in this lovely country people thought they had to rush away somewhere for a change.

But there was always Work. The author attacked it vigorously.

She was coming in, one evening at dusk, from watering the garden (no one to help her now) when Miss Poppe called agitatedly from a front window:

"Abagail, who is that man, coming down Brook Road with a bag?... Oh, my goodness, Abagail Ormsbee, it's your father!"

CHAPTER XVI

August Intrusions

HER father. Almost sixteen years older than when she had last set eyes on him. Still jaunty, with straw hat a bit aslant on curly hair now quite gray. Still with the blue eyes and thick lashes that she had inherited. But a puffiness now around those blue eyes of Randolph Ormsbee's, a blurriness in them — almost a teariness — that told a story. A flabbiness in the once alert figure. Natty, Randolph Ormsbee would always be, whatever ill fortune overtook him: his shabby suit was well pressed, his slightly broken shoes well polished. He carried his scuffed pigskin bag in a thin, veined hand that wore a becoming seal ring.

Ill fortune had overtaken him now; Gail soon found that out. Not a cent in his pockets except what was left of his railroad fare. He'd borrowed even that, he confided, to get east. Rheumatic fever last winter. His job gone. Once out, no hope — at his age. Only young, husky fellows got the jobs now.

"So I thought I'd come home," he said.

Gail's eyes regarded him without enthusiasm. "Whose home?"

"To my daughter's home," he stated with simple dignity.

He looked around him approvingly. Nice little place she had. Must be several bedrooms upstairs.

"How did you find out where I lived?" For one

furious moment she had suspected Rosamund. But he absolved Rosamund. He'd met a traveling man, he said. Cloak and suit salesman. Fellow said he knew a Miss Gail Ormsbee who did mighty clever fashion copy for the Buyer and Retailer in New York — made good money at it. She had eyes something like Randolph Ormsbee's, might be some relation. So Mr. Ormsbee had dropped a line to the Buyer and Retailer and they'd written him that Miss Ormsbee was no longer with them but they would forward any communication he desired to send her.

Good old Joe Bussing! thought Gail.

But when Mr. Ormsbee had reached New York he had dropped in at the place and the telephone switchboard girl — pretty kid — had told him Miss Ormsbee was living out at Shadow Hills. Gail could see silly Mamie Meecham, flattered by nice manners and attractive blue eyes.

"So I hopped a train," Mr. Ormsbee said affably, "and here I am."

Here he was, indeed. "You are just east for a visit, I suppose — father?" It was impossible to say the once easy and intimate "papa" to this interloper.

"I've left the west for good," he told her solemnly. "When you get on, my dear, you crave the old affections. Blood ties — nothing like 'em. I'm an old man, Gailie!" Old and sick and lonesome, those once expressive eyes conveyed. Gail was untouched.

"You're not old at all. You're scarcely sixty. What was your idea — to settle down here and let me support you?"

Well, she wouldn't begrudge her father shelter, he

supposed. At any rate until he'd got his strength back and was, so to speak, on his feet. "You were always my favorite," he told her benevolently. "You were my little pal, you know. Rosamund and your mother were always leagued against me —"

"There isn't a word of truth in it!" cried Miss Poppe from across the room. "Don't you believe it, Abagail. Rosamund stood by her mamma. You were too little to understand ... I know a thing or two about what went on, Randolph Ormsbee —"

"Now Prunella — you who were always such a good friend of mine!" He fixed her with a once engaging smile. "Tut, tut, Pruny — remember how I called you that? And the Christmas night you gave me a kiss back of the dining-room screen? And the songs we sang together —"

"Well, we're not singing songs together now!" Miss Poppe flounced out of the room.

"How long is she going to stay?" inquired Mr. Ormsbee.

"She is not 'staying'," Gail said firmly, "she is living here. And I'm sorry, father, but there is absolutely not room for anyone else. Of course I can put you up for the night —"

"Let her go," recommended Mr. Ormsbee. "Silly old maid — always was one to stir up trouble." He appended in a genial way, "I'd like right well to settle down here and spend my last days with you, daughter."

"But you won't!" was Gail's inward reflection as she carried the scuffed pigskin bag upstairs. She slapped sheets viciously on the guest room bed. Downstairs, the guest lounged comfortably, legs outstretched on an ottoman, while he smoked a contented cigar. Randolph Ormsbee was the sort who always managed to have a cigar in a waistcoat pocket, however untoward circumstance.

What should she do? What should she do? Gail thought distractedly, whisking out fresh towels for the bathroom, a fresh cake of the dainty soap she kept for guests... just enough soap to last nicely over a weekend. What had she done that Fate should burden her with this incubus? Was it for this she had achieved her lovely little home: to supply refuge to a down-at-heels father of whom she was ashamed? It was unfair, Gail protested passionately. Unfair!

Yet one could not turn a father, approaching age and incapacitated by recent illness, out on the world — when one did possess a comfortable home. It wasn't done. He would have to go to work... But well did she know Randolph Ormsbee's disinclination for work. If there were anyone else he could rely on for sustenance.

Why couldn't he have gone to Rosamund? Yet it would have been pretty hard on Rosamund, running a boarding-house and putting five children through school. Of course if he had to be taken care of, Rosamund must help. Keep him part of the year at least. "I can't do everything, in this family," Gail said to herself rebelliously.

"That man," reported Miss Poppe, putting her head in at Gail's door later, "is reading in bed. He has left his door open a crack and I could see in, coming from the bathroom. I hope to goodness he won't set fire to the place with that cigar."

Hair in crimpers and meager figure wrapped in a

cotton kimono, Miss Poppe dropped down on the edge of Gail's bed. Gail had not been reading, but figuring, her eyebrows drawn together in a deep frown. The light of the bedside lamp glowed softly on the blue silk bed-jacket that was exactly the color of her eyes, and on the rippling, yet unrumpled wave of her hair, brushed back as she always wore it, from her forehead. Something pathetically youthful and feminine about Gail — the competent business woman — sitting up in bed, figuring; that distracted little frown between her eyes. Still frowning, she glanced up at Miss Poppe.

"It's just terrible," breathed Miss Poppe sympathetically. "I know what your poor mother went through. Did he say how long he planned to stay?"

"Forever I guess! He does look sick, cousin Prunella —"

"He always had a pasty look," said Miss Poppe unfeelingly. "It used to be romantic, sort of, when he was younger and his hair was black. Couldn't you give him some money, Abagail, and ship him back west again?"

"How can I, cousin Prunella? I'm helping Rosamund now — and there's this house to pay for. Rosamund and I gave him two thousand when the Brooklyn house was sold. He told the lawyer we should never see him again."

"Where's that lawyer now?"

"Dead. It was just after my twenty-first birthday and Mr. Sickles died the next year. He had always handled mamma's business. She left the house to Rosamund and me, but papa got something out of the rent each month till I came of age. Then the house was sold and the whole sum came to Rosamund and me. It makes just a tiny income, not enough to live on."

Miss Poppe nodded. "Your mother had a head on her shoulders, for all her lackadaisical ways. He'd have had that house sold within a year and gone through the money. What became of that woman —" Miss Poppe flushed delicately — "The one he traipsed out west after?"

"He says her husband came back and her son has grown up now and they objected to having him boarding there."

"Kicked him out, most likely. Where's he been, since?"

"Boarding somewhere else I suppose," said Gail wearily.

"And getting cream for his coffee and the tenderloin of the steak. The world is full of fools when a man has long eyelashes." Miss Poppe closed her mouth with a snap.

"What shall I do, cousin Prunella?"

Gail had dropped her face on her hands and the wave of hair tumbled forward over them. It gave her, usually so neat, so trim, a dishevelled look. Huddled among her pillows in the blue silk bedjacket, she looked frightened and little and alone — to be bearer of such heavy responsibilities.

"I could let you have a hundred dollars, Abagail. I've been saving up for a summer at Chautauqua. But if it would help to get rid of him —"

Gail felt deeply ashamed, remembering how ungracious had been her acceptance of cousin Prunella. She reached over and caught the thin hand resting on the coverlet. "That's sweet of you, cousin Prunella. It wouldn't do any good, but thank you for offering. It would pay his fare back to the west, but he wouldn't stay there. The only solution would be a regular allowance. I can't do that — and help Rosamund too. And Rosamund certainly couldn't contribute anything. If he had money, of course he'd stay away; this is the first time he has been heard of —"

"Not by me, it isn't," said Miss Poppe tartly. "He has written me four or five times, trying to borrow —"

"Cousin Prunella! You didn't lend him money?"

"I certainly did not. Do you think a few eyelashes could get around me? That was all there ever was between us." With this vague but sufficient assurance, Miss Poppe rose, drew her kimono around her and tiptoed to the door. "His light's out and I don't smell anything burning. I guess now it's safe for us womenfolks to get to bed."

She came back and looked sympathetically at the huddled figure in the blue bed-jacket. "I feel dreadfully sorry for you, Abagail. We Methodists would call it a Discipline. If I were you I'd pray over it some . . . Of course, after all, he's your father!" She turned, in the doorway, and offered, helpfully.

"Maybe Mr. Ingram can think of something."

If only John were home! That thought had been at the back of Gail's mind all evening.

But what could John do? She must not get the habit of putting all her problems up to John Ingram, just because he —

Here another thought intruded: She wouldn't have

to worry any more about John's pestering her to give up her work and come and share his responsibilities. Not with a derelict father who had to be supported as part of the bargain!

This, however, lifted no burden from her spirit. Rather the contrary. As any woman will admit, there is something comforting about devotion in the offing. Even if one cannot make up her mind she wants it; distinct comfort in knowing it is there.

It was irritating, unreasonably so, perhaps, to have Bill develop enthusiastic regard for the newcomer. Like his daughter, Mr. Ormsbee was fond of dogs but found children disturbing. Bill being, as has been said, no one-man dog, followed his new admirer slavishly; and it does seem churlish to whistle off your dog when he bounds out joyously for a walk with your father. Mr. Ormsbee liked to stroll downtown (as he called the village) and with hat a little on one side, jauntily, he would twirl his cane and glance approvingly at pleasant houses set back under trees — and at attractive ladies who happened to be on porch or lawn. He soon knew the druggist and various other tradesmen by their first names; he was an affable fellow and had a fund of good stories. Later, Gail found he had opened a charge account at the drug store. A gentleman may do without many things, but he must have shaving cream and cigars.

The Perfect Treasure liked him — until on the third day he chucked her under the chin. Regina was an earnest Episcopalian, she had no time for triflers. She put him out of the kitchen with a rolling-pin. But by this time Regina was attached to Lilac

Cottage which was an agreeable place to work with many privileges that the average mistress did not think of offering, so when Gail, fearful, went to the kitchen after the incident and the considerable racket that had attended it, she was reassured.

"We not mind him — if he keep out of our kitchen." Regina added darkly, "We bigger than he is."

"I don't know how long he'll stay, Regina." Gail, in honor bound, reported the worst.

"Well, he your father!" One couldn't do much, when it was a father, Regina's tone implied. But she appended encouragement: "That kind gemplams not stay long in place quiet like this."

Indeed at the end of a week Mr. Ormsbee showed sign of restiveness. Good country air and nourishing food had taken a little of the pastiness out of his face. His eyes were less blurry and he carolled in his bath. The mellow tenor that had once done solo bits in the Apollo Club was, though rusty, still efficient. As soon as he got on his feet, he announced to his daughter, he would step over to New York and find some little thing to do. The commuting was just far enough to be pleasant — for one who had easy hours.

It was a pity, he thought, that Gail didn't have a car—small roadsters cost so little. And that she didn't belong to the country club. Mr. Ormsbee's social gifts had made him a welcome addition to any gathering, back in the days before he made a mess of things. The clubhouse looked a pleasant place to while away idle afternoons — if one had the clothes. He hinted delicately to his daughter that rubber-soled oxfords and knickers were almost essential to a gentleman's comfort and correctness in a country community in midsummer.

He really did need clothes. When asked whether the pigskin bag contained all he possessed, he admitted that a trunk, unfeelingly held by a hotel proprietor in Omaha, would be forwarded on receipt of a check to cover a little matter of indebtedness — eighty dollars, to be exact.

Gail asked with canny prescience, "Is your winter overcoat in it?"

Unfortunately, she was told, it was not. In early spring it had seemed advisable to part with an unrequired garment in interest of more pressing needs.

It seemed advisable now, to put the eighty dollars in new habiliments. One couldn't have a father going around in broken shoes, or in blue serge frayed at the cuffs and shiny at the seams. Gail had been saving, here and there, for a squirrel fur coat. She had meant to take advantage of August sales. A squirrel fur coat next winter — she could see it! With pleated wool skirts and a little pull-on red felt hat. Squirrel looked so pretty with snow on it. With a sigh she drew a hundred dollars from the bank and sent Randolph Ormsbee to the city to replenish his wardrobe. If she had to provide clothes, from now on, for her father the monthly remittance to Rosamund could not be kept up. It would be hard on Rosamund, but one person simply couldn't do everything.

Mr. Ormsbee, in new shoes, new suit and a new pearl gray felt hat (because fall was on the way) arrived home at three-thirty A.M., having come on the milk train. Gail and Miss Poppe, wondering if perhaps he had vanished with the hundred dollars, had finally retired, leaving the front door unlocked and Bill on guard, on the landing. No taxis ran from the station after midnight, but they heard the homecomer from afar and knew that his return was joyous; for all the way down Brook Road he carolled in a rollicking tenor "Rolling down to Rio."

Bill's tail thumped the floor and then he growled — at an unfamiliar, stumbling step in the hall below.

Miss Poppe's door opened an inch and Gail put her head out of hers.

"Is that you, father?"

"Yesh, m'dear. L'l delayed. Met some friends. Trished m'main — what mean is, mished m'train. Got new clo'es. Wannasee 'em?"

"He's drunk, Abagail!" Miss Poppe's voice quavered, out of the darkness.

"Now, now, Pruny," adjured Mr. Ormsbee, making hard going of it, up the stairs. "You, who were al'ays sush goo' friend o' mine!" Arrived at the landing, he rapped on her swiftly closed door. "Come on out an' talk to me. Not soul roun' t'welcome feller home."

After that he sat on the top step and sang plaintively, "In the gloaming, oh my darling, think not bitterly of me..." After awhile he went to sleep. Gail and Miss Poppe succeeded in getting him to his room before Regina came down.

There wasn't a cent left of the money except a lonely ten cent piece which, virtuously, he handed next day to his daughter. "I bought a fifty-trip ticket, Gailie. Be running in to town now, to look up that little job." He smiled ingratiatingly. All afternoon he made extra effort to be helpful, pushing the lawn mower and clipping the hedge.

Gail was heartsick. If only John were home. Just talking things over with John bucked you up. He was so whimsical and made you see exasperating things in a humorous light. Marigolds gleamed golden in the garden and queen's lace dotted the roadside, but Gail did not notice them, preoccupied with her worries.

She heard several times from John. Postcards. One with a view of the beach: "How's the book coming on?" ... One picturing people playing tennis: "Don't work too hard." ... And a blue-black night scene with two people silhouetted against a rising moon: "Why don't you send a fellow a line?" The last he enclosed in an envelope with a snap-shot of the whole Ingram family in bathing suits. John, tanned and grinning. Fiske, scowling at the camera. Freddy, plump as a partridge in brief woolen garment, smiling through tumbled curls.

"She is cute," thought Gail, "the little tyke!"

Possible to be lonesome, she discovered, for even things that pestered one.

She felt distinct pleasure one afternoon while listlessly weeding the zinnia bed, at sight of two small figures lurking in the gap of the hedge. The children had arrived with Katie, ahead of their father who had stopped at his office.

"Hello, youngsters! So here you are, back again." The tone was so hospitable that they advanced promptly through the gap. Fiske was carrying a large pasteboard box.

"My, how tanned you are!" said the lady, admiringly. "And I do believe Fiske has grown an inch. Have a good time?"

"We bwought you a pwethent."

"You did?"

Fiske shoved the box into her arms. "Father said to wait till he came, but we couldn't."

"Open it. Open it. Open!" shrieked Freddy.

"Maybe I'd better wait for father —"

"No," Fiske insisted, "it's from us. He said so."

They pressed against her while she knelt on the grass and untied strings. Within tissue wrapping was a gorgeous fringed shawl; apricot color, splashed with great embroidered roses in mauve, magenta and black. Gail held it up and the sun shimmered on it. The garden flowers were dimmed by its splendor.

"We got it at a nauction place," Fiske informed her. "The man had 'em in all colors. I liked a pink one but father said they must have made this one specially for you." He inquired anxiously, "Do you like it?"

"Fiske, I can't speak, I'm so pleased."

"Put 'ton. Put 'ton." Freddy jumped up and down.

Gail stood up and wrapped the shawl around her. The long fringe trailed on the grass. She walked up and down, soliciting the children's approval. Fiske regarded her judicially.

"Gee — you're pretty!... I never noticed it before, d'ju, Freddy?"

"Come on," invited the wearer of the shawl gaily — the first moment of light-heartedness she had experienced in two dreary weeks. She extended a hand to each of the children. "Come on, we'll have a party. We'll find some layer-cake —"

"That's the way I like to see you," said John Ingram, coming through the gap. "You're worth looking at, now!"

She turned, the children's hands in hers, and laughed at him over her shoulder.

John was back. John was back. Things would be better now.

John Ingram looked at Randolph Ormsbee — up and down — and didn't care for him. "If he's going to stay on," John said to Gail, (they were watering the garden together) "we'll have to find him something to do. I might fit him in somewhere, over at our office. You can't have him on your hands all day."

She had known that John would tackle the problem in a capable way!

"But if you really want to get rid of him —" John was continuing.

"If I want to get rid of him —?" She laughed shortly.

"If you really want to get rid of him," John repeated, "and two thousand would send him off again for another spell of years, it could be managed. You could raise the money with a second mortgage — or, better still, let me lend it to you."

She shook her head, pointing the hose-nozzle firmly at the bird bath. "Not that, John. I couldn't." But she felt grateful. Cousin Prunella, and now John; people were so kind, offering to help her get rid of a worrisome burden.

"I think myself," John was lifting loops of hose

over a bed of foxglove, "if he had two thousand dollars and no one to tie to, he'd drink himself to death in a year."

"Well, let him!" said Gail.

"After all, he's your father —"

"John! You don't know what I've been through or you wouldn't be — soft — like that. It's pure sentimentalism!" She flung down the hose and the spurting water made a freshet among the sweet alyssum.

John went and shut off the water. When he came back Gail was staring at the bird bath which gleamed delicately pink in the dusk. A flaming sunset had made a rosy afterglow that bathed all the garden in a lovely light. John said:

"You are something like him, you know, Gail."

"I? — like him —"

"Yes. You have his eyes and his smile — with that dimple. And that sort of alert grace when you move suddenly. From somewhere along the line of ancestors you picked up more steadiness and stamina and principle. But you've got a quality he has: both of you can be ruthless."

She turned and stared at him.

"Both of you," he repeated, "can be ruthless. In pursuing what you think you want for your own personal gratification, regardless of the feelings or needs of people who love you. With him, it is selfishness; with you, it is — what is it, Gail?"

She walked past him with her head high. She felt rigid all over with a numb coldness, and at the same time seething with hot rage.

"Please remember," she said icily, "that my

father's derelictions were toward people who had some claim on his affection!"

"Gail —" He stood there with the looped hose in his hands.

"You've reminded me —" she stopped on the lower step of the porch. Her face looked white in spite of its tan — "of my duty — to a poor broken down old father; that's how you look at it, I suppose, being a man also, for whom women were created to serve and sacrifice. Well, he's another duty that will keep me very tightly tied — and indefinitely — to that typewriter you so disapprove of —"

She called Bill and went into the house.

She glanced back, through the glass doors, when she had them closed behind her — to see if John Ingram were following. She half expected him to knock at once on the closed doors. But he was walking toward the gap in the hedge and the hose lay where he had dropped it.

CHAPTER XVII

Leafy Shadows

SHE wrote to Rosamund.

Rosamund at least would understand. Rosamund at least had sympathy with literary ambition. (Hadn't Gail Ormsbee's achievements thus far lightened considerably the burden on Rosamund's own shoulders?) Rosamund would perceive the imperative need of unfretted atmosphere for an author. And of unhampered hours for work.

Rosamund (she wrote) would realize how much better it would be if she herself undertook Randolph Ormsbee for the first six months, while the author completed her important job. Train fare of course to be furnished and the regular sum sent each month, since Randolph Ormsbee would require some spending money — though very little. (Trenchant sisterly warning.) And of course one more at a boarding house table would make no appreciable difference, where his food was concerned.

Gail fixed it all up very reasonably and practically. After the letter had been mailed she felt better. There would be peace again at Lilac Cottage and that solitude so essential to creative work.

She put in a good afternoon at her desk. Randolph Ormsbee, these hot days, took the paper upstairs after luncheon and dozed in his room. And Miss Poppe also retired to her chamber and negligible costume. But Gail worked hard, turning off first, a thousand words of copy on Warm Sport Togs For the Thanksgiving Weekend and then attacking a chapter of the novel that had been left in that up-in-the-air situation that keeps an author so mentally disturbed until the thing can be rounded off.

Insects buzzed outside the screens and heat waves quivered over the garden. Gail continually thrust back damp hair from a damp forehead. Nobody, today, on the golf links. They were all under the clubhouse awnings probably, drinking things in which ice clinked. Perhaps because she was a little ashamed of herself (the feeling certainly nagged somewhere at the back of her consciousness) she felt virtuous self approval that she thus labored while others weakly relaxed. People were always telling you how busy they were. It was what you accomplished, being "busy," that counted.

That evening she watered the garden. Alone. Once or twice she glanced toward the gap. It gave you an exhausted feeling inside — having had words with a friend. Of course no constitutional peace lover relishes a row. Such things are upsetting.

Though John had undoubtedly been right, (looking at it from the purely ethical standpoint) if she could talk it over with him and lead him to view the matter from the practical side, he would realize that she was not — what was that unpleasant word he had used? — ruthless; but merely possessed of plain every day common sense.

So many people, unjustly called ruthless, were really only using their good common sense, unhampered by sentimentality.

No one, however, appeared to talk things over.

Randolph Ormsbee, refreshed by his bath, and very natty in his new clothes, wandered down town after dinner. Having discovered a congenial spirit — one Gus Abbott, proprietor of the single hotel of the village, a not engaging edifice known as the commercial house and located near the railroad station — he whiled away many an evening in the billiard and pool parlor back of Gus Abbott's office. At least, his daughter hoped, it kept him out of worse mischief. Returning about ten, Mr. Ormsbee mentioned that he had seen the Ingram fellow driving with the Vernon girl. Good looking girl, that. Snappy little roadster she had, too. They had waved to him.

Instead of a letter from Rosamund, arrived a telegram. Rosamund couldn't possibly take father — explanation in letter following. But she was sending Lucy to help Gail.

To a tormented author, Lucy represented the last straw. While Miss Ormsbee was hotly composing a return telegram about the absolute impossibility of entertaining Lucy or anybody else at this present moment, a second message arrived: Lucy had already started and would Gail meet her train next day in New York? Time of train arrival was appended.

On top of this, Miss Poppe, who had received a letter in the morning mail, came into the study all aflutter. Her sub-tenant was departing and her landlady wrote that the bird was droopy. Hadn't Miss Poppe better come home?

"Oh, Cousin Prunella, you are not going to desert me?"

"I wouldn't, Abagail, except for Dickie. When he gets these droopy spells nobody can do a thing with him but me. At any rate if Lucy Lovelace is coming, you'll need the extra bed. Neither you nor I would relish taking a restless young thing her age in with us. But Lucy'll brighten you up," encouraged Miss Poppe. "She'll draw young folks around the place."

The author groaned.

"And she'll help entertain her grandpa at meals." Miss Poppe was doing her best, according to her code, to make things pleasant. "She must be an affectionate little thing and she's so fond of children; Rosamund has often written about the way she has with the younger ones. She's pretty as a picture too — if that snap-shot her mother sent last winter is to be believed. She looks like the old-fashioned kind. Homelike and quiet —"

"Let's hope!" said Gail devoutly. Someone else to get out guest room towels and soap for. Was her life never to be blessed with the halcyon humdrum of unshattered routine?

She had mentioned, of course, when she bought the house that later on she hoped to have Lucy for a nice long visit. But it was unfeeling of Rosamund to take advantage of that just now.

Gail helped Miss Poppe tie up paper bundles. Once she had despised those bundles; now she felt real regret in seeing them depart. "Maybe," said Miss Poppe hopefully, "I can come for another spell next winter. I sort of hate leaving the Methodist minister, here. He's so understanding. I wish you'd go to that church, Abagail, and get your father to go. Randolph has a nice voice for hymns; — full of feeling. And choir practice would help keep him steady."

While they were waiting on the platform for mail to be loaded on the train, Miss Poppe had another thought. "Lucy Lovelace is so fond of children, she'd be just the one for Mr. Ingram. Her mother would be tickled — with those five on her hands — to have Lucy comfortably fixed."

Gail was amused. "But she's a child, Cousin Prunella."

"She's seventeen, almost. Those southern girls grow up faster than girls do, here. I've kind of hoped you and he, Abagail — But I know you can't abide those young ones. It would be a real help to Rosamund if you could engineer something like that for Lucy."

"Whatever else I am," thought Miss Ormsbee, waving a handkerchief as the train pulled out, "I'm no engineer!"

She watered the garden that evening, again alone. Afar off could be heard a piano. A lively tune, full of gaiety and spirit; the player was evidently in carefree mood. John was playing Percy Grainger's *Country Garden* but Gail did not know that. To a lot of people it is a lively tune and they never get the undertone of wistfulness.

Randolph Ormsbee, perhaps in celebration of the departure of one of the spinsters eternally watching him, (his own comic expression recently confided to the druggist who was a humorous fellow) had departed for town. And Regina was making one of her all-night visits to the cousins in Newark. The house was beautifully still, what coolness there was in the summer night wafting sweetly in at open doors and windows.

Gail sat on the porch step and looked at the garden, steeped in moonlight. There is nothing constructive about moonlight meditation. Especially when your own spirit is irritably unserene. The moonlight might have been soothing. But the music that crashed through it was not. Fugues of Bach that actually hurt the lovely night. A Crescendo of somebody's that had no peace in it. A Prelude of Rachmaninoff — all terrific chords plucked from the bass. Music that, considering the environment and the hour, made you nervous. It sounded as though the player were fighting something that had to be pounded and banged at and punished ... And then, when you yourself were all strung up and quivering, the whole business ended with a lovely little tone poem of Thomé's — *Under the Leaves*, a thing you had always loved — which, after the pounding and banging, and because of the environment and the hour, made you suddenly want to cry.

Thus it was that Mr. Ingram, about midnight, strolling outdoors with his before-bedtime pipe — and strolling, as he frequently did at such time, down through his diminutive orchard to a gap in a hedge whence he could view unlighted windows of a dwelling on adjoining property, discovered Miss Ormsbee huddled on the seat under her grape arbor, crying.

Now Gail, crying, was a most disconcerting spectacle. Gail never cried. She despised women inclined to easy tears — that Mr. Ingram knew. She despised feminine weakness of any sort, she had frequently expressed herself to that effect. If women, she had often asserted, would use their sense of logic and — more important — their sense of humor, crying would be as infrequent with them as it was with men. The only possible excuse for tears, in Miss Ormsbee's opinion, was profound and devastating sorrow.

Yet here was she, at twelve o'clock at night, huddled on a bench at the back of her garden — crying!

Mr. Ingram didn't stop to ask why or how or wherefore. Having made sure that it wasn't Mimi Holbrook, (whom he had glimpsed on other occasions at this hour in this spot) he simply dropped down on the bench and took the weeper in his arms.

Very close in his arms. For having divined by some inexplicable feminine process (since she did not look up) whose were the arms, Miss Ormsbee with a long, relieved sigh, cried it out on the fortuitously offered shoulder. So preoccupied they were, she with her woe and he with necessity of easing it, that twice he kissed her (once on the mouth) and neither of them, apparently, noticed it.

Conversation was naturally halting.

"I m-miss cousin Prunella."

"I know!"

"And f-father hasn't come home. I'm worried."

"Of course!"

"And Regina's out and I was all alone in the house —"

"Poor little girl!"

"I came down here where I could hear you playing; it didn't seem so f-forlorn."

(It was here that he kissed her on the mouth.)

And I want to be understood, not misjudged; and sympathized with and made to feel I'm perfectly right ... but this was not sobbed out audibly though it might have been said to contain the gist of the matter. Instead, she sobbed out: "And I hate the idea of one more relation descending on me tomorrow—"

"Who's that?"

"My sister's little girl. That is, she's sixteen. I'll have to be looking after her every minute."

"The dickens! That's too bad. Cheer up, I'll help." A generous offer, from Mr. Ingram who could not abide flappers. It made Gail laugh. How much better was everything in the world when you were not all alone, carrying your worries, but had an understanding pal to share things with! She sat up and wiped her eyes — though not with John's handkerchief. For all her weakly feminine tears Gail was not the kind who relied on masculine handkerchiefs; she had two neatly folded fresh ones in her sport frock pocket.

"I guess the thing that really upset me," she said, and believed it to be the truth, "was father's not getting home on the 11.29; and not knowing now how he'll be when he does come."

"Don't worry," said Mr. Ingram. "I shall be right here with you when he comes."

"But, John," she protested, "you can't stay all night, you know. Last time it was almost four in the morning. He came out on the milk train." She glanced over a shoulder at the unlighted house. "Regina's away and I'm frightened."

His arm, along the back of the bench, tightened around her shoulders. "It's an outrageous situation for you. Gail — let me take charge. Just say the word. Give me the right —"

Almost, again, she was tempted. So very hard and muscular and comfortably dependable that arm felt, gripping her shoulders. Pleasant, to be a protected woman; somebody else undertaking all your problems. His coat sleeve smelled of tobacco, a nice soothing smell. She could smell also the wet earth of the garden borders — a cool night smell. Leaves of the vine on the arbor made sharply defined shifting shadows on the brick floor. Outside was the white loveliness of August moonlight. The strong yet so tender arm held her close. John whispered, "Gail! Give me the right —"

From afar off the whistle of a train . . . The theater train from town. Randolph Ormsbee might be on it. Unconsciously she braced herself and the familiar action made her feel cool again and self poised. She drew away from the encircling arm.

"The right to what? To support my father? That's what it would amount to. John, would you honestly be willing to have Fiske, for instance, see his — his step-grandpa come home intoxicated? If you would, I wouldn't. No child ought to share in household apprehension of that sort. Your children must not be brought up under that shadow —"

"I thoroughly agree with you," said John Ingram. "But in this case things might be arranged some other way —"

Her sudden laugh had an edge. "Don't forget, John dear, you reminded me only three nights ago that after all, he is my father! My willingness to dispense with his company didn't seem to endear me to you."

"Oh, Gail," he implored her, "you always argue so —"

"So reasonably," she told him. "Men do hate it I know, from us women. No, my dear, I have refused to take on your responsibilities; why should I allow you to shoulder mine?"

"Because I love you," he told her simply.

She was silent. She looked down at the flickering leaf-shadows on the brick floor and he looked at her. After a moment he said, "If you loved me you'd feel that way too. Responsibilities wouldn't matter. It would be just you and me —"

"If it would —" she hesitated. He leaned nearer and said quickly:

"What do you mean by that?"

"It wouldn't be just you and me ... I don't believe I love you enough, John."

He said gloomily, "I guess you don't, Gail. If you did, you'd be sure about it."

"I can't take care of two children," she said obstinately. They were back at the old barrier again.

"But you wouldn't have to —"

"Wouldn't I? What sort of person do you think I am? If I made up my mind to undertake anything like that I'd see it through — all the way. And it would be too big a job to allow time for anything else. If it were done right. Those two children deserve better than just left-handed care while somebody's right hand is doing something more congenial..."

She got up from the bench. Suddenly she felt very tired. How many times had they thrashed this out? She hoped he wouldn't put his arm around her again. She felt so — sort of disorganized, tonight. She couldn't see values. She wanted to work. And to succeed in her work. But everything of late had made work so exhaustingly up-hill. If John should put his arm around her now, with this scent of the garden coming to them and leaf shadows quivering all over them, it would be so easy to yield. Something in her, ridiculously weak and undependable, wanted to yield. Wanted to most awfully. She hoped John wouldn't put his arm around her again. She hoped he would . . .

He didn't. He put his hands in his coat pockets and followed her across the garden to the porch steps. The world was very still. Almost one o'clock now. A little breeze of morning rustled the hollyhocks and made them scrape against the house clapboards.

"When that book is done —" his tone said plainly: When that confounded distraction is off your mind — "will you think about it, Gail?"

"I have thought about it."

"No you haven't. Not with your heart, only with that cool mind of yours. There's a sheath of hard self-protectiveness that mind has built up. If anyone — if I, or Fiske, or Freddy — could get through it to your heart —"

"You are always getting through it to my heart — all of you!" — was on the tip of her tongue to answer him. But aloud she said, "I'll promise — to think about it — if you will promise not to speak of the thing again until I have finished my book. I must do that, John!"

"I know. All right. Then that's a go." They

were standing now by the porch steps and he added wistfully, "Do you think you could give me a kiss to bind the bargain?"

A voice spoke humorously from the shadows, the voice of Mr. Randolph Ormsbee, proceeding from the depths of a wicker chair:

"Hate t' dishturb young folksh spoonin' in the moonlight — or neckin', guesh they call it now. But itsh pretty late."

He was by no means sober as a judge, but there was nothing in the least terrorizing about him — merely intensely obnoxious. Mr. Ingram bade a dignified goodnight and went home, by way of the gap.

"Hang it all," he reflected, walking up through his own back yard in the moonlight, "I ought to have grabbed her, there in that arbor, and kissed her into giving in."

The trouble was, John understood perfectly Gail's feeling about her work. Time had been when he had throttled literary ambition to give himself to work that would support a family. He knew what a sturdy proposition he was asking Gail to accept in lieu of her dream.

He knew the heart of Gail — under that self-protective shell she had built around herself... Her courage... Her loyalty to an ideal; or to a decision. Into whatever she undertook, as Hilda Braithwaite had said, she would put that whole courageous self. He knew what a pal she could be — times when her laughter and those eyelashes and that dimple were allowed their chance. And he knew the sweetness of her in a man's arms (twice had he known it) when for one moment the Gail who was all impulse and all woman let herself shine through.

Well, the writing of no book could take forever. With any luck she ought to have the thing done by Christmas...

CHAPTER XVIII

Summer Lightning

TO MISS Ormsbee, nieces, it will be remembered, were no treat. The hardest five years of her life had been spent taking care of nieces. Pushing their little go-carts when other girls strolled in pairs and shared secrets and had sundaes. Washing out their little garments. Fixing their bottles. (Rosamund's twins had been babies then.) And entertaining them when they were peevish with whooping cough and mumps. Nieces had been the strongly impelling incentive that had started Gail on a business career.

Yet, standing outside the train gate waiting for Lucy, Gail experienced thrill of upsurging affection for this little daughter of Rosamund's who was coming to her. Rosamund's oldest girl whom Gail had not seen in almost nine years. Lucy had been seven or eight then, a slim legged little thing with a crop of chestnut curls that never would stay brushed. Cousin Prunella said Lucy was now pretty as a picture, an old-fashioned girl. Maybe Lucy would be a real comfort to have around. Rosamund was evidently sending her for that purpose. "I am always too quick," Gail told herself rebukingly, waiting at the train gate, "to take for granted that things will be the very worst. I've got to get over it and grow more sunny."

There was no doubt that Lucy was pretty. Her prettiness took Gail's breath away. She was tiny and dainty and made you think, in the big, noisy station with its crowds of drabbish hurrying humanity, of a lovely little flower that had somehow gotten into that cavernous place. She had the Ormsbee eyes and lashes and the winsome Ormsbee smile with the dimple. But her hair was a rich chestnut with auburn lights. And every man on the train platform turned and stared at her — because she was so pretty and little and flowerlike; and because that hair (in an era when every young feminine head was bobbed) tumbled in curls over each shoulder.

"My goodness," thought Gail, "she looks like a copy of a movie star playing an ingenue part."

When Lucy's hat came off, at Lilac Cottage, the curls were enchanting, caught back at the nape of her neck with a little shell clasp. And the dark chestnut tresses, parted meekly in the middle, gave her the effect of a girl in an old-fashioned daguerreotype. One almost looked for a flounced skirt and pantalettes. Lucy was old-fashioned all right. She was a Victorian mother's dream of winsome girlhood. Though her little frocks were brief and slim like frocks of other young girls of her age, most of them managed to have ruffles and the skirts seemed to fall more modestly than other youthful skirts when she sat in a low chair, ankles demurely crossed. An upholstered ottoman in Gail's living-room she pre-empted for her own. And Lucy, on that ottoman, with ruffled skirt and little crossed strap-slippers, and a curl trailing forward over each shoulder was something to see!

Immediately the house became full of boys. Gail had not realized there were so many lads, home for college vacations, in Shadow Hills. They sprawled on the living-room chairs and lounged on the front steps, and played ukuleles on the porch, evenings. Like bees around a honey pot they swarmed around this darling of a girl, so merry and fun-loving yet with something about her ... A quality that none of these short haired, frank legged, plain spoken maidens they palled with, possessed. A girl that roused something protective and gallant in a fellow. No oblique allusions, no raw wisecracks made conversational exchange where she was. She just opened wide, long-lashed eyes and stared, and then bit her little red lip and looked uncomfortable. And said confidentially to the boy who happened to be nearest: "Oh, I don't like that! Let's go somewhere by ourselves." She was the kind of girl whom other girls called the "twosing sort." Yet other girls couldn't help liking her, she was such an ingenuous little thing and so happy when everybody was having a good time. And so ready, because she was the youngest, to let others do the leading while she just fitted in.

The boys offered her cigarettes just to see her refuse them. That quick shake of a little head that made curls fly about, followed by demure indrawing of dimpled chin and shy, "Oh, no! But thank you." A real girl, sweet as honey. Not dumb — far from it — but not eternally trying to put it over that she knew as much about everything as a man.

"It's just her line," said Mimi Holbrook, "and she gets by with it because she looks that way. She's got a good bean on her shoulders all right. She knows what she's about."

Mimi, back from Maine and brown as a butternut,

had been pressed into service by a discouraged author who had to get her work done somehow and implored Miss Holbrook to convey a disturbing element (because of the train of followers) temporarily off the premises. Gail laughed at Mimi's privately expressed opinion.

"She's not seventeen yet, remember. You take her to the club to watch the tennis and I'll be eternally obliged. If I have to listen to that ukulele through another afternoon I shall throw something at somebody."

"Leave it to me," promised Mimi helpfully. "She's wild to get to the club. I'll give her a card for a month. That'll be a rest for you. It's a riot, the way the boys fall for her. Sweet little southern girl. Really-truly feminine sort, no fooling. Gets 'em every time. Men do adore being concentrated on — with lashes like that. I'm not afraid of her vamping Jimmie. He gave her the once-over and said 'Nothing doing!' Horse-and-buggy stuff, he calls that line of hers. All she needs is a rose in her bosom — to be perfect."

There were years and years between aunt Gail, successful business woman and householder, and little Lucy, not quite seventeen. Lucy made that evident from the start.

"You don't have to rise every time I come into the room," said Gail, a little nettled. "And you needn't call me 'Aunt Gail,' you know." (She was sick to death of being Aunt Gailed all over the place.) "Just say 'Gail.'"

Lucy opened wide eyes. "Oh, I couldn't, Aunt Gail! It would seem so — so disrespectful. Mamma told me how marvelous you were — so intellectual and all — and she said I was to treat you with greatest consideration, Aunt Gail."

Randolph Ormsbee also had his sensitiveness. Never having encountered any of Rosamund's offspring in a period of family-tree adventuring out west, he hadn't grown gradually accustomed to privileges of riper years. The first "Grandfather" ingenuously uttered in liquid southern syllables, smote him like a thunderclap. He turned very red and flung down his fork.

"Suffering Saints! Don't let me hear you say that again, young lady."

Lucy opened big eyes. "Say what, grandfather?"

"That — epithet. Cut it out."

Lucy laughed mischievously. Pleasing the male is Lesson Number 1 in a southern girl's lexicon of behaviour. "Very well. What shall I call you — just 'Randolph'?"

"Any pet name you like," said Mr. Ormsbee. "But I'm doggoned if I'll be called grandfather by a strapping female your size."

"How about 'father'?" said Gail from her end of the breakfast table. "Does that also offend your sense of juvenility?"

"No need to be sarcastic, Gailie." His blurry blue eyes rested on his daughter with something that approached fondness. "I have no objection to being called father by you, my dear. I regard it as a privilege."

Gail was touched. She must be nicer to her father.

John forestalled any appeal for sympathy about another relative inflicted on busy working hours of an author: "Don't ask me to regret anything so pretty being around."

Lucy thought Mr. Ingram just wonderful, and told him so. She reproached her aunt Gail: "You never said a word about him in your letters to mamma!" If she had ever known there was anything so attractive next door, she protested, she'd have been up here months ago.

Over John's constituents she went into raptures.

If there was anything in this world she did dote on, she averred — she was kneeling on the grass with an arm about each of the children — it was "big boys like this" . . . and she kissed Fiske. "And fat little girls like this" . . . and she snuggled her face into Freddy's dimpled neck.

"I like you too," vouchsafed Freddy who adored being petted.

"Do you, honeypie? Well, I love you! I reckon the angels were just plumb sorry when they had to bring you down here and leave you with your daddy. They couldn't bear to let anything like you go."

John looked on, Gail observed, with fatuous delight. Cuddling arms and kisses — how children did respond to them; and fathers too, beholding the pretty sight. All you had to do, to enchant a man, was to cuddle his children. Gail lugged the garden hose further along and soused the salvias. Tormented petals gave up trying to hold on and spattered the ground in a scarlet shower.

Fiske came running. "You got it caught in the zinnias." He lifted the hose for her helpfully.

"Thank you, Fiske!"

"I'll do it for you, you're getting your feet wet."

"That is very nice of you, Fiske." She surrendered the hose.

He stood sturdily, short legs well apart, directing the spray of water at the salvias. "I like girls who don't mush," he confided.

Gail felt ridiculously pleased.

She and Fiske finished watering the border. John didn't notice; he had his back turned, laughing down at Lucy who was sitting on the grass with Freddy in her arms.

There was no doubt that Lucy loved children. And she had a way with them. Without exerting herself at all she attracted them to her. And if there were a child anywhere about she couldn't keep her hands off it; — had to fondle it, lift it to her lap. The kind of woman, Gail reflected ironically, that man inevitably thinks of reverently as "the mother-type" and enshrines in a special place in his soul. The kind of female who goes into raptures over soft little bodies and dewy baby mouths and gets more delight out of the cuddling and fondling than ever she does out of unfolding intelligence and personality. The kind who adores her babies, but later, encountering wills, resorts to spats and slaps and sudden pounces. And still later, nags. With continued plaint to sympathetic ears: "They were so darling when they were babies but I simply can't cope with them now."

There was a lot more to motherhood than cuddling — though a man didn't think of it, watching a pretty woman with a baby. A woman, to bring up sons, would have to have a strain of sternness in her, wouldn't she? ... Of — ruthlessness. That would be able to deny and even to hurt, when temporary suffering meant sterner sinews of resistance for real temptations later on.

But one day Gail had to cuddle Freddy herself, and she learned something about that, too. She had been working all afternoon over a troublesome chapter. A hot, breathless Saturday in early September, but for once the house was blissfully quiet. Randolph Ormsbee was upstairs, taking his afternoon doze and Lucy had driven over to Ridge Fells with John Ingram. A dog show was being held at the Ridge Fells country club with entries from all the surrounding villages. Jule Vernon had called for Bill that morning. Earlier in the week she had dropped in to beg Gail to enter Bill in the show. Jule Vernon wasn't a bad sort of person when one got to know her. Crisp and forthright, likely to say anything — no nonsense about her. But friendly. You couldn't be aloof and chilly toward one who seemed really to like you and who took your liking for granted.

"You mustn't work so hard on that book," Jule Vernon had said, taking leave. "John has told me about it — that lad thinks the sun rises and sets on you. I have known old John since he was knee-high; long before he brought that blonde baby doll bride into our midst. No offense to the dead intended, but, alive, she was the awfullest bore I ever met. No kind of a pal for a man with brains. John's a lamb and she never found it out. But I do want something better for him next time... Oh, about the book: you will leave it for once, won't you, and come to the dog show?"

"I don't know whether I want to see Bill chained up and unhappy —"

"He won't be unhappy, he'll be proud as punch. This isn't one of those city shows with gangs of people and putrid air and a rackety jazz band. It's outdoors and the dogs are walked around on leashes. They enjoy it. You'll come?"

Gail had promised. John was to drive Lucy and herself over in his car. But when he arrived, Lucy, dancing out in fluttery peach chiffon, with curls tumbling under a shady black hat, (where Rosamund procured such clothes for her Gail could not imagine unless the whole monthly remittance went on Lucy's back,) climbed nimbly into the front seat.

"I'm going to ride with Mr. Ingram." Eyelashes made play at John. "Can't I?"

He laughed indulgently. Such a spoiled child! the indulgent smile said. "If your aunt Gail doesn't mind sitting back there by herself."

Gail saw herself: old auntie, sedately alone in the back seat chaperoning hilarious youth. Some emotion — obstinacy, indignation, she did not define it — rose up within her and she said she had no idea of going to any dog show; she had a chapter to finish that day. The only reason she had her hat on, she mentioned, was because there was some last minute Saturday marketing to be done — if they would be so kind as to drop her in the village.

When she got back with an unnecessary pound of butter she attacked Lucy's room. It hurt her to have such a deplorable mess in any part of her neat little house. But she remembered Rosamund's flat in Brooklyn; children grew up the way they were started.

It was almost five when, deep in literary labyrinth,

she glanced up to see why the afternoon was suddenly so dark. Colors in the garden were sharply defined and the bird bath had a spectral whiteness. Against a lead-black sky trees in the ravine were bending away from the wind. Gail flew upstairs to close bedroom windows. When she came down, she stood at the open doors of the study and looked anxiously at her garden, threatened by this pelting hail. All in a moment the paths had become torrents and her larkspur stood in a lake. Lightning darted and thunder crashed. The storm would spoil the dog show, and all the refreshment tables set out of doors. Too bad.

The gate on the ravine side flew open and a little bedraggled figure came running toward the porch. Freddy — frenzied with terror of the lightning and the wind-driven rain.

"Luthee!" she shrieked, "Luthee!"

"It isn't Lucy, dear, it's Gail. Why baby, where have you come from? Where's brother?"

Freddy couldn't answer. She sobbed and shivered and clung. Lucy or Gail, it didn't matter; to be taken care of in a universe that had turned to chaos — that was all she craved. Her arms closed in a stranglehold around Gail's neck.

Fiske was at the dog show, with Jule Vernon, Gail managed to elicit that. And Freddy had been playing down by the brook. "I lef' my dolly. She'th dwonded."

"No indeed," comforted Gail. "After the storm is over we'll go find her and wash her face and Gail will make her a bee-utiful new dress. And now we'll get Freddy's wet things off and wrap her up tight in Gail's big bathrobe. Won't that be fun?"

"I dravver have Luthee," said Freddy with frankness.

But she submitted to being undressed and rubbed with a big bathtowel and then wrapped in the soft corduroy dressing-gown that had fur on it. She loved the fur. "Like a kitty," she said delightedly to Gail. And Gail, who always frowned when very intent and busy, had to laugh also. Her hands were very gentle; there was something about the white little body, so trustfully submitted to her ministrations, that was touchingly innocent and appealing.

With the warmly wrapped child in her arms she went down to the telephone and called up the Ingram house. The O'Hara person had been properly frightened. "Of course," appended Miss Ormsbee before hanging up the receiver, "Freddy should not have been out by herself, playing in the ravine. Especially with a storm coming up. Mr. Ingram will be very angry. Somebody ought to be taking better care of those children."

Miss O'Hara had the high spirit of one who hails from County Galway. Before Miss Ormsbee could get her receiver on its hook she heard a muttered, "Sure, an' since there's some as would like to do it, why don't they?"

Regina brought the hot milk she had been asked to have ready, and for an hour Gail sat in a low chair with Freddy cuddled in her arms. There wasn't a rocker in Lilac Cottage. (Miss Poppe had deplored it.) You really ought to have a rocker in the house, Gail reflected, in case of emergencies like this. It was more natural to rock — holding a baby.

"The lightning won't hurt you, darling," she said,

feeling Freddy quiver. "It can't get in here."

"Katie tol' me it would stwike you dead if Dod don' like you."

That stupid woman. What was she doing to these plastic little souls?

"Nonsense, Freddy. God doesn't strike people with lightning. They just get hit if they run out outdoors in the lightning's way. Anyhow God loves a little girl like you."

Freddy was doubtful. "But I'm in your houthe."

"Don't you think God likes me?"

"Not much," said Freddy. "Katie don' think tho. Katie thed: 'Dod fordive th' liketh o' her!' — when you thent uth home, yeth'day."

"Gail has to work. You like me, don't you, Freddy?"

"Ye-eth. I do if you'll tell me a sto'wy."

So Gail told a story. The thunder ceased after a while and pelting of rain on the windows. Warmed by the furry bathrobe and the hot drink Freddy grew drowsy. The little body relaxed in Gail's arms.

"Poor neglected baby." Gail looked down at the small face. Freddy, asleep, had a look of John. Gail hadn't noticed it before. John's nose and that turn of the jaw. She would be exactly like John when she grew up and lost the baby chubbiness. John's little daughter.

If she did come to love these children — really love them — wouldn't it be, thought Gail, because they were part of John? Very near to him and therefore precious.

Suppose this little warm, soft thing, sleeping so trustingly here in her arms were — John's and hers!

A wave of some emotion, big and deeply moving, swept over Gail. A curiously thrilling emotion that left her a little breathless... Made her clutch the bundle in her arms and press it close against her breast.

She rose and laid Freddy on the sofa and tucked a blanket around her.

"If I ever *did*," said Gail, hands very gentle and careful, tucking in the blanket, "I'd have to be just as good to Freddy — to both of them — as if they *were*."

CHAPTER XIX

Bittersweet and Butternuts

GAIL loved the katydids. She lingered by the bridge, evenings while giving Bill his run, to listen to the staccato antiphonal chorus that filled the dark with clamor. Nothing relaxing about katydids. They made you feel in a hurry, and at the same time brisk and energetic... Is the woodpile stacked? Is the corncrib full? Are the chinks all tight? Potatoes in the cellar, onions in the bins? Call the critters back from the hills and get your lantern ready; soon chores must be done in the dark... Winter was coming, the katydids did not let you forget.

Gail had to put on a heavy sweater now for her tramp with Bill. And dusk drew in early. Orion was swinging up in the east and maples in the swamp over beyond the golf meadow were turning red cheeks to the north. From the gnarled tree at the foot of the garden dropped speckly looking pears that had a tough skin but were sweet as honey inside. Gail carried them rapturously to Regina. Apples would be ready soon for pies, and there were already glasses and glasses of grape jelly on the cellar shelves. Fruit from your own place for your table; — it gave you an expansive, complacent feeling that people who bought things at delicatessens never knew.

Fiske was going to school. He came over to display his new suit. Exactly like father's with knickers and wool stockings turned down at the top — no more babyish socks! — and stout-soled shoes with laces. He called attention to their beautiful shine.

Lucy wanted to pat the new coat and turn Fiske round and round. He went and stood in front of Gail. "What do you think of 'em?"

"They're grand, Fiske. I'll say you look grown up. Shouldn't be surprised if you were on the football team soon. How about this red pencil to stick in that breast pocket?" She reached for it on her desk.

"Well — if you say they are all right. Father told me you'd know." He accepted the pencil with enthusiasm.

"You are going to learn a lot, aren't you, Fiske — to please me?"

"And father," he included.

Lucy wanted to kiss him for luck.

"Aw, I don't kiss girls," he told her contemptuously and stamped away in the stout new shoes, through the gap.

"He's getting rough," said Lucy. "School will ruin him the way it does all of them."

But Gail realized with warming satisfaction that Fiske liked her best and that Lucy was jealous. Lucy couldn't bear it if every male in her vicinity, irrespective of age, didn't offer adulation.

But that, Gail had to admit, was unfair. "What's the matter with me?" she chided herself. Lucy really did love children — sacrificed her time to them. She had offered to sit with the Ingram youngsters on John's bridge tournament evening which unfortunately fell on the same night as Miss O'Hara's progressive euchre club.

"She's a generous hearted little thing," John said

to Gail.

And Lucy had spent two whole days fashioning a delectable bonnet for Freddy. Blue velvet, shirred around the face and with little French rosebuds tucked under the brim. John promised to buy Freddy a winter coat to go with it — if Lucy would help him pick out the coat. It was arranged that Lucy should take Freddy to town some Saturday and they would have lunch before the shopping expedition.

"You come too, Gail," John invited. But she said she had enough to do that week, writing copy about children's fall clothes, without shopping for them too.

Lucy was always running through the gap to chatter with Katie O'Hara: about the children's diet and their baths and their wardrobes. She persuaded John to take Fiske to the dentist and to have Freddy's playroom redecorated in gayer colors. She personally supervised the stenciling of ducks and nursery rhyme pictures on the walls.

"Oh, let her do it," Gail said to John, laughing. "It keeps her out of the house, mornings."

"You see Aunt Gail and I are so different," Lucy confided to John when, stricken with admiration, he viewed the new decorative scheme and properly thanked the laborer. "I reckon," admitted Lucy humbly, "I'm only the domestic sort. Aunt Gail has such a wonderful brain she ought to be a man."

John was amused. "You think women don't need brains?"

Lucy laughed merrily. "I reckon I haven't many; I'm such a silly little thing. But you know —" with intense seriousness — "I do think children are heaps more important than a lot of other things."

Gail was really accomplishing good work on the novel. There was less to do in the garden now, and Randolph Ormsbee was going into town every day. He was on the track of a likely job, he said, and if he landed it they would all be on Easy Street. At least he came home sober and at a reasonable hour and Gail was thankful now for the extravagance of that fifty-trip ticket.

Regina's protective attitude toward the book and its author touched Gail. Regina could be heard at the front door explaining to callers who had the temerity to lift an author's knocker during morning hours, "She's writing. Not talk to peoples till afternoons." Gail was discovering that the scribe who dwells in a lay community has to fight for every hour of her working time, and if she fights too hard she cannot hope to be popular. People could be made to respect your work and to leave you alone . . . but you would be likely to find yourself alone when, work completed, you yearned to play. Neighborliness was the thing that counted, not genius. Gail had no desire to hold herself aloof. She had come out here to Shadow Hills, she told herself, to enjoy a home and a garden and pleasant neighbors, to establish congenial contacts. But if the pleasant neighbors would only not call, mornings!

It had helped, having the telephone moved to the hall. Gail had grown tired of stopping work for long intervals while Lucy perched on a corner of the table-desk, twinkling eye on an inwardly seething author, and exchanging converse with one or another of the college lads who were eternally calling up. But now

Regina stood guard. Sometimes it seemed to Gail that Regina had more respect for the developing novel than anybody else in its vicinity. What the gratified author overlooked was that the Perfect Treasure, liking well to work for professional ladies who were not fussy or interfering, was in her own way protecting the goose that laid the golden egg. Success of that book, Regina comprehended, would safeguard a position whose permanence she coveted. And one or two things, of late, had seemed to threaten it. By the same token she approved of Miss Lucy Lovelace who was, from the Regina angle, a lucky red herring drawn across the trail of outside distractions.

The author was grateful to John for keeping Lucy busy. Lucy had no qualms about using the country club without regular membership privilege. She would go with anybody who asked her. Glancing out of front windows, Gail would see the little scarlet sweater and beret cap on the links among the other players. Bending over a teed ball, long driver grimly clutched in small hands and a curl dropping forward over her shoulder, Lucy was a cunning thing. John came home early, afternoons, to keep up the lessons. "I could make a player of her if she'd keep her eyes on the ball," he said in the amused, indulgent way he always spoke of little Lucy. "I wish you'd come out and learn too, Gail." She had no time for golf, she protested. Later perhaps. He nodded. She had informed him the book was approaching completion and he knew no author at such a time had patience with people who tried to pull her away from her work.

John was an understanding person, she told herself. One could always depend on him.

All at once it was October. Maples outside the hedge were saffron and sienna with slim black branches showing through. The birches were rich gold with a golden carpet underneath — where the buttercup path had been. The big beech in the Ingram yard was deep wine color, and woodbine on the Holbrook porch gleamed crimson in the morning sun. Down in the ravine the brook floated on armada of brilliant little leaf ships. And the mountains revealed hitherto unperceived slopes and crests and ledges because of contrasting color in foliage.

In early morning the roof gutter held brittle slivers of ice that looked like broken glass and in the garden only the marigolds were left, with scarlet flags of the salvia gallantly waving behind them. But the cosmos by the gate was beautiful. Gail loved the pale, starry blossoms gleaming at night against the hedge. Nun of the garden, the cosmos that had no fragrance, no sentimental appeal. You could not love cosmos as you did deep hearted roses, or heliotrope or mignonette. Not a flower to send to one in sorrow, or to lay on a coffin. But a great jar of it in a dark corner of the room was exquisite, with delicate ghostly reminder of springtime in the woods.

Lucy and Randolph Ormsbee made breakfast conversation about furnace heat. The coal was in, but Gail, like all householders in October, developed that sturdy feeling. Brisk, bracing cold was good for you after relaxing heat of summer; there was the wood fire to take the chill off, evenings — and of course a kitchen range really warmed the lower part of a house. She wore a sweater, working in the study. When finally her father asked to have his breakfast carried up because bed was the only place, he said, where old bones could keep warm, and Lucy took to sneezing at regular intervals, (she really felt acutely the first nip of a northern winter) Gail had old Jenkins, the neighborhood handy man, start a fire in the furnace. And the sudden change from numbing chill to mellow warmth was so delicious that one's very soul expanded. The outdoor prospect, instead of looking nipped and frostbitten became interesting and gorgeous; and Bill stretched luxuriously in a patch of sunshine crossbarred on the study floor by the closed glass doors. After that, Gail would have sold her cherished antiques to keep coal in the cellar.

It might be necessary, she thought grimly — if she had to buy any more little items like winter overcoats for Randolph Ormsbee. She had worked down her house budget to what she considered the irreducible minimum, but these extra expenses were terrifying. When the novel was placed, (a pleasanter word than "accepted") there would be an advance royalty. She must finish as soon as she could. How miserable, to have financial pressure affect what ought to be happy and leisurely creative achievement!

Doctor Holbrook and Mr. Heddon and lonesome Mr. Swain had taken to dropping in again evenings, now that the season of hearth fires had arrived. John Ingram came also. Lucy made rarebits, looking very cunning with a white pinafore tied back over a ruffly frock. Often they played bridge while Gail shut herself into the study to catch up with fashion copy, neglected in a deep preoccupation with the novel.

One morning, letting Bill out before breakfast, she picked up in the porch swing a gay little magenta striped handkerchief. It had "M.H." embroidered in a corner. And Randolph Ormsbee at breakfast remarked facetiously: "Heard you and your fellow out on the porch pretty late last night, Gail. Which of your boy friends was it? Not Ingram, I met him in the village on my way home."

"It better not be Mr. Heddon," said Lucy mischievously. "I don't think his wife cares much about his running over here evenings."

"You know very well, Lucy," Gail said, "that I was not on the porch last night. I went upstairs when you did."

"But you might have come down, mightn't you?" Lucy twinkled at her grandfather. He looked at her with disfavor.

"You might," he retorted. "But if Gail says she wasn't out there, she wasn't. It must have been the wind, creaking the swing."

"See what it is," sighed Lucy, "to have an unassailable reputation!"

But after Randolph Ormsbee had departed she said to Gail, "Of course I have often seen you in the grape arbor, Aunt Gail. In that gray cape of yours. But why should I say anything? It isn't my business."

"And you needn't make it your business," Gail longed to retort. She knew the prattling tongue of little Lucy. Undoubtedly Mimi had borrowed the old cape, frequently left out on the porch; and had probably been sitting on the porch with her Jimmie, now that the vine over the arbor had shed its leaves. If Randolph Ormsbee found out about the secret engagement and stolen meetings he might make jovial comment down at Gus Abbott's pool room — he was quite capable of it. And Lucy might let out the secret to Mrs. Jessup or Mrs. Holbrook. She had been flitting across to see both.

"She fits in perfectly, here," thought Gail. "People admire her though she doesn't do a constructively useful thing. Pity John didn't meet her first; he evidently considers her a born mother and I'll say she's a perfect suburban neighbor."

She went out and greased the pullies of the porch swing. If Mimi and Jimmie were going to sit in it, at least it needn't squeak.

Jule Vernon called up and begged Gail to come to the Hallowe'en dance at the country club. John added his persuasions. "Everybody will turn out and if you are ever going to take your place in this community it's time you began."

"But I can't do frivolous things like that, John, until I get the book off my mind."

"Oh, hang the book! You come and have a good time — for once. And I speak for the supper dance."

Lucy stared. "Aunt Gail dance?" An amusing idea, her look said.

"She danced before you were born," John told Lucy crisply.

Lucy's merry laughter rippled. "I reckon that's true all right," she admitted.

Gail decided to go the the Hallowe'en dance.

Lucy planned a new frock for the dance. Lavender chiffon, all fluttery little ruffles. She sewed on it steadily. John hitched his chair over, one evening, and picked up one end of a ruffle. She was snipping through a line of hemstitching to make the picot edge.

"That's a pretty color. You are a smart little girl, to make your own dress."

"I make all my own clothes," Lucy said virtuously. She held the material up against her chin. "I think I'll wear violets with this — cotton ones of course."

"Of course not," said John. "They ought to be real ones. I'll bring some out from town." He turned to Gail. "What color is your dress?"

"Oh, I'm wearing my old blue. It has done service at several Buyer and Retailer banquets, but it will have to do. I haven't time to think of clothes — until the book is done."

"How about pink roses with that?"

Gail laughed. "They'd only show up its lack of freshness. Don't bother, John. I detest real flowers with an evening dress — the stems all sopping wet. I prefer my flowers in a garden."

But for Gail arrived white gardenias which looked charming on the blue frock. It was shabby — and limp — Gail perceived when she lifted it from its hanger. She ought to have gone to town for a new one. She had Regina press out the crumpled costume while she dashed to the village to have her hair trimmed. Of course the trim just missed the smartness her town barber would have given the severe haircut and Gail felt that night that she did not look her best. It made her diffident and stiff. She told herself, standing a little aloof from the chattering crowd in the dressing-room that an author, concentrating on absorbing work, had no business to enter into gambols of this sort. These people were bent on a frolic and she didn't fit in.

But Gail loved to dance and presently began to enjoy herself. The club house was gay with pumpkin lanterns, and black paper bats and witches were tacked against the walls. There were haystacks in the corners of the dance floor and in the center a pen with geese and chickens that made weird noises above the bleat of the saxophones. Everybody was hilarious. This was fun, thought Gail, who was young and light footed — if only one had nothing more serious to think about.

John and Jule Vernon kept bringing up new partners. Some of them she had noticed on the golf course during the summer.

"Where have you been keeping yourself all this time?" asked one man who approved the new girl's blue eyes. And the dimple.

"I've been working. I'm starting a garden. And I — I write —"

"Oh lord!" His voice fell a whole note. "Are you that literary lady in our midst? Wouldn't have dreamed it." Immediately he began to converse, instead of being casual and jolly; and when the dancing stopped he asked her if she had read that book about philosophy by what's-his-name. She did not see him again during the evening.

It was going to spoil all her fun, Gail realized, if in this community she talked about her writing. In a lay gathering you had to hide your talent like a secret sin — if you wanted to have a good time.

"It's sweet of you," she said, dancing with John, "to give the infant department such a happy evening."

"Who — little Lucy? Cute, isn't she, in that lavender get-up. It's like dancing with a fairy. One thing they do teach girls, down south."

Lucy in ruffled lavender chiffon was cute, no doubt of it. She wore the deep purple violets, not as other girls wore flowers, at the shoulder, but below the V of her bodice in quaint, old-time fashion. And over the shoulder strayed a curl.

"The rose-at-her-bosom effect," whispered Mimi, stopping for a moment beside Gail. "She makes every man in the room think of Annie Laurie. Womanhood — before the Vote spoiled it."

"I wish," Gail whispered back, "she would refrain from piping out 'Aunt Gail' every time she comes near me. It makes me feel a hundred."

"Don't you think perhaps she does it purposely?"

"Oh, come now, Mimi. Why should she deliberately try to annoy me? It's just her babyish way."

"Well, my advice to you," said Mimi cryptically, as she prepared to foxtrot away with Jimmie Jessup, "is to watch her!"

It was a little provoking of Lucy to ask John, just before the supper dance, to run around to Lilac Cottage in his car for a forgotten scarf. Gail went in to supper with the Heddons rather than remain in the ball room, alone.

Sunday afternoon John strolled through the gap and asked Gail to go for a tramp. "Bring Bill," he said. "Too nice a day to waste indoors. Bound to be a break in this weather soon. Come along; it'll do you good."

Gail looked out at the gorgeous autumn afternoon.

Distances were misty with Indian summer and golden leaves fluttered down in the still air. Lucy had gone to the club with Mimi, and Randolph Ormsbee was dozing upstairs over the Sunday paper. It would be pleasant to have a walk with John. They had not had a pally time alone together in weeks. John was an understanding person, he was letting her finish her book as he had promised. But a little walk this perfect afternoon—

"I have to get supper on Sunday." She hesitated. "How far are you going?"

"Not far. Through the meadow beyond the bridge and up into Dickman's woods. Butternuts in there and I promised the youngsters I would take them this Sunday."

"Oh —!" said Gail. (She might have remembered that Katy O'Hara had Sunday afternoons off!)

She told John she had letters she simply must write; it was a crime, the way she had neglected Hilda and Arlene of late. He'd better run along and get his walk — and come over that evening. She'd be free then.

But she had an uncomfortable certainty, after he had gone back through the gap, that he had seen her expression change when she learned the children were to be part of the walking party. He hadn't looked provoked — just sorry. And had gone away without urging her further.

She was finishing up her letters at five o'clock when Jule Vernon in riding breeches and coat ran up the porch steps and tapped on the glass door.

"I came around by your garden gate. Hope you don't mind. Tied my nag to a tree outside your hedge. Glorious day. What you doing indoors?"

"I had letters to write." Gail began clearing a chair of books and papers, but Jule perched on a corner of the table-desk. She switched at her ankles with her riding crop as they talked. She hadn't come, it appeared, for any special reason; the others had ridden on to the club, but she had taken the notion to drop off here.

"I'm glad you did. Won't you let me give you some tea?"

"Never touch the stuff, thanks. I'll have a cigarette and then be off."

When the cigarette was finished she tamped it out in Gail's pen tray and locked her hands around an updrawn knee. She grinned at her hostess. "I had an idea when I came in here that I'd favor you with a piece of my mind. But I guess I won't."

Gail smiled back at her. "Go ahead — say it."

Jule looked at the other girl speculatively. Then she reached over and touched with a fingertip the neat pile of manuscript on the desk blotter.

"Say, lady, does that book mean more to you than anything in the world?"

Gail laughed. "Well — pretty nearly."

"There's nothing that matters so much as — say: getting it finished by a certain date?"

"I wouldn't say that." Gail was an accurate person. She glanced at her visitor curiously. "Why?"

Suddenly she was aware that Jule Vernon, who was not smiling, was trying to convey some sort of warning. "Why?" she asked again.

"Because," said Jule, "I thought, not long ago, I saw you holding something — rather precious. I wouldn't want to see you lose it — if it did happen to be worth more than a book to you."

"Just what do you mean?" Gail heard her own voice, stiff with dignity. She had that little cold feeling all over that was anger — and barrier of pride swiftly erected to protect invasion of an inner citadel.

Jule Vernon laughed and sprang off the table. "I've said too much. I told you I'd better keep still. You're angry. I don't blame you, I guess I would be too. I've got the most indecent way of being too frank with people I like —"

She caught up gloves and riding crop and then suddenly rested her hands on Gail's shoulders.

"And I like you very much, my dear," she said. "I like you — enough, not to want to see you make any silly mistakes ... for that." She turned and brought down the little whip smartly on Gail's stacked up manuscript. And ran out of the room.

From the gate she called, laughing. "Drop over and see me — when you manage to forgive me."

Gail still stood, petrified, by the study table when Jule's horse clattered out on the turnpike from Brook Road. Gail stared at her manuscript, flicked by Jule's whip. The top pages had been disarranged and she straightened them.

Her book — slashed at by a whip. As though it were something worthless besides —

Besides what?

Jule Vernon was meddlesome. And impertinent. What business was it of hers how long an author took to finish a book? Or for that matter, what interests she might have outside the writing of it? Gail felt again Jule's hands on her shoulders; saw the friendly eyes smiling into hers.

"And I could have liked that girl!" Gail sighed, with regret.

She slipped into her sport coat, pulled a felt hat down on her head and whistled to Bill. The house was stuffy, too hot. A run down the road before attacking supper preparation would do her good. She saw Mimi and Jimmie in the ravine and waved to them. They wouldn't be able to meet there much longer, the leaves were getting too thin... Why, where was Lucy? She and Mimi had gone to the club together. Lucy must have slipped in at the front door while she herself came through the garden gate.

Gail went as far as the bridge where she encountered Doctor Holbrook returning from a solitary tramp. Recalling that Mimi and Jimmie were in the ravine, Gail held him chatting on the bridge while Bill rustled about among the heaped up leaves.

Doctor Holbrook pointed with his cane. "Pretty sight, that!"

Gail looked at a tangle of bare twigs through which gleamed the rich scarlet of bittersweet. Then she saw that he was pointing, not at the bushes, but beyond them. Through the tangle of briars could be seen a little group advancing out of the Dickman woods into the meadow beyond the bridge... Lucy Lovelace, holding Freddy by the hand and laughing back over a shoulder at John Ingram who was whittling busily as he walked. Beside him, Fiske, intent on John's handiwork. They were all laughing. John's cap was pushed back on his head and Lucy was carrying her hat.

Quite a jolly little family group out for a Sunday afternoon stroll, had been Doctor Holbrook's implication. Nobody could miss it! Gail stood rigid. Something sharp and hurting stabbed at her heart.

John — and Lucy!

There recurred something Cousin Prunella had said that day at the station, waiting with her bundles for the train: "Lucy Lovelace is so fond of children, she'd be just the one for Mr. Ingram."

Doctor Holbrook had evidently the same idea. He remarked, "Now if they could fix that up. She's a winsome thing. And a born little mother."

The group had arrived at the fence that bordered the road. So lovely was the evening they seemed loath to end their outing. They could not see the observers behind the tangle of briars down by the bridge and Gail had unconsciously slipped the leash on Bill's collar. John swung Lucy to the top rail of the old fence and set Freddy beside her. Then he lifted Fiske to her other side and, dropping his cap on Lucy's lap, leaned on the fence, steadying her — and Freddy — with his arm. The sun was setting behind bars of black that had luminous edges of pure gold and the still air had a quality of filtered gold shot through with rosy light. Grasses in the meadow were pink and maples at the edge of the wood stood out in fiery splendor. The radiant, rosy light rested on the group: on Lucy's chestnut curls, on Fiske, bending over the newly whittled toy in his hands, on John's face, upraised to Lucy's while he steadied her and his little daughter with careful hands.

Down on the bridge where dusk had already settled

Gail felt suddenly a chill of autumn and of loneliness.
She made some murmured excuse to Doctor Holbrook about supper, spoke sharply to Bill and hurried up Brook Road toward home.

CHAPTER XX

Frost

UNBELIEVABLE! That John Ingram with his shrewd intelligence, his cultivated mind and intellectual taste, could be seriously attracted toward an immature person like Lucy Lovelace, a pretty little chatterbox, not out of her teens and in no sense a companion for him.

But was it so impossible? Men did such things. Serious men married girls like Lucy and seemed happy with them. John's wife had been, if reports were to be credited, the babyish, appealing sort who wept to get what she wanted and could converse about nothing much but her "big man" and her babies. Her babies —! Cousin Prunella had said Lucy would be just the one for John Ingram because she was so fond of children. Maybe he thought so too.

The born little mother. The born domestic type. Infallibly admirable type in man's opinion for wifehood. All men adored little cuddling women. Times changed, and manners, but masculine nature did not change. Even in this advanced and intelligent age didn't the very music of the dance halls stress that quality in man? ... "L'il honey gal" ... "She's mah baby" ... "Pril'l thing" ... "Where'd you get those great big eyes?" ... Cunning women-dolls that big boys longed to play with; little darlings they could protect, and protecting, feel how strong they were!

Something that hurt — in the memory of John swinging Lucy up on the fence and then steadying her with solicitous arm while he smiled up at her. The taken-care-of woman. Gail's stout independence had always professed to despise them. Snuggling, secure, behind walls that somebody else upheld. Women whom harsh winds did not touch, who had always shelter to fly to. Who did nothing worrisome and exhausting for their own sustenance. They ran homes — oh yes, they talked about that nerve-racking strain! But women who ran homes with one hand while with the other they earned their daily bread could smile at that. They bore children — yes. And countless thousands of them chose the childbearing lot rather than labor of self-support. And thousands more, soul-sick with conditions of their chosen lot, elected to stick things out rather than come to grips with that — to them — more terrifying bogie: self-responsibility.

But something . . . a symbolism . . . about John's lifting of Lucy and standing by, steadying her, the while they laughed together, had made Gail see this matter of protectedness in new light. A light that was, though hurting, illuminating. Deep in her soul Gail knew that here, in this thing she had seen symbolized, was best happiness for any woman creature: to laugh, or to cry if need be, to suffer if must be — protected! Taken care of. Safe within barriers that greater strength than her own put around her.

There were the hedges within which a woman should make her garden!

Lucy knew it by instinct. They hadn't brains enough, the lucky Lucys, to be led astray by urge of self-expression or ambition. Undistracted, their feminine instinct led them surely to their goal.

"She shan't have him!" Gail told herself angrily.

John Ingram was hers. Nobody should take him from her. True, she hadn't been sure she wanted him. She hadn't been sure she didn't want other things more — She looked at the almost completed manuscript and thought of Jule Vernon's whip, flicking it, Jule's quiet question: "Are you sure this means more to you than anything else in the world?"

She looked around her cosy study and out at her garden — even in its winter drabs and browns and with leaves raked over the beds, a place of peace. She could go on here and each year have a lovelier garden. And if Lucy and John were married the children would run through the gap with little presents. Aunt Gail, always interested. In their school triumphs. Their commencements. And their weddings. After a while John's little grandchildren would come running through the gap to show things to old Aunt Gail . . .

"I won't do it!" said Miss Ormsbee aloud and indignantly, as though somebody else had presented this pleasant panorama for her consideration.

But what could she do about it? She could ship Lucy Lovelace back home; — but if John were really attracted there was nothing in the world to keep him from boarding a train and going down to Georgia after her. You couldn't manage men like that; they had a perfect right to choose their mates.

"But he chose me!" Gail told herself resentfully.

"Yes — and how much proof have you given him that you were the one he wanted?" retorted an inner critical self that seemed now to look on, amused but exasperated, at this new emotional Gail who had waked up. For as every author must be two beings: the creator, imbued with warmth and ardor, and also the chill and relentless critic who can sit back and slash at achieved effort, so is every balanced human two selves: the one impelled by headstrong will and the other curbed by reasoning intelligence. After all, Gail's perfectly sound intelligence told her, there was nothing much to be done but wait and watch events. When she began to calm down from a rage that had stirred inner forces of which, in pleasant pursuit of life as she had arranged it, she had been unsuspecting, she saw that she was perhaps imagining things for which there was no basis of fact.

John had invited her to go for a walk. She had refused. He had taken Lucy. Why all this excitement?

John had asked her, that night in the arbor, if she would "think about it" when the book was finished. And she had promised. An author would be allowed to finish her book in peace. After that, business of thinking about other matters.

And meanwhile, Lucy Lovelace was doing everything feminine ingenuity could suggest to captivate John Ingram. Gail admitted it now. She didn't need Mimi Holbrook's warning. Lucy was a cunning little southern thing but she would indeed bear watching. Gail sighed. Nice work for an author whose whole mind at this critical juncture should be on completion of her book!

Ought she not, perhaps show a more beautiful spirit: be willing to sacrifice her own claim, if any, and yield the whole field to Lucy if such were for John's best happiness?

"Fudge!" said Miss Ormsbee so distinctly that Bill opened an eye and looked up, alarmed.

It wasn't for John's happiness — not if she knew John Ingram as she believed she did; his mental and spiritual needs in companionship; his dislike of triviality; his love of order. (If he could see Miss Lucy Lovelace's room as Miss Ormsbee had seen it, mornings!) If he knew about the little white lies Lucy's Aunt Gail had more than once caught her in. Of course one could not tell John these things: it would be unsporting. But there they were.

"I'll not let it upset me," Gail told herself firmly. "I'll go right on and finish the book and not think about it. Probably there is nothing in it at all but my own imagination."

But she knew Mimi would not have given that warning and Jule Vernon would not have flicked the manuscript with a whip if there had been nothing in it at all.

She plodded on with the novel but her heart was not in the work. Fortunately all there was to do now was revision and final polishing up, details that required concentrated attention, but demanded no fine frenzy of creative effort. But she fussed and rewrote and fretted, impelled by a feverish desire to get through. She almost begrudged the few hours she had to spend in the garden, planting bulbs — which the garden manual insisted must be set out before the second week in November. Hyacinths, pink and blue. A hundred Darwin tulips in the borders around the bird bath. She planted them all carefully, as the garden manual instructed, an inch and a half below their depth, but she felt no thrill of anticipation about their blooming next spring. When those tulips came up, maybe she'd be so unhappy she wouldn't care whether she had them or not.

It was perhaps fortunate for the literary production that John Ingram departed on his autumn trip to the western office. For a fortnight work on the novel went well. Lucy made pretty business of writing John long letters. Reports about the children, she mentioned. "He knew you wouldn't have time, Aunt Gail, or see as much of them as I do."

Lucy asked if there were any objection to having Fiske and Fredricka continue to come for the before-bedtime story hour. This charming custom had been inaugurated back in September when the story had been told in the arbor. Then, colder weather arriving, and earlier dusk, the before-bedtime story had been related before the living-room fire in Lilac Cottage, the children running home afterward, carefully muffled up by Lucy who watched from the gap until they were safe inside the Ingram house. Sometimes John came for them and listened to the end of the story from a deep chair back in the shadows. The story-telling group was a pretty sight: Freddy on Lucy's lap and Fiske curled on the floor at her knee, the firelight playing over them. Gail, who took Bill for his evening run at this hour, usually came in just as the story ended.

"That's a ridiculous yarn," she commented once. The story-teller and her audience looked up, shocked.

"Don't you see," Gail, brisk from her walk in the keen air, breezed into a firelit atmosphere of romance with crude fact, "you are telling them, Lucy, that the mother kept a candle lighted in the window to guide her sons, out at sea, home through the fog. The biggest lighthouse on the coast hasn't a flash that could be seen ten miles out at sea in a thick fog. Even on a clear night you'd have hard work to see a candle-glimmer at that distance. Why fool children for the sake of a pretty sentiment? That's what makes all the disillusionment in this world — sentimentality of that sort."

Fiske turned anxiously to the infallible authority. "Couldn't it be true, father?"

"Well," said John, back in the shadows with his pipe, "it's nice to believe the little mother's prayer, when she set her candle there for her boys, might have helped."

Freddy flung soft arms about the story-teller's neck and looked truculently at the critic. "I fink it wath a lovelly sto'wy and I love you, Luthee."

But one night when Lucy had to beg off because one of the college lads, home for a weekend, had invited her to join a party driving over to Millington for a dance, Gail amiably offered to tell the story. Fiske was enchanted. "Gee, I wish you'd do it every time!" he confided while his father buttoned Freddy's little reefer. "I druther hear about real tigers in a jungle than those silly dragons Lucy's always makin' up. What you tell a feller is true and he knows it."

Gail's eyes and John's had met over Fiske's head in a look that she remembered now with a stab of loneliness ... "My girl — and Fiske's!" the look had said.

That had been a month ago. She couldn't recall any exchanged pally looks between John and herself for — how long had it been? She had been so absorbed in the book, she hadn't noticed.

She told Lucy now to go ahead with the children's story hour. But she stayed out later with Bill, tramping fast up the turnpike under the incredibly bright November stars so that she need not come in to find that group before the fire; — Freddy's sleepy little face against Lucy's breast and Fiske's head alertly uplifted. Whatever the story, Fiske loved a story.

"I could tell him a lot better one," Gail thought, closing the study door to shut out sound of honeyed southern drawl. But she couldn't offer. Lucy had started the story hour and it was her established prerogative.

Randolph Ormsbee had a job. He went to town every day and came back with the other commuters, the evening paper tucked under an arm. A new company, Gail was informed. Recently incorporated to market an industrial product. A practical invention (patent pending) that would revolutionize kitchen labor. Everything in the recurrent task of dishwashing could be accomplished without touching hands to water — except wringing out the old dish-mop at the end. And here was a tricky little contraption that gripped the dish-mop and with one twist wrung it dry as a bone. No more red hands at bridge parties. Maidless housewives all over the U. S. A. would leap at the treasure. There would be a fortune in it when —

Where had the company been incorporated, Gail

wanted to know. And when the new assistant manager mentioned a far western state that had a reputation for leniency toward ambitious but not so very well financed fledgling enterprises, his daughter remarked, "I thought so. Well, I hope it's all right. Don't let them use your name on any company documents. Where's the factory?"

The plant, he admitted was yet mostly on paper. He submitted the company's letterhead. A handsome plant indeed, expensively engraved at the top. Smoke rising from chimneys that obviously spread themselves over many acres. Of course, explained Mr. Ormsbee, they had to sell the stock before manufacturing could begin on a large scale. "I suppose you wouldn't take a little block, Gail — get in on the ground floor?"

"No thank you. And don't you try to sell any of it around here, father."

He refrained from mentioning that he had already let in on the ground floor John Ingram, Doctor Holbrook, Mr. Heddon and Jule Vernon. None of them had much faith in the stock but hoped the purchase would ease things for Mr. Ormsbee's daughter for whom they felt sorry. Gail, beholding the first crisp twenty-dollar bill tendered as paternal board money, fondly hoped the project would turn out better than she feared.

"By the way," said Mr. Ormsbee, who with solid ground of earned increment under his feet, expanded with mellow sense of parental responsibility, "I'd cut out sitting up so late with Whosis on the porch, nights. Now the leaves are off the trees —"

"Father, who —"

Mr. Ormsbee held up a protesting hand. "I'm not asking which one it is. That's your business. I'd hoped it was Ingram; he's free and he is earning a good income, but he has his eye on little Lucy Lovelace, I can see that. She makes a fuss over the kids and that's what he's looking for I expect. If you don't want to get married, that's your business too — I understand the artistic temperament. You take after me. But folks in a place like this don't look at things the broad way we do and people are talking —"

"Who is talking?"

"Well, Lucy was prattling, last evening while you had the dog out, about old lady Holbrook's asking her who it was, in our garden, night before last. Bright moonlight now and she can see a strip of the garden, sitting up in bed. She told Lucy she saw some chap going down past the bird bath and turning around to wave at the house. Wanted to know if Ingram was back. Trust Lucy to look coy, denying that Ingram came over here to see anybody but herself. So the dame concluded it must be Heddon or Swain — they have both been hanging around this summer — and she tried to pump Lucy about you: what you'd been doing before you came here —"

"I hope Lucy told her what I was doing. Helping support her mother, for one thing!"

"Well, that little trick is something of a pussy cat; seemed to think it a good joke, passing it on to me. She told Mrs. Holbrook her mother had always worried about your living so alone, but of course they were sure everything must have been all right. Lucy didn't want me to tell you, but she thought I ought to say something to Swain or Heddon —"

"You'd better not!" his daughter warned him. It was a little too much that through Mimi's mother, from whom she was generously guarding Mimi's secret, should be spread abroad ugly misconstruction of her own behaviour. Gail resolved that the thing must stop. And that night she put an end to it.

It was unusually late when she was roused by Bill, making the familiar movements that apprized his mistress of visitors below on the porch. Bill, climbing out of his warm basket, stole silently out into the hall, returned after a moment, scratched himself negligently and with a grunt climbed back into his cosy nest. Nothing for his watchfulness to worry about; only two good friends again making conversation at this odd hour on the porch. Gail switched on the bed lamp, glanced at her watch, and then, slipping on a warm bathrobe, tiptoed down to the study.

"Mimi, I want to speak to you!"

At the sudden opening of the glass door, two muffled figures rose from a wooden bench back in the shadow. The porch swing and the wicker chairs had long since been brought indoors.

"It's almost two o'clock, Mimi Holbrook. You promised me —"

"There was a dance at the club, Gail —"

"I know. I heard the cars going home an hour ago. You have no business here now and you know it. It isn't respectable. If you haven't sense enough, Jimmie Jessup ought to realize. He ought to take better care of you —"

"Oh, come now," said young Jimmie, "I'm taking

care of Mimi all right, Miss Ormsbee, and I can prove it. You don't have to worry."

Mimi caught his arm. "Let's tell her."

"Go ahead," responded young Jimmie. "She's a good sport; she won't blab."

"We're married," said Mimi. And she tucked her arm through Jimmie's.

"Married! When?"

"Six weeks ago. We were both twenty-one in September, you know. Not a soul knows about it."

"We certainly put something over on 'em," mentioned young Mr. Jessup with satisfaction.

"It's a — a companionate marriage," announced Mimi complacently.

"What do you mean by that?" demanded Miss Ormsbee. They looked like a couple of mischievous children discovered rifling the jam closet.

"Well, you see," explained Mimi who was obviously the major mind of the enterprise, "if we tell the glad news we'll have to spend every last cent Jimmie earns, supporting ourselves. My mother wouldn't have me in the house, and Jimmie's mother wouldn't tolerate me around. We'd just naturally have to shift for ourselves. And ten-to-one, Jimmie couldn't stay on at the mill. We simply can't be married and not have a house and a car and belong to the club. We'd pass out of the picture. So we thought what they didn't know wouldn't worry them. I'm working part-time in the library and Jimmie's salting away every penny he can save. When we get enough to stage the thing properly we'll open the cut-out and let 'em know we're arriving."

"That's the dope." Jimmie lighted a cigarette

and tucked the match carefully in his overcoat pocket. Tell-tale matchends, he had been warned, must not be flung about during nocturnal trysts on other people's property.

"And meanwhile," said Gail, "you are deceiving your parents, living on their bounty while you take advantage of them, and behaving like a couple of sneaks — instead of an honest man and woman, willing to face your own responsibilities."

"Oh, come now, Miss Ormsbee, that's a bit raw, isn't it? Mimi and I have a right to be married. We're free, white and twenty-one. It's our own life, isn't it?"

Gail swung round on him. "It would be your own life — if you made it so. If you came out honestly and admitted that you were married. You two are afraid to face a row — that's what's the matter. And if you are too soft to endure a few hardships for the sake of being together, I don't know whether you have the right to be married. If I were Mr. Syd Jessup I don't know whether I'd think so — or if I were Doctor Holbrook. My advice is, to tell them at once."

"You're not going to say anything?" anxiously inquired Mimi.

"I won't tell. But you can't make use of me any more."

"Oh, Gail!" Mimi put wheedling arms around the other girl. "I never thought you'd go back on us! I thought you were modern and a sport. You let us meet here —"

"I didn't know you were going to do anything like this, Mimi: use me, and use your father and Jimmie's father. It's — underhanded."

"All right," said young Mr. Jessup crisply. "Sorry. We don't meet here any more, that's understood. Come along, Mimi."

"But where'll we meet?" forlornly protested young Mrs. Jessup. "This was such a perfect place — right between our two houses. You know we can't sit in your car, Jimmie. That chauffeur sleeps over the garage."

Miss Ormsbee's sense of the ridiculous overtook her, in spite of her indignation and the fact that she was shivering in the biting chill of the November night. "Why not try the Ingram porch?" she suggested.

"Yes — and have that O'Hara woman tooting about it all over the neighborhood. Besides, John Ingram wouldn't let us — he has terrifically old-fashioned notions."

"Oh, has he?" said Gail. "Well, so have I — when it comes to two o'clock in the morning! I have felt sorry for you children — though you are not children any more, you are a man and a woman, shirking grown up responsibilities. And I have to think about myself." She told them about Lucy's conversation with Mrs. Holbrook, as reported by her father.

"Hot dog!" Jimmie was remorseful. "I never thought about you being implicated — you seem so much older and everything. Why didn't you say that in the first place, instead of shooting off the sermon?"

They couldn't meet here; that settled it. Miss Ormsbee had been a peach but they saw her position.

"Of course, as far as Mimi goes," said young Jimmie stoutly, "I can look out for Mimi. Nobody'd dare say a word about her. Gosh, let 'em try it!" But of course a single woman ... unprotected ... It wouldn't do, he saw that.

They went away together, separating at the gate. (Because it was moonlight, Mr. Jessup could not escort Mrs. Jessup across the ravine.) Gail saw them exchange a long kiss in the shadow of the hedge, before Mimi slipped through the gate and Jimmie vanished through the gap, into the Ingram yard. Gail watched from the porch, the bathrobe hugged tight about her shivering figure. Preposterous children, making a game of marriage. How quickly they had sensed that though gossip might hurt her it couldn't touch Mimi. Mimi was married! How safe it must feel to be married! The whole of humanity could yapp and yelp around you, but you and one other would be safe within a little magic circle. Everything else would be outside and you could snap your fingers at it.

She went back into the house and with Bill, whom she found shivering just inside the glass doors, climbed noiselessly upstairs.

When she had snapped off the light she pulled the covers over her head, to get warm. She tucked them in all around and under her. It was a wide bed — the kind with two pillows, the sort of bed that after years of hard and narrow boarding-house "singles" had seemed to befit the dignity of a property owner, head of her own household. Tonight, in it, she felt small and cold and pathetically alone in the world. Presently, thrusting one bare arm out into the nipping cold, she made a sound with thumb and forefinger.

Jumping on beds was a privilege rarely extended to Bill and he lost no time now, availing himself of the invitation. He curled around at the foot of the coverlet exactly over Gail's feet.

Comforted by Bill's undeviating devotion, the author drifted into slumber.

CHAPTER XXI

In the Town Tradition

WALKING up Fifth Avenue, Gail had that gloriously free yet slightly lost feeling of the author whose long effort is ended and whose brain child has been, for better or for worse, consigned to other keeping. There was all the time in the world and time felt curiously empty.

Town was gay and crowded and noisy. You didn't realize how noisy until you had dwelt for months amid country stillness. Yet there was something stimulating about the crowds and hurry and incessant motion. The shops were bright with football colors and enormous yellow chrysanthemums blazed in florists' windows. All the women were muffled in furs from chin to knee. Between the book and the garden, Gail had almost forgotten the vital matter of clothes. She looked wistfully at a squirrel fur coat in a furrier's window — she had so wanted that squirrel coat this year! But she bought a new hat (the invariable procedure, had she but known it, of any feminine author the instant a book is done). And then had a modest orgy of shopping. Shoes and a silk slip, two blouses and a soft green wool jumper.

She strolled into a toy department and looked speculatively at a handsome aeroplane and a white fur cat with yellow glass eyes.

"A Lucy trick!" she told herself, and walked out of the place. But down on the main floor she stepped back into the elevator and had herself carried up again. "They brought me that shawl for a present," she reminded herself. "And I have to celebrate getting that book done, some way."

After that, a long conference at the Buyer and Retailer office to talk over the Spring Styles Supplement which was coming along soon. How familiar the old place looked! And what a clatter of typewriters! Had she ever spent five years of her life in that cubby hole shut off with ground-glass partitions?

Joe Bussing accompanied her to the elevator. This time last year he hadn't troubled to remove his feet from the desk when she stepped into his sanctum with a batch of copy. She hadn't minded then; she knew she would, now.

"How is Hickville? Sick of it yet?"

"Not yet." Gail laughed.

He looked at her approvingly. "That tan is becoming — makes your eyes bluer. See much of Ingram? Out his way, aren't you?"

"We meet occasionally."

"Who's the baby doll he is taking out to lunch? Understand she is a relative of yours. Some little fairy! She had Ingram's kid in here one day — got in our office by mistake. And last week, in she trotted again, all by herself. Elevator put her off at the wrong floor, she said. Kind of a dumb-bell in an office building I'd say, but easy to look at. Couldn't persuade her to pose for our misses' style number, could you? That demure type is hard to get, these days."

So that was why Lucy had been so vague about where she'd had lunch the day she came in to the dentist's! John had dropped over that night to say goodbye before starting on his trip and he hadn't mentioned the lunch either. If they were doing things like that — making a secret of their meetings ...

Gail had regretted, earlier that morning, that John was out of town. It would be fun, she had reflected, to surprise him after she finished her interview at the Buyer and Retailer office — make him take her out to lunch. Ages, since they had eaten together across a little restaurant table. But now she was glad he was out of town. When the elevator paused at the fifth floor she kept herself from glancing at the familiar door with black lettering on a ground-glass panel: Editorial Department. Keep Out.

Down on the street floor she went by the magazine stand with a mien so icily aloof that the lame boy to whom she had always cheerily nodded opined with regret: "She's got snifty since she had an estate in the country. Nice girl she used to be, too."

Hilda's welcome was warming. There was cinnamon toast and tea with lemon, and Hilda's cat, curled into a yellow muff, was on the only sunny windowsill. Arlene would be there for dinner and there was a party on for the evening — in Miss Ormsbee's honor.

And — big news! Arlene was going to be married. An artist she had met last summer on Cape Ann, Hilda reported. A real one, too — no commercial stuff. Landscapes and pastorals, on exhibition now at an uptown gallery. "Five hundred apiece, my child — when he sells them! Someday he'll be buying Arlene a limousine. Just now they are going Dutch on dinners at Bruccoli's. And they will live at her studio. You see," Hilda reasonably pointed out, "Arlene has steady pay with that costume design work, and of course he never knows what he'll have — or when. But he has the talent, his time will come. And they are happy; that's the main thing, isn't it?"

Hilda felt concerned about Gail. She thought Gail, in spite of her becoming tan, looked less sturdy and blooming than she should, after a country summer.

"I have been working hard on the book," Gail said, defensively.

"Nothing worrying you, is there, old dear?"

What should worry her, Gail protested; — aside from trying to do a book in a houseful of relatives, with a Perfect Treasure who must be kept contented?

"How's John?"

"Oh, flourishing," Gail said. And changed the subject.

Arlene breezed in and accused them of talking her over behind her back. "I surprised you, didn't I, Gail? For all your devoted Steady, I'm going to be a missus first. Hope Hilda's told you what a sheik he is... And how distinguished his work is too. I never hope to do anything approaching it." Arlene's voice had an unwonted humility and gentleness. Her amber eyes had lost their restlessness and were full of a bright content.

Gail told them about the book. It was agreeable to discuss it with people who were more than politely interested. The three good pals spent two hours in happy shop-talk and it did Gail good; — the spirited talk of books and pictures, of publishers and editors, of reviewers and critics, of who was doing this and who had achieved that. She felt stimulated and rested, as though an invigorating breeze had blown a lot of musty cobwebs out of her brain. Petty household economies, irritating relatives, and secret, gnawing worries faded, temporarily at least, into their proper perspective: nagging personal problems in no way vital, compared with the real business and constructive activities of a professional career.

She had missed this sort of thing. "I wonder," she said, "whether I shall ever really fit in — out there."

Hilda looked up alertly. "What's wrong?"

Gail laughed in a rather rueful way. "I haven't any social talent I guess. The women don't care for me."

"Have you tried to make them?"

"Why should I try, Hilda? I can only be myself. We don't speak the same language, that's all. What you do doesn't count in a place like that; it's how valuable you are as a social unit. You are expected to accomplish all the things they do, even if you give eight hours a day to your work. They don't want to know anything about the eight hours — you just have to get it in somehow."

"How much do women want to know," inquired Hilda, "about the eight hours of work men put in every day?"

"But they don't expect men to be chatty and hospitable at any hour of the morning when they call up, or drop in. Or to be punctilious about returning every little invitation. Or to send flowers when somebody has a sore throat. Or remember to ask after Grandma's bronchitis or little Willie's earache.

Or return grape jelly for the plum jam they sent over. If you don't do all these things you are no neighbor. And how on earth are you going to get your work done and be a neighbor too?"

"You would try it," reminded Arlene.

"Oh, I'm not sorry!" said Gail quickly. "I'd stifle in the city now. I guess —" she smiled rather pathetically at Hilda — "I miss my garden, now winter has come."

"You miss something!" Hilda thought. Aloud, she said, "You don't get out enough. Did you go to Maud Atchison's luncheon?"

"Yes. She sent the car for me. I could have had a lovely time — they were all jolly women. But the minute they found out I was doing a novel, that ended it. They stopped being informal and chatty and started talking about the books they had been reading... You know, Hilda —!"

"I do indeed," assented Miss Braithwaite. "About as cheerful as it would be to a mother, if a whole roomful of women began raving about how clever and handsome and well behaved other people's children are. When they start books I always switch the conversation to 'permanents'."

"They wouldn't switch," said Gail mournfully. "They kept on books, and one woman asked if I wrote under my own name —"

Hilda chortled. "Meaning of course: if you did she had never heard of you. That's always cheering too."

"After that," said Gail, "they talked about educational reforms in the training of youth. But I got quite pally with one nice old lady — the Atchison grandma — about gardens. She's coming to have lunch with me someday. While I was upstairs with her, looking at a garden magazine, I could hear them chattering below, sixty-to-the-dozen — as though a blight had been lifted from their midst."

Hilda looked compassionately at Gail. "You can't," she said, "hold people off with one hand and expect them to reach out to grasp the other. You resent it when they won't respect your hours of work — and revere the work. And you also resent it when they won't accept you as an irresponsible playmate, familiar with all the shibboleths of their play. I warned you long ago: you can't run with the hare and hunt with the hounds."

"It was why," Arlene inserted, "I left Pleasant Avenue, Ohio."

"But I could do it," Gail protested, "if they'd let me." She looked down at her hands so that Hilda might not see the tears that had sprung to her eyes. "I don't want to be lonely."

"If you are lonely," said Hilda succinctly, "it's your own fault!"

Gail sought to evade admission of Hilda's meaning. She laughed. "I guess it is. I'm too direct. I'm not suave enough. Mrs. Atchison's cook was ill and one of those women said, 'It's a shame, Maudie, for you to take all this trouble for us.' Maudie came back brightly, 'Why it didn't take me half an hour to scrabble this little lunch together!' Of course everybody there knew she had been on her feet since dawn, preparing those croquettes and mushrooms and salad dressing, and helping the waitress wash the best china. And she knew they knew it. A business woman, in Maud Atchison's place, would have said, 'Of course I worked all night, dear hearts — but it's worth it, to see you enjoy the feed.' If she had, those women would have told each other on the way home: 'Maudie's an awfully whole-souled person — but a little abrupt, don't you think?' ... What they are so deadly afraid of, is abruptness. I can't get used to it."

"You'll have to," said Hilda. "Remember you're not a business woman any more, but a social unit. You'll have to learn to swim in the waters the other fish find salubrious if you hope to enjoy yourself."

"You want to get married," advised Arlene. "That'll sweeten you up. You're entirely too caustic for a person with eyelashes like yours. That bucolic existence has got on your subconscious."

But Hilda did not think it was that. "How are the Ingram youngsters?" she inquired. "Obnoxious as ever?"

"Who said they were obnoxious?" asked Miss Ormsbee. "They are perfectly normal children." She related, with evidence of personal gratification, a recent accomplishment of Fiske's at school. Miss Braithwaite flashed a warning glance at Arlene who, unnoted by the visitor, had just sent her a prodigious wink.

If it wasn't the children, thought Hilda, then what was it? John Ingram? Now what had John done? Or failed to do. Not all her diplomatic efforts, however, could persuade Miss Ormsbee to mention Mr. Ingram in any but the briefest way.

"I'll have to go out there and spend a night on that living-room sofa I suppose," reflected Hilda who disliked the country in November. "And it did seem as though everything were going so well!"

Dinner was fun, sitting on benches in Hilda's "breakfast nook" that let down from the wall, and with everything crowded on the narrow slab-table: potato chips and chops cooked in a skillet over a gas flame and a pie from the delicatessen. After dinner there was one of Hilda's famous parties. Half the company sat on the floor because there were not enough chairs, and everybody talked at once. Two novelists were there; and a reviewer who had a reputation for biting wit; and a young man who could play the banjo; and a famous entertainer who did an extemporaneous monologue that it would have been worth five dollars a seat any time, to hear; and an almost-famous baritone who sang without accompaniment something that wrought a spell in the room so that no one spoke for minutes after he got through.

The reviewer brought Gail coffee and sandwiches. "Hilda Braithwaite says you have been doing a novel. Your first?"

When she admitted it he looked pitying. "Hope it's not reeking with sentiment. They so often are."

She showed him the dimple. "You'll have your knife in it, if it is, won't you?" She mentioned a recent novel, a best-seller on two continents. "There is plenty of sentiment in that book. I suppose you disapprove of it?"

"Gush, my dear child, pure, unadulterated gush. He merely pleased his public. You don't want to write like that."

"I'd give my soul to," said Gail.

He favored her with the Mona Lisa smile which the

sophisticated reserve for less completely aware persons. And drifted away to munch sandwiches with a lady in long earrings.

"I must tell John about that," Gail reminded herself.

Suddenly a wave of homesickness overtook her. For her little house and her garden. For the wide spaces of the golf meadows and beyond them the clean hills. For the brook singing in the ravine. For Bill — watching at a front window. For Doctor Holbrook, trudging down the road with a book under his arm. For Mimi, hanging over the gate. For Jule Vernon, clattering by on her sorrel horse and waving a friendly whip. For John, coming through the gap in golf kit and grinning apologetically because it was a short cut to the links. For Fiske and Freddy, smiling up at her: "We've brought you a present."

"I love them all," thought Gail. "Why, I care a million times more for them than I ever could, for this sort of thing!"

She couldn't wait to get back to them.

It was good to find herself on the train, after a bumpy night on Hilda's spare cot and a morning of intensive last-minute shopping in department stores that were too hot and too crowded; and nerve-racking with incessant ringing of bells — diabolical invention of some efficiency expert for summoning minions to a central office. From the train window she gazed out contentedly at the brown November landscape. Here and there an oak stood forth in still glorious crimson. And the far hills were densely blue under a brooding November sky.

She got out of the taxi and went up her own front

walk. She must rake leaves this afternoon. Somebody was burning them over at the Jessup place, the pungent odor came deliciously through the still air. And there was Bill, ears pricked, eager eyes yearning through a window pane. She could hear his yelp of ecstasy as he disappeared from view, making for the front door.

Her own front door and her own adorable brass knocker... And on the step two small, bundled-up figures.

She stooped and hugged Freddy and answered Fiske's trusting, expectant gaze: "Of course Gail brought you each a present. They're coming on the delivery truck. I hope you didn't think Gail would forget you."

"Luthee thaid you would," reported Fredricka.

"But I knew you wouldn't," Fiske assured her.

She went into the house, laughing, a child hanging on either arm.

CHAPTER XXII

East Winds Blowing

HILDA came for Thanksgiving and she did not have to occupy the living-room sofa. Gail insisted on doing that, and was up before even Regina was astir. This was Gail's first dinner party and everything must be perfect. There would be quite a tableful: she had asked Mr. Swain whose mother was visiting a married daughter in Boston, and dinner was to be at two so John could bring the children. It had been Gail who invited them — no suggestion of Lucy's. John was pleased.

"They'll bother you."

"No. I want them, John. Fiske can sit at my end and you can look after Freddy. I'll put her between you and Lucy."

"It will be a real Thanksgiving," he told her. "All of us having turkey together. Now don't go to too much trouble."

Gail's eyes twinkled. "I expect to be up all night, getting things ready, but it will be worth it: to see you enjoy the feed."

"You bet it will," said John enthusiastically. Men were a comfort.

He had inquired the first thing, on his return, how the book was coming along. "Fine!" Gail said. She did not tell him it was in a publisher's hands. "I'll wait and surprise him," she thought, "with my big news." There had been a little matter whose settlement was contingent on completion of the novel and she was not going to be the one to bring things to an issue by heralding glad tidings that the book was done and others might now present their propositions for earnest consideration. (The thought of that luncheon she had never been told about, rankled.)

She had come home from the little visit at Hilda's, resolved to be less resentful and suspicious. John had promised to look after Lucy while the novel was being completed, and he had done his best. Man-like, he hadn't considered it necessary to report all the details. There was no doubt but that Lucy was maneuvering to get John, but in all probability John had no inkling of it. Gail had taken invigorating tramps with Bill in the frosty air and felt better for it. At dusk there was a fiery streak low in the west with bare branches of trees silhouetted against it. And the world was very still, with all the insect clamor hushed. November was a delightful month in the country.

"Miss me?" John had asked, one hand clasping hers while the other was affectionately held by Lucy who had rushed to greet him, childlike, joyous countenance uplifted to his. Did Lucy expect the man to kiss them, thought Miss Ormsbee, just because he was back after a three weeks' absence? So she said, crisply, by way of rebuke to Lucy's foolish exuberance:

"No. Why should I? I've been busy."

She had been instantly sorry — there was no reason for being curt like that with John. He had inquired, then, about progress of the book.

After all, on Thanksgiving day, he came to dinner without the children.

Bad colds, he reported. The youngsters had been fretful for twenty-four hours and he had been up all night with them. He'd have to eat and run. Too bad. But Katie had been promised Thanksgiving afternoon off; and Freddy seemed to have a slight temperature.

"She would," said Gail who was removing the two extra chairs and re-arranging her dinner table. It held things up, of course, at the last moment. "Children always do run temperatures when their parents are going anywhere."

Lucy was indignant. "Aunt Gail! As though darling little Freddy would do a thing like that on purpose!"

"Who said she did?" retorted Gail. "Can't you ever see humor in an abstract assertion, Lucy Lovelace? It's instinct, that's all: the instinct to retain the slave and keep the upper hand. Children are just little expanding egos, bound, sooner or later, to choke us older ones into the background. Why be a sticky sentimentalist? If you see facts the way they are, some of them are entirely amusing."

Lucy, in a little yellow crepe frock that made her, with her bronze curls and one of the big golden chrysanthemums John had sent for the party tucked in her belt, a perfect harmony with the Thanksgiving decorative scheme, looked across at John — an intimate, deprecating little look that said as plainly as words could have articulated it: "Unfortunate — the way Aunt Gail feels about children!" Hilda saw the look and it gave her the key to something that had been puzzling her.

"So that's it," she decided. "Little Lucy is a

minx. And Gail knows it and it is getting on her nerves."

But Hilda frowned anxiously. All men liked to be adored and a little cuddling, insinuating thing like Lucy could do a lot of mischief in a situation that was trembling in a balance of uncertainty. John Ingram was a lonely man. Gail hadn't been too kind. If Gail had held him off just the unfortunate moment too long . . .

The dinner was a great success. Randolph Ormsbee carved the turkey with many a facetious pleasantry. And Regina's pumpkin pie was beyond compare. Gail was proud of her beautifully set table. She was sorry Cousin Prunella couldn't be there too. She found herself, while chatting amiably with Mr. Swain about recent football scores, envisioning a Thanksgiving dinner table . . . On one side, Cousin Prunella and Hilda — dear Hilda who would always be included in holiday parties, wherever Gail's home. On the other side, two shining-eyed children. Herself at one end; at the other —

It was just here that, glancing up, she met John's eyes smiling at her. The smile was so exactly the one in the vision — that beaming, proud smile a man sends up a dinner table to one who is presiding beautifully and perfectly in the place where he likes to see her — that Gail sent back exactly the sort of smile the vision called for. And the little exchanged smile somehow glorified the day.

But why should she, Gail reflected, ten minutes later, be so foolishly thrilled by a casual grin? . . . Like a dog, wagging joyous tail because a bone was thrown at him. John Ingram flung those genial smiles of his around with too much prodigality, that was the trouble with him.

But when John rose to go, immediately after dinner, she slipped out to the pantry and brought back two of the little pumpkin baskets of candies that had served as place-favors. The children must have these, she said: it was a tiny bit of the party he could take home to them.

"I'll carry them," said Lucy brightly. She had slipped on Gail's gray cape and was going over with John, she explained, to help tuck the youngsters in. "I want to have a look at that temperature of Freddy's. You'll have four for bridge without me."

Hilda observed that until Lucy returned, an hour later, Gail gave little attention to the bridge game.

"Send that girl home," counselled Hilda, before her departure next morning.

"She's going — after New Year's, Hilda."

"Then tell John Ingram tomorrow you'll have him. You have kept that man dangling long enough, Gail Ormsbee. And, mark my words, Lucy Lovelace will marry him if you don't."

Gail laughed — not with any effect of spontaneity. "She'd be welcome! Do you think I'd want a man whom either of two women could get — depending on who made the most effort?"

"Better men than he have been married that way," mentioned Miss Braithwaite.

"But not by me," Miss Ormsbee retorted. "I have my work, as you know very well. I'm not pining to marry any man."

"Well, you're pining about something," was Miss Braithwaite's reflection as the taxi took her away.

She glanced out of the rear window. The author sat on the doorstep, both arms tight about Bill. There was a rather desolate look in her eyes that were fixed on the far away hills. She did not suggest a person enthusiastically concerned with beckoning labor.

But Hilda knew better than to say anything to John. It didn't do to put ideas in a man's head — and if they were already there, all your arguments and advice would only serve to fix them deeper.

Three weeks from the day it had been submitted, the book came back.

Gail was out in the garden, raking leaves over the beds, when the expressman drove up with the package. She had to go upstairs for her purse because (crowning indignity) the manuscript had been sent "collect."

Then she shut herself in her study and only an author who has labored six long months and then waited with hope and prayer in her heart can appreciate the bleakness of the rest of that day.

But the flame that burns intensely for months on end, through weariness and discouragement, is a flame of courage. It may flicker and be beaten down, but it does not go out. On the following day Gail got her manuscript ready for its second venture. She resisted temptation to do the whole thing over. Only one opinion had pronounced against the book. It was good. She had put her best into it. She knew how to write; — for almost six years she had supported herself, writing. And in this book she had thought she had something to say. There were other publishers — dozens of publishers. Why back down and confess herself a failure because a single one refused to be convinced?

But faring forth with the manuscript the second time she felt more of belligerent determination and less of exultant thrill. It was a raw day with gusts of east wind swirling leaves in mad little witch dances on the lawns, and rain had been coming down in those intermittent spurts that to the weather-wise foretell a downpour by night. Gail donned her good country galoshes and raincoat and took along the big storm umbrella. And told Bill that this time he must stay at home. There was nothing more depressing than Bill, plodding home in the rain. He got no joy at all out of fighting a downpour.

By the time she had finished her business at the express office rain was coming down in earnest. The early December dusk was closing in and Gail decided to take a taxi back to Brook Road. All the available taxis at this hour would be at the railroad station where commuters' trains were coming in. The Jessup's chauffeur would have the closed car down there on a night like this. Perhaps Mr. Syd Jessup would give her a lift.

Umbrella slanted into the wind, Gail arrived at the station just as the 5.57 pulled in. Umbrellaless passengers swarmed out and dashed for any available conveyance... And there, huddled against a pillar, obviously awaiting someone's arrival, was Lucy... Lucy, slippered thinly as was her wont and garbed in the dainty tan suit in which, against Gail's counsel, she had set out two hours ago.

So that was why Lucy got home every afternoon just in time for dinner. She met the 5.57 and walked as far as the turnpike with John Ingram! Even when she left the house early, to play bridge at the club; or went down town to exchange a book or match embroidery silks, (foolishly taking her walk as Gail had pointed out to her, after the brief winter sunshine was gone,) she invariably turned up, Gail recalled now, just about dinner time.

Today, Gail saw the meeting; saw John leap off the car step, give one look at the drenching storm and make for the line of taxis — and then, at Lucy's call, halt and turn back. Of two things Gail was certain: he had not expected Lucy to be there; and he was a little exasperated that she was. He was most obviously giving Lucy a sound scolding for being out in such a storm in the sort of clothes she had on. But nobody scolded Lucy very long or very hard. Her penitence was too disarming. In a moment John was laughing down at her, reproving but indulgent. They stood by the pillar and he had the effect of guarding her solicitously from the rain, the crowd and all the discomfort of the draughty platform. When an empty taxi drew up he hurried her into it. And they drove away.

"I could have gone back with them," Gail reminded herself too late. Why on earth hadn't she dashed forward and claimed a place in that taxi? — there was plenty of room. Well, why hadn't she? John hadn't beamed with delight, finding Lucy waiting for him; he had looked distinctly impatient. But having Lucy on his hands, he had of course taken care of her. (There was a sting in the recollection of John's protective arm, rushing pretty Lucy in her dainty costume, out of the wet, into the taxi.) It was just John's way. He never let uncomfortable things come near you when you were with him. If it had been Miss Prunella Poppe he would have hurried her into a taxi with his arm around her just the same way.

But he wouldn't have scolded Miss Poppe — indulgently, as though she were a naughty little girl — because she happened to be at the station when his train came in! Lucy Lovelace evidently "happened" to be there frequently; — John hadn't looked surprised, come to think of it, merely concerned that Lucy should be out in such a storm.

The platform was deserted. All the taxis had gone and all the private cars too. Gail, with her umbrella, plodded homeward: up the village street, shining with wet in which shop lights were reflected, along the turnpike where cars sped by, spattering her, and down Brook Road where frozen ruts had softened to mud. The storm drove across the open golf links and bare tree branches writhed in the gale. "Good thing I put on my galoshes," thought Gail ... And then remembered that it had been Lucy, in thin slippers, who was the one solicitously taken care of. "That's where girls like me lose out," reflected Miss Ormsbee, trudging along in her galoshes, "—by being so well able to take care of ourselves!" Lucy knew her line all right, as Mimi had declared. It won a man every time — having to be taken care of. Appeal to his tenderness was what won and held any man strong enough to be worth wanting.

But though she might, Gail decided, fighting the wind with her big umbrella, be hypocritical enough to pretend dependent meekness, she could never be such a dumb fool as to don slippers in face of a brewing December northeaster.

When she reached home, her father was on one side of the fire with his evening paper and on the other side, Lucy in a raspberry wool frock and dry stockings and slippers, was turning the pages of a magazine. She looked up reproachfully:

"You're late, Aunt Gail. Regina has been holding back dinner."

"How did you get home?" Miss Ormsbee inquired. "You went out without an umbrella."

"I stopped at the station where there were taxis," reported Lucy. "And I've changed my shoes and stockings."

"Very sensible," said her aunt Gail. They went in to dinner.

Half truths. Reservations. Slyness. Pretense that you did not know for sake of keeping things pleasant. Gail hated it. She hated herself. People ought to be direct and forthright with each other; not sneak and keep watch and suspect.

What she ought to do, right now, was to have it out with Lucy Lovelace. And with John Ingram too. Clear the air.

To Lucy, she could say: "Look here, keep your paws off my man. He was mine before you ever set eyes on him and I won't stand for interference — see?" If they were two business women she would do it. But Lucy was not a business woman: she was one of the protected women who fight with different weapons. Lucy wouldn't fight fair. Lucy would go straight to John and tell him all about how her aunt Gail had misunderstood her. And misconstrued their pleasant friendship. And had implied that he had no right to be pally with anybody but Gail Ormsbee who owned him. And what had they better do about it?

Then the fat would be in the fire for certain! Even if John's sentiment toward little Lucy were (one still hoped it) friendliness and nothing more, he would be given the idea that Gail was jealous and suspicious and possessive. No, impossible to talk to Lucy!

She could have it out with John; in the frank and courageous way modern girls were supposed—according to fiction of the moment — to deal with heart problems. To John, she could say: "The book is done. Do you still want me, or have you become interested in Lucy Lovelace?" ... And exhibit good-tempered willingness to relinquish whatever prior claim she might have thought she had.

No, she couldn't tell John that she herself was ready — if his own interest had been diverted into other channels.

And John would want to know all about the book. She'd have to confess it had gone out and come back and gone out again. A stubborn pride in Gail flinched at that. She couldn't admit to John that her book was, perhaps, a failure ... after posing complacently as an author, and holding off John — and everybody else — because her superior status of authorship gave her the right to be exacting.

It would be one thing, with a publisher's enthusiastic acceptance in her hand, to go to John and say: "You see, I made good. But you mean more than any book — and here I am, John."

It would be quite another,to go to John, defeated, and say to him: "Well, I didn't make good, John — but anyhow there is *you*, so here I am."

No. If the book proved a failure John Ingram would have to come to her. She couldn't go to him!

Oh dear! So much depended on the wretched book! If only, meanwhile, John would give her some inkling of how he felt. If only, occasionally, he would exchange with her a glance of understanding — or a surreptitious handclasp. Why didn't he? If only he would flick her a glance even, of cynical amusement at Lucy's transparent little wiles. But he never did. He seemed to be pleased and amused by Lucy as one would be by a winsome child.

Gail overlooked the fact that she had never encouraged surreptitious handclasps. And that she gave John no opportunity for tenderly understanding glances. When she met his eyes nowadays it was always with a laugh, or with quick, sensitive withdrawal of her own gaze. John must not catch eyes fixed on him wistfully! So if John followed with a puzzled frown her endless flittings on household errands: to put Bill out, or to let Bill in, or to speak to Regina in the kitchen, she was unaware of it.

It was unfortunate that when she did call John up — on sudden, desperate impulse — asking him if she might have luncheon with him next day in town, he could not arrange it. The book had come back again. This time, out only a week, and returned with no word except an abominable little printed slip stating that it was "not available." Gail cried all night; and next day went around the house with the feeling that she had been kicked. She had to tell somebody about it. She had to tell John, of whose sympathy, at least, she was sure! Lucy was always calling him up evenings: How was Freddy's scraped knee — had the bandage been changed?... What was that three-letter word that meant Australian bird? She had the old cross-word all but that... Couldn't he come over and play Russian Bank or something?... There was no reason why Gail should not call him up. And it was silly of her, she knew, not to want Lucy to hear her do it; and to lower her voice cautiously when she used the telephone out in the hall.

"Hello there." John's cherry voice came over the wire. "That you, Gail? Quite a treat to be called up by the busy author!"

It was the devil's own luck about next day, he said. Atchison had made an appointment for him with their biggest middle-west customer. Lunch, and discussion of a new advertising campaign. He couldn't very well get out of it —"

"How about Thursday?" said Gail.

Well, Thursday, Lucy was bringing Freddy in to be fitted with that bunny suit or whatever they called 'em — made of worsted, for playing in the snow. Of course that could be done another day —

"Oh, no!" Gail said hastily. "Never mind. Some other time, John."

"Look here, Gail, what's up? Anything gone wrong? I'll run right over now —"

"We could not do any talking here — you know that."

"No," agreed John, "I suppose not. The dickens of it is, I have to go to Chicago, Thursday night. Be out there a week. Look here, you come, Thursday, for lunch and tell Lucy she and Freddy will have to wait till I get back —"

"I couldn't think of it," said Miss Ormsbee. (She had just glanced over her shoulder at a bright little face in the living-room doorway.) "Here's **Lucy** now; I think she wants to speak to you."

CHAPTER XXIII

Christmas Candles

SNOW. The garden asleep under a still, white blanket. The arbor topped with a bulging white canopy. Tracery of fairy lace where the climbing rose sprawled on the trellis. All day Gail looked out at the snow. From the study window, at new, mysterious vistas in the ravine where the brook was hidden somewhere under that undulating carpet of white. From her bedroom window, at snow whirling and driving across the golf meadow and obliterating the hills. Snow, muffling the hedges and the roof of the Holbrook house. Not an angle left in the world! Humans, fighting their way down Brook Road, just dark lumps. You felt yourself the only creature in the universe, so still the world, so vague everything outside your own withdrawn horizon.

Within doors, radiators simmering. No fear of callers. A day to work! But Gail could not work, she watched the snow. She had dreamed of the loveliness of snow, blanketing her garden. But now the anticipated loveliness was sad. A dead garden spread with a white pall. A great drift blocked the gap in the hedge; the Ingram house was far away now — the long distance around by road. The bird bath with a dome of rounded white looked more than ever like a little tombstone. Gail remembered that summer night ... How silly she had been, jealous of Jule Vernon! Jealous, she realized now, of whatever had threatened her possession. The precious possession that had been within her hands and that she had been too self-absorbed to safeguard.

She had made the mistake of banking too much on a good-comrade relationship. She had always been wrong where men were concerned, she saw that now. Men didn't crave comradeship of women; fair and square understanding; mutual exchange of opinion. Palship. All wrong. The idea was to encourage them in their masculine belief that they knew much more than you did — and to listen respectfully, profiting by their wisdom. So they could feel important and wise, affectionately tolerant of your foolishness and benevolent toward your dependent intelligence. You mustn't be too lucid about anything; or too keen about grasping ideas — it left them nothing to explain, patiently and kindly to you. The more illogical you were, the more feminine you were. The more you needed their solicitous care, (lest you hurt your silly little self against something you didn't understand) the more precious you were. If you were perfectly well able to take care of yourself and let all and sundry know it, you could go ahead and do it. Nobody would prevent you . . .

If this storm would let up she could take Bill for a run. Dogs had the right idea about storms, they curled up and snoozed away the hours; they didn't spend the time gazing out of windows and getting restless. If the book were not finished she would have something to do. Authors ought to keep something stiff to work on all the time; when they were at a loose end they got broody . . . Of course there was that Spring Supplement copy to tackle — but how undiverting to write about bathing suits and parasols with a snow blanketed world outside. She hated that fashion copy anyhow. She detested all writing of any sort. She wished she need never look at a typewriter again as long as she lived . . .

Lucy Lovelace was busy and happy this shut-in day — not roaming round the house and gazing out of windows. Lucy had sent for eight yards of pale pink tulle and was making a dress for the Christmas dance at the club. Yards of pink tulle attached in fluttery ruffles to a trifling little sleeveless bodice that fitted like a sheath. Lucy would be ravishing in that pale pink tulle — like a just-opened June rose.

Miss Ormsbee roamed upstairs and inspected her own costume for the Christmas dance. No limp and shabby blue silk pressed out by Regina for this event! Though squandering of substantial sums on party regalia is farthest from sane calculations of any author whose manuscript has just been declined, that pink tulle had decided Miss Ormsbee. This time she would look as well as a hundred dollars could make her! Whether there were money to keep the lawn mowed next summer or not!

Her clothes were all too stern, she had decided after critical contemplation of her wardrobe. She had ever hated sashes and jabots and tagging ends of this and that. There were two kinds of women: the ones who adored lace and the ones who loathed it, and she had always hated an inch of it on even her underthings. Very best fabrics cut on simplest lines: Gail's inflexible rule, and Arlene had once said that Gail's hair epitomized her idea in costume: thick and soft and shining hair severely cut to outline the shape of a beautiful head.

The Christmas party frock now gave splendor to the clothes closet. A delectable frock of shimmering gold tissue with veiling clouds of sheer black net. Sleeveless. And crushed at the hip; gorgeous twin roses, black and magenta, with gold leaves trailing over the skirt. To wear with it gold slippers with little twinkling toes and heels of criminal and fascinating tallness. She had felt really light-hearted, buying this outfit, as does any woman who is being wickedly extravagant, acquiring clothes for an occasion. Now she regarded the splendor with gloom. She had been a fool to spend that money — the price of six tons of coal. She would probably have a deadly time at the dance. She slammed the closet door and roamed downstairs again — to the study, from habit. It had stopped snowing and a streak of pale lemon spread low across the west — lovely, above the white line of snow enwrapped hills. Doctor Holbrook and Mimi were out shovelling paths, their voices coming with odd clarity through air no longer muffled by snow. Gail flew for galoshes and the brand new snow shovel. She would clean off the doorstep and front walk herself. Fun! All her young vigor and love of energetic work leaped to the task.

Fiske came ploughing through the gap in proud, new rubber boots, dragging Freddy on a sled. Gail hailed them with joy.

"We'll build a snow man!"

Freddy had come to exhibit her bunny suit. In it she was like a funny little fat blue gnome, only her rosy face visible in the round opening of the cap. Gail knelt on the floor and pulled down the snug sweater and hitched up the nether garment. "Wait a minute baby, let Gail fix you."

But Freddy pulled away. "Wanna thow Luthee."

She came out presently, however, and helped build the snow man. Fiske and Gail worked furiously to finish him before dark. Lucy applauded from an upstairs window; she detested snow and nothing could tempt her to plunge about in it but she was a wonderful encourager from a window.

"He's grand, Fiske." Gail leaned on the handle of her snow shovel and admired their achievement.

Fiske was equally enraptured. "Gee, I wish father could see him!"

They made a charming picture: the flushed, bright-eyed girl and the sturdy small boy. And little bunny-suited Freddy delving in the snow with a griddle cake turner that Gail, to Regina's disgruntlement, had filched from the kitchen. It was too bad indeed that John could not see them.

Everybody hoped the snow would last till Christmas. It didn't, but more was coming down, softly, not in a swirling smother, when on Christmas Eve Gail and Lucy ran across, through the gap to the Ingram house.

John had implored them to come and help dress the children's tree. Mimi and Jimmie Jessup were there, and lonesome Mr. Swain, tempted by lighted windows and experimental Christmas tree twinklings, also dropped in. They trimmed the tree and piled toys beneath it and stuffed the small stockings that hung so trustingly from the mantel shelf. Pathos in those little stockings — stockings of two motherless children on Christmas Eve. Gail found herself looking at them, tears in her eyes. She had filled Fiske's herself and had stuffed in the new jack-knife she knew he wanted and the box of pencils for school. An orange bulged in the toe and a candy cane stood up jauntily from the top.

John saw her standing back in the shadows looking at the small Christmas stockings with tears in her eyes.

"Why for, lady?" He touched her elbow. "This is a glad occasion."

"Oh, I don't know, John — they look so much like Fiske and Freddy. Such little stockings — so sort of little and lonely in this big room."

"No more lonely than I am, Gail."

The hand on her elbow gripped tighter. "But next Christmas!" he said in a voice that had a warm thrill in its undertones.

It might have been because Lucy called at this moment that his eyes turned toward her. But Gail's glance flashing up had seen John's glance go to Lucy.

Lucy's summons had been peremptory. "John! Where shall we put this Santa Claus? I think he ought to go at the top of the tree."

If Lucy hadn't called . . . But she had. Would John have looked her way if she hadn't called? Gail's breath was coming hard. She would not be a dog, wagging a tail because somebody tossed a bone, she told herself angrily. It was indecent to feel so upset and queer — dizzy — because a friend touched your arm and made a remark that very likely had nothing to do with you at all.

She had dropped limply on the nearest chair. Now she too called — peremptorily. "John! Do you think that Santa Claus ought to go at the top of the tree? Shouldn't it be the silver star?"

"Gail's right." John removed the Santa Claus and affixed the little shining cardboard ornament. "Of course it ought to be the star."

After the tree was finished they had supper, a larky, scrambled affair, all of them foraging in the big Ingram kitchen. Lucy's little air of responsibility was amusing. She had on Katie's apron and was like a cunning child "playing hostess." . . . "You sit here, Aunt Gail, next to Mr. Swain . . . Mimi, would you mind beating those eggs? . . . John, I need milk for this rarebit, it's in the icebox . . . Aunt Gail, better not touch that stove draught, you don't know how it works . . . John, have we any Worcestershire sauce? It ought to be on that top shelf."

It was John, here, John, there, and he fetched and carried obediently; got out table napkins, cracked ice. It was wonderful, how Lucy knew where everything was; she must, thought Gail, have absorbed the whole working formula of the Ingram house, running in and out, chatting with Katie. During supper she reminded John to go up and see if the children were well covered. "Wait —" she was out of her chair before he could rise — "I'll run up myself. I thought I heard Freddy sneeze."

But John went with her. When they came down, Gail and Mimi had the table cleared and dishes piled ready for Katie.

John played for them — softly, not to wake the little folks upstairs. There was only the firelight and flickering gleam of the candles. Gail had set one candle in a window, carefully looping curtains away from the flame. John looked at the candle and at her, and smiled. One of those exchanged, understanding glances that Gail stubbornly thought of as bones to a tail-wagging dog, and from which she looked quickly away with a hardening of her mouth quite unguessed by herself.

John played a Berceuse of Chopin. *The Old Refrain*. Cadman's lovely *At Dawning*. Gail stared hard at the flickering firelight. The first time John had let her know he cared they had been playing that Cadman thing — in the luncheon room at the Hotel Astor. The violins had breathed the recurring refrain, "I . . . love . . . you . . ." She could hear them now, feel John's hands suddenly enclosing her hands, clasped on the table. His eyes had said what the violins were saying . . . A year ago — a year and four months ago.

He sat now, playing dreamily, head thrown back, eyes not on the keyboard. If he looked at her when he finished, it would show he remembered . . .

But he did not look. He swept into the great chords of the *Adeste Fideles*. They all gathered around the piano and sang Christmas hymns. All but Lucy, who with finger on lip went about closing doors. Lucy never let you forget how important were children.

"Oh little town of Bethlehem, how still we see thee lie . . ." Gail could hear her own alto following John's baritone. But though she kept her voice true her eyes swam with tears. The homelike circle singing the old hymns. The red glow of the fire. The flickering candles. The little bulging stockings. The tall tree with the shining star . . . Peace. Protection.

Happiness. Full, sweet happiness — not self-accomplished, self-gratifying happiness, but shared happiness.

"Oh, I want it!" Gail's heart ached with the want of it. Fiske and Freddy and John — next Christmas; this room and the world shut out. Good neighbors, first, to enjoy the fun of dressing the tree and then John shutting the door on cheery Merry Christmases. And they two alone, here by the dying fire with the little stockings hanging there and that same gigantic shadow of a star-topped tree flickering up the wall. She shut her eyes: "Oh please let me have it. Never mind the book. Never mind anything else. Let me have this!"

When they came out the snow had ceased falling and the air was frosty and still. A pale December moon rode high overhead and down in the east, Sirius shone with that unearthly brilliance the star always seems to have at the Christmas season. John drove them home by way of the village so they could see the Christmas lights on the lawns. Little fir trees with blue and red and orange lights strung in the branches, and loops and festoons of colored lights around doorways. Windows silhouetted with holly wreaths, and a big holly wreath on each hospitable door. Gail loved it. This was her abiding place. Here was home.

She had wanted to hear John's admiring comment, beholding the mammoth wreath on her door knocker, but it was Mr. Swain who went with her up the stepping-stone walk. At the last minute Lucy lost her slipper among the rugs in the car and John had to find it. Lucy had not, like her Aunt Gail, had the sense to wear rubbers, so John, laughing, carried her through the snow and set her on the doorstep.

"She's a fairy. She doesn't weigh as much as my fat Freddy. I'll drop you at your house, Swain, if you're coming along. Well, Merry Christmas, everybody."

He hadn't even noticed the holly wreath on the knocker.

The Christmas dance was very gay. Mellow candlelight in the clubhouse. Festoons of holly. Great masses of hemlock. Red ribbon-tied favors for everybody. Lucy never stopped dancing. All the college lads were home for Christmas and Lucy, in pink tulle, and with the curls, was easily the girl of the evening.

"The rose-in-her-bosom!" murmured Mimi to Gail. "Where'd she get it? Roses like that don't grow out here in December."

Gail laughed. "Where I got mine. John sent us each a dozen; Lucy's, those little pink ones and mine, American Beauties."

"Whoopee!" said Mimi. "A dozen A. B.'s at Christmas time. I hope you realize what that stood him — you cold blooded author. Any girl would be thrilled."

But Gail hadn't thrilled at the roses — she hadn't cared for the cards. On Lucy's John had scrawled, "These, for a fairy." And on Gail's, "These, for a queen." Somehow a fairy sounded more intimately lovable than a queen. And Lucy had offered information, sniffing hers: "The florists call these little pink ones 'sweetheart roses.'"

Gail knew she looked well in the gold and black

dress. John told her so. "Some queen!" he whispered, during their first dance together. But two other men said the same thing: Jimmie Jessup and Mr. Swain.

"When are you going to tell the world about you and Mimi?" Gail asked Jimmie.

"New Year's. We can't stick it any longer. I've landed a job. At Bridgeport. Mimi and I are going to clear out together and when the storm breaks it won't be on our benighted heads."

"I'll help pick up the pieces," promised Gail. It was the proper thing to be casual, but she felt sorry for Doctor Holbrook. She couldn't have treated him that way, she thought. She hoped Mimi and Jimmie would be back — Jimmie in the Jessup mill again — by this time next year. Next year... how problematical next year's happiness was for everybody!

Gail did not enjoy the dance. She hadn't expected to. There was too much on her mind for brief frolic to change her mood or lift her depression. These people were nice to her — but they were nicer to Lucy. They had taken Lucy to their hearts. Gail, they treated with more formal courtesy. It was, as Hilda had pointed out, her own fault. She had held them off, protecting her work from intrusion.

"I'll make them like me," she said to herself. "I'll make them like me and take me in. I'll do it — if I never write another line as long as I live!"

Just before midnight she went up to the dressing-room to have one of her tulle draperies, torn loose, pinned back in place. She and Lucy were to have supper with John and Mr. Swain, it had been arranged last night while they trimmed the tree. Descending the stairs, she could see into the supper room — all red candles and snapping mottoes and bunches of red balloons ready to set loose. What fun people could have when they were lighthearted!

Disliking to enter the ballroom partnerless during progress of a dance, she slipped into the sun porch to wait. The big glassed-in place, furnished with palms and wicker chairs, was a favorite retreat between dances because it was dimly lighted. It was deserted now . . . no — a man and a girl were standing over in the shadows. The man's back was toward the doorway — but Gail knew that back very well indeed. And the girl was a little fairy in pink tulle. Gail could not see John's face, but she could see Lucy's, upturned, laughing; and white arms wreathed about John's neck. Lucy had to stand on tiptoe.

Hands at either side of the little pink bodice that fitted like a sheath, John lifted her up — little fairy girl that she was — lifted her clear of the floor and then, laughing, kissed her.

CHAPTER XXIV

Snow and Flame

GAIL found herself walking down the hall. Blindly, and without sense of direction. "So that's that!" she said to herself. And thought she said it with nonchalant bitterness. And finality. The sensible closing of a door on something that must not be allowed to hurt.

But her hurt was that of a blinded thing whose impulse is to flee from the horror that has smitten it. She neither saw nor felt the three people she bumped into and who stared at her with amazement. She wrenched open a door that opened on a side porch of the clubhouse and stepped out into the freezing night. Leagues and leagues of snow-covered golf course. Millions and millions of stars, gem-bright, over the whiteness. All whirling and running together. And hurting — hurting. Everything hurt. There was no getting away from the hurt. The night was filled with it. It pressed in on you, so you could not see — or breathe. Gail clenched her hands and stared steadily before her until undulating meadow and spinning stars swung back into normal perspective.

She found her eyes focusing on a red glare that somehow stayed in the same place. It rose and fell, but it stayed where it was. It shot up to the stars and died down again. Queer. There was no such red light as that...

Then, through the icy air, a recognizable sound:

the long wailing note of the village fire siren. Four
... two. Four ... two. She associated that number
with something. There it was again: four ... two.

And then other sounds. Shriek of the fire engine
whistle. Clang of the hook-and-ladder gong. On
the turnpike. Coming this way. No — turning
down Brook Road ...

Jimmie Jessup leaped past her. Huddled in thick
coats, he and Mimi had been out here on the porch.
"It's our house!" Jimmie yelled, dashing for his
parked car.

Mimi was flying after him. "Ours! My mother —!"

Gail was on the running-board, climbing in.
"It might be Lilac Cottage —"

Unmindful that she was wrapless in the freezing
air, she strained her eyes ahead. Jimmie drove the
roadster at breakneck speed. Up the turnpike,
skidding round the corner into Brook Road. Bouncing over snow covered ruts. It wasn't the Jessup
place. It wasn't — oh, thank God! — Lilac Cottage,
still and dark within its hedges.

But it was the Holbrook house. The whole rear
wing seemed to be ablaze. Mimi kept moaning,
"My mother!" and urging Jimmie to drive faster.

Brook Road was jammed with people and with
parked cars. There was the dreadful thudding of the
fire engine. Men's voices, shouting. Crackle of
flames. Crash of falling timbers. A lurid red light
on the trampled snow and on gaunt tree branches
overhead. The rear wing was already collapsing and
smoke was pouring from front windows.

Men were dashing in and out of the front door, salvaging what they could of Holbrook possessions. On the lawn, a great pile of furniture had been covered with a soaked dining-room rug. Gail saw her father tottering down the steps under a load of framed pictures and calling out untimely jests. (Having celebrated Christmas, it was all too apparent, with cronies down at Gus Abbott's pool room.) But he was doing his best to help. So was little Mr. Heddon. So were a dozen other neighbors. Among a group of women Katie O'Hara stood chattering, a shawl over her head. Gail frowned, remembering the Ingram children left alone in the house.

Mimi ran about in thin slippers in the snow. "Father!... Where's my dad? Did they get my mother out? Oh, somebody tell me!"

They drew her aside and told her, Jimmie and Gail standing on either side of her. And then Mimi buried her head in Jimmie's shoulder, close held by his arms.

Doctor Holbrook was over at the Heddons' house where Mrs. Holbrook's body had been taken. No one knew how the fire had started. It was thought, from an overturned alcohol lamp in the invalid's room. Doctor Holbrook had gone to the drug store for something — it was Christmas night and the druggist had no one to send. The invalid had complained of pain—

"Her neuritis," sobbed Mimi. "It has been bad. She must have sent dad for more sleeping tablets. And then lighted that stove to heat her milk... I shouldn't have gone to the dance." Mimi sobbed more wildly. "We never left her alone in the house. We always warned her not to light that lamp herself. But she would do it..."

Mrs. Syd Jessup had run around on foot to a

neighbor's — just beyond the bridge. And, passing the Holbrook house on her return, must have heard screams. On no ordinary occasion would Mrs. Syd Jessup have set foot across that threshold, but terrified screams may not be ignored. She must have rung the bell, they thought, and while waiting, smelled the smoke. Doctor Holbrook had left the door on the latch, the invalid was never left in a locked-up house. At any rate Mrs. Jessup had gone in. And she had tried to carry the invalid out of the blazing wing. Both women had been found on the stairs, suffocated by smoke. The bodies had been carried, one to the Jessup home, the other around to the Heddons'.

These two bitter enemies — for fifteen years neither able to speak of the other except as "that woman" — had died in each other's arms, one trying to rescue the other. Mrs. Jessup had gone into that inferno of flame and smoke and had lifted helpless, screaming Mrs. Holbrook out of bed and tried to carry her down the stairs. It was unbelievable. But it was true.

Gail felt very humble and solemn and abased. Fat, tiresome Mrs. Jessup whom she had despised as a nagger and a gossip, had risen to these heights of courage and self sacrifice. Mrs. Jessup had given her life for one who had done her most grievous wrong. Never again, Gail Ormsbee told herself solemnly, would she judge any human being by her own arrogant opinion, or by any trivial surface characteristic! You never knew what human nature was capable of. Or how big people might be, whom you had thought of, smugly, as less admirable than yourself.

SNOW AND FLAME 313

She helped put poor little overwrought Mimi back in Jimmie's roadster. Before going home to his own father he was taking Mimi to hers. "He'll have to know about Mimi and me now," said Jimmie, sober and shaken, but with young shoulders squared to his responsibilities in face of this disaster that had overtaken both families. "No more cheating. My mother's gone. I wish I'd told her about it. I wish we hadn't sneaked because we were afraid of a few scenes. I wish I had half the courage my mother had!"

When the car drove away Gail found herself shivering under the overcoat somebody had wrapped around her. Jimmie Jessup's coat she thought, though she had no memory of putting it on. Her feet in the ruined gold slippers were icy cold and soaked from the slush made by puddles of water in the snow. They had the fire under control now. The front part of the house would be saved, and Doctor Holbrook's books and papers. The engine kept up its thudding but some of the parked cars were being driven away. The wind was blowing the smoke away from the ravine; Lilac Cottage was quite safe. Gail glanced across and saw lights in the windows. Lucy must be home, for Regina was away for the night, and Randolph Ormsbee was still over here, helping. Gail saw John too, carrying out books. Just that glimpse of John, and pain started again, fiercely. Gail thrust it away. This was no time to think of one's own pain. "I'll run over and make coffee," she decided. "Gallons of coffee. For the firemen and everybody."

In the ravine the snow would not be deep and her slippers were past hope anyway. She might as well clamber down and across that way. She pushed through the brambles, but something caught at her — gripped her round the knees. Almost tripped her.

"Dail! Take care me. I fwaid."

Freddy —! In little bedraggled pink pajamas. Face grimy and tear-streaked. Slippers gone, bare feet in the snow. The little body shaken by terrified sobs.

"Baby! How did you get here?" Gail gathered her up; huddled the overcoat round her. Tight little arms clung about Gail's neck, as they had that day of the thunder storm.

"I want my favver!" wailed Freddy.

"We'll find him. Did Fiske bring you out here, Freddy?"

"We came to thee fire. I loth my slipperth. I loth Fifke. I hurted my foot. I want my favver!"

Gail did not wait to find John. Or Fiske. Or Katie O'Hara. If nobody in the Ingram household was capable of taking care of a baby girl better than this, she was! Freddy — out in the snow in bare feet on a December night!

Gail tore off the overcoat and bundled Freddy into it and, bare-armed herself in the filmy evening frock, struggled with the bundle down through the ravine, across the frozen brook and up to her garden gate. And from there, through the gap to the Ingram back door. She fumbled for and found light-switches. Put a kettle of water on the gas stove; (no time to bring up the range fire) carried Freddy upstairs, wrapped her in blankets; had her in a warm bath and out, snuggled under a mound of comfortables rifled from any beds available, a hot water bottle at her feet and a cup of warm milk inside her — when Katie O'Hara, frightened out of her wits and dragging a sneezing Fiske, arrived at the house.

Chilled to the bone, nervously overwrought and in a temper that had to take itself out on somebody or something, for once Miss Ormsbee herself let go. She gave the Ingram housekeeper that night a tongue-lashing that the woman never forgot — and never forgave.

Miss O'Hara, however, was too taken aback and too honestly frightened to attempt adequate retort; and after sharp command to put Fiske also in a hot bath and under blankets, Gail swept down the back walk in the borrowed overcoat, still in mood of righteous indignation.

She entered her own house by the back door and found lights on in her kitchen and a confusion of piled up dishes. Lucy had attended to the coffee. And had also thriftily changed her costume. In a homelike little blue frock and ruffled apron she was sitting on the kitchen table, swinging small strap-slippered feet and chatting cheerily with her grandsire and John Ingram. Strenuous activity and much coffee had sobered up Mr. Ormsbee. Both men looked tired and dishevelled, with smudges of soot across their faces. John's evening clothes were completely and irretrievably wrecked.

He sprang to his feet. "Gail! Lucy said you were in bed."

"I thought she must be," amended Lucy. "She got home first and she wasn't anywhere around."

"Where have you been?" demanded John. He

saw the white tiredness of Gail's face, her ruined and soaked slippers, the masculine overcoat over her bedraggled evening frock. "Where have you been?" he repeated, blocking her way as she moved toward the door that led to the hall.

She glared at him. At that moment she hated John Ingram. Kissing in secluded corners. Cosily drinking coffee in this warm kitchen while his baby daughter wandered, barefooted, in the snow at one o'clock in the morning. And now pretending concern for herself. Concern!

"Let me pass," she said.

"Gail —!"

"Let me pass."

"Why so hoity-toity?" inquired Randolph Ormsbee amiably. "We are not stealing the spoons." He winked at John Ingram. "Let the lady alone, John, that's good feller. You'n I worked hard. Poor old Swain worked hard. If she wan'ed to say g'night to him, what business ours?"

John made a gesture of distaste. He had no notion that Gail Ormsbee had been philandering at this hour with Mr. William Swain or anybody else, the impatient movement conveyed. He stepped away from the door. But he followed her out into the hall.

She ran past him, up the stairs.

"Go home and look after your children," she flung down at him. "If they are both dead of pneumonia tomorrow morning it's your fault, not mine. You ought to be ashamed of yourself. I never want to speak to you again!"

And in the ruined party frock and borrowed overcoat she threw herself on her bed and wept.

Bill scratched at the door and whimpered, but she never heard him. She wept until from sheer exhaustion she fell asleep.

CHAPTER XXV

In the Grip of Winter

THE children were ill — as might have been expected! Just bad colds, but Freddy had temperature and bronchitis symptoms. The practical nurse was there again and John looked anxious and tired. The nurse had to have her sleep at night and somebody had to be up and down. Of course Miss O'Hara, on her feet all day long as she frequently averred, couldn't be expected to sacrifice her night's rest.

Lucy was over at the Ingram house continually. She had a way with children, the nurse said gratefully. Gail wondered how soon Lucy would be over there, to stay. Lucy was going south after New Year's — but of course she could return. She wouldn't be going now but for an insistent telegram. Rosamund had hurt her knee and was confined to her room. Old Mammy Sutterlee was doing her best, but the boarders were getting restive; Lucy must come back and attend to things.

Lucy was distressed about having to go. "I don't see how I can start till the children are better," she said to Gail. "It just tears my heart to desert them — they need me so. Would you go, Aunt Gail?"

"You'll have to do as you think best, Lucy," said Gail wearily.

She kept away from Lucy as much as she could, shutting herself in the study all day and working furiously at the Spring Fashion Supplement. And

IN THE GRIP OF THE WINTER 319

after Bill's evening run she retired to her bedroom. The college lads would not depart until New Year's so there was plenty of company for Lucy downstairs. The ukulele again wailed and snappy roadsters were parked in Brook Road. Gail controlled her tongue. Spiteful words, bitter allusions — they would only bare her own hurt, expose it in indecent nakedness for Lucy to spy upon. And then, inevitably, for John Ingram to discover and be sorry about. She did not want John's sorrow, or his regret, on her account. If she had been hurt it was her own fault. And spiteful remark would only reveal how hurt she was. The stern pride that had made it impossible to refer to unreported luncheons and pally meetings when commuters' trains got in, made it even more impossible to mention spied-upon kisses in secluded nooks.

Anyhow it was too late. Nonchalant mention of such matters has to come immediately — otherwise there is suggestion of brooding resentment.

She kept away from John too. What had she to say to him? Or he to her? On the day after the fire (a Sunday) he had come over and asked for Gail. Regina took up the message. But Gail, who had heard his voice below stairs, pretended to be aroused from a comfortable Sunday afternoon nap and sent word that she was completely done up after last night and could not possibly dress and come down.

On two evenings, after that, he telephoned; and Lucy — who was always at the phone the moment it tinkled — was requested to tell him that Miss Ormsbee was in bed, reading. There was perfectly good excuse for not coming downstairs: people do not dash, in kimonos, down to a telephone when college lads are sprawled all over the place. John himself because of the college invasion, kept away, evenings. And he was fully occupied with troubles in his own domain.

John wanted to offer profuse thanks to one who had saved his daughter's life, Miss Ormsbee opined. Well, she wouldn't give him the chance. Why should she be thanked for ministering to little Freddy whom she loved dearly — and of whom she was better able to take proper care than he was?

The week dragged along. Snow fell incessantly. Drifts banked high against the hedges. The shiftless gray squirrels who do not lay up winter stores like their provident red cousins, came tamely to the kitchen door — when Bill was safe inside the house. Gail fed them and went out in galoshes to tie lumps of suet to tree branches for the starving birds. The garden was buried deep under trackless snow. Only one path, from the gap to the porch steps, made a dent in the unbroken whiteness — and now that was almost obliterated.

The village snow plough cleared Brook Road for the Jessup funeral. Mimi and Jimmie rode with Syd Jessup out to the cemetery, and the day after, rode with Doctor Holbrook. Mimi was living at the Jessup house now and Jimmie would not take the Bridgeport position. Doctor Holbrook was staying on with the Heddons for a while. Everybody said it was so fortunate — in a way — that the tragedy had happened during holiday time so poor Doctor Holbrook could get himself together before resuming his duties at the school. Gail saw him walking down Brook Road with Syd Jessup. The old friendship had copy was again valiantly attacked. But when the copy was finished there wasn't a thing to do. And not a soul to talk to.

For instance, one couldn't run to John with news of Randolph Ormsbee's departure and preposterous plans. What was one going to do without John to run to, about everything? It gave one the most ghastly feeling of loneliness: not to be able to.

And to whom could one talk about the loneliness? Not to Arlene, who was enjoying her honeymoon. Not to Hilda, who was at this moment in Cairo, in the middle of a Mediterranean cruise. Not to Jule Vernon, just back from a visit in Washington and only this morning extending cheery greeting over the telephone ... Oh, especially not to Jule Vernon who had flicked the manuscript with her whip!

Gail almost wished the manuscript would come back, (it was about due again) for that would give her something concrete and excusable to brood over and feel furious about. Not that the fate of the novel was of vital consequence. There was only one thing in the world worth having and she could not have that ...

Gail looked out at the snow which was falling again, thick flakes drifting down through bare tree branches. Small foot-tracks showed where Lucy had floundered through the path to the gap. Only deep affection for little sick children (or some other strong incentive) could have impelled Lucy Lovelace who detested snow to wade that long distance through it. And she had borrowed her aunt Gail's galoshes — much too big, of course. But one couldn't refuse; it would appear too ungracious.

When Mimi dropped in about four o'clock Gail welcomed her with enthusiasm. They sat by the fire in the living-room and Regina brought tea and little crisp buttered scones. Mimi looked very sweet and subdued in her new black.

"It seems awful to say it, Gail, but I'm so happy. Jimmie and I together! And our two dads friendly ... talking about chess last night — imagine. They used to have battles over it, years ago. The poor dears long to take up that old friendship; — they grew up together, you know, and went to college together, before those two women came into their lives. But they are scared of what people may say. It's pathetic. Jimmie says: when the two wives went — together — and may be friends again now, how silly for those of us who are left to continue the old antagonism!" Mimi looked across at Gail, her little face radiant. "Jimmie and I are going to have a baby just as soon as we can — to give our dads a good excuse to enjoy something together. I suppose," she added regretfully, "I couldn't play in the tennis tournament this year... But wouldn't it be glorious, Gail?"

Gail agreed that it would be. Why should anybody worry, she thought, about these youngsters of the much railed-at generation? That was a beautiful thing young Jimmie had said about the two mothers. When it came right down to the big things of life, the profoundly moving things, were not the reactions of these youngsters — for all their pretense of flippant sophistry — much the same as those of their forebears? Here was Jimmie, taking hold at the Jessup mills; and Mimi, planning to have a baby — and give up all her good times. Shining-eyed about it.

But young Mrs. Jessup hadn't come to talk about her own affairs.

"Gail — have you lost a telegram lately?"

Miss Ormsbee recollected. "Yes. From the Buyer and Retailer office. About some copy. Did you find it?"

"No. But somebody else did. It was in Mrs. Syd Jessup's desk."

Gail stared. "Why on earth didn't she return it to me. I lost that telegram weeks ago."

"Do you remember what was in it?"

"Something about copy for my juvenile page. I had to telephone over because I forgot how many extra words they wanted."

Mimi produced the telegram from her handbag. "I'm going to read it to you. Listen: 'Must have more for children. Coats, shoes, school frocks needed. About two hundred will do. Can you send by return mail. J. B.'"

"Well?"

"Yes — well! Don't you get it? The nice moral, high-minded dame who picked up that telegram ... No, I won't tell you who it was. One of that Ladies Aid bunch ... drew her own conclusions. And they were plenty! She went right around to ask Mrs. Syd Jessup if she didn't think something ought to be done about it; — you coming here all by yourself, and none of your relatives seeming to know what you had been up to for years and years. It seems Mrs. Syd showed this telegram to her husband and he ordered her to hush up that woman and not to breathe a word herself to anybody of a matter she didn't know a thing about. He told me last night when we came across this telegram, clearing out her desk. He said he knew it was all bunk but that Mrs. Syd had been much distressed — 'distressed' was the word he used. She thought you had some man visitor here, evenings. You see when the Jessup's car turns at a certain curve in the drive, the headlights shoot a ray of light across your hedge right into the arbor. The drive up there is on higher ground than this house. And several times Mrs. Syd had seen two people in the arbor —"

"Oh — Mimi!"

"Yes, I know, Gail. It was Jimmie and I. And believe me, I'm telling everybody I know that we did our courting in that arbor, all summer. And this morning I went to see that high-minded dame who found the telegram and concluded it was a spot-light illuminating your dark past. She knows better now! I'll take care of this. Don't you worry."

"It's so absurd." Gail tried to laugh.

"It is absurd. And when I get through with them — if that woman did do any gossiping — they'll know how absurd it is. You see, Gail, in a place like this it isn't always comfortable for a woman who is attractive and — well, unprotected, you know. Why, even Jule Vernon who has lived here all her life, can't have a new man out to dinner without everybody in the village commenting on it next day."

Mimi leaned forward in her chair by the fire. "Gail — why don't you marry John Ingram?"

Instantly Miss Ormsbee stiffened. She produced what she thought was a merry laugh. "John seems to be very well occupied, don't you think?"

"You could have him by snapping your finger, and you know it."

"Could I?" Gail laughed again. "What are you trying to do, Mimi Jessup, get me married-and-protected? Because of the tongues of a few gossipy old women?" She drew herself up with convincing dignity. "I have my work; that is enough for me."

But was it? And had she her work — if the book again came back? After Mimi had gone she sat forlornly in the study, clasped hands stretched out on the empty desk blotter, eyes staring unseeingly in front of her.

It was all absurd of course, and Mimi's explanations would soon clear everything up. But how easily one could be misjudged and how quick women were with unkind suspicions. These women. Not her own kind — business and professional women who concentrated on work. Like men, they would give you the benefit of the doubt. They would be more concerned with what you accomplished and achieved than with how you behaved.

In a community of protected women, you also had to be protected. If not, you were an outsider; somebody to be watched and speculated about, and reported upon. And if you didn't conform to their pattern of behaviour, something must "be done about it." In other words, you'd be talked over and ostracized by the clan . . . Whether your work were successful or not.

It had been a mistake to come out here. If you intended to make work your first preoccupation, you ought to stay in the atmosphere where work was the important thing, and success in it was reverenced.

Out here your whole scale of values got awry. In a place like this — where home and things that had to do with home were the paramount interest — you, also, began to want things that had somehow come to seem more important than mental accomplishment and professional success... And your mental independence got so sapped that you could see the point of view of these women and feel a sneaking sympathy with it, instead of being able to rise above it and ignore it. You felt hurt instead of contemptuously amused.

You felt defeated.

And the irony of it was, Gail reflected, staring out at the winter landscape, tranquil in the dusk, that if she hadn't come out here — trying to barge in all by herself with no qualification but her vain self-sufficiency; fatuously envisioning herself in the graceful role of householder and author — if she had stuck it out in town and been satisfied with her boarding-house room and those little restaurant dinners for two, by this time she and John might be...

Suddenly, head down on outstretched arms, she sobbed desolately: "I want to be a protected woman too. I want to be taken care of. I don't want to be independent. I can't bear it — being so lonely!"

Bill came and laid his head on her knee. She sat up and dried her eyes, switched on the desk light. The room was almost dark.

Somebody was rapping. She tried hard to steady her voice.

Regina came in and laid a bulky package on the desk blotter pretending not to notice sign of recent tears. Regina was a person of exquisite tact.

"You not see this, may be. On hall table since expressmans bring at noon."

It was the novel. Back home again.

CHAPTER XXVI

January Stars

ONE of the things an author learns is not to be completely cast down by sight of a returned manuscript — until the very worst has been made sure of. Many a screed has been chucked into a desk drawer because of sheer inability to look at the unhappy thing, when within the wrappings nestled a priceless pearl of hope.

Miss Ormsbee, snipping string and folding up wrapping paper next morning, solely because she was a systematic person, discovered not only her by now dog-eared literary offspring, but also a letter. If the author (said the letter) would be willing to cut ten thousand words out of her novel and rewrite the last four chapters, giving a slightly different twist to the ending, (suggestions appended) the publisher (and the name on the letter-head was the name of a very big publisher) would be glad to handle the book and would like to talk with the author concerning a contract for future books.

Gail sat, stunned, staring at the letter.

Her book was accepted. Accepted! For taking ten thousand words out of ninety thousand would be no job at all for a practised copy-writer, accustomed to measuring work by number of words. And the changes — her eye glanced over the list of suggestions — would not be difficult to make.

A publisher wouldn't be interested in a contract

for future books unless he saw promise of commercial profit.

She had made good. She was accepted into the ranks. She was An Author. All that was essential now was unremitting work. Undeviating attention to it. Sacrifice of all else. And the fruits of authorship, so passing sweet when yearned for, just out of reach, would be hers.

Why was there no savor, now, in their anticipation?

She stared at the manuscript. She didn't actually dislike it; she had labored over it too long and too lovingly. But its new aura of promise brought no thrill. Her preoccupation with it had lost to her a treasure of infinitely greater worth. It was as though she had made of it an idol, and now the religion the idol symbolized had lost power to comfort or satisfy.

She took up the letter and re-read it. John Ingram's eyes would glow at sight of this letter. He would be sincerely happy about her success ... But not the way she wanted him to be happy; — *with* her, not merely *for* her. Not rejoicing merely in the luck of his good friend!

She flung the letter on top of the manuscript and, pushing back her chair, walked restlessly about the room. Between the windows that looked out on the ravine was a narrow framed motto: a line of Carlyle's in illuminated text. She had hung it opposite the table-desk to be a constant inspiration. She stood before the motto now and read it:

"Blessed is the man who has found his work;
let him ask no other blessedness."

"Asinine!" said Miss Ormsbee. And savagely ripped Mr. Carlyle's philosophy from the wall.

What was a book? What were twenty books — and all the things, mentally and materially gratifying, that they might bring — if you were lonely?

But by afternoon, neither loneliness nor success, nor any personal consideration, mattered. Only John's trouble loomed large. Freddy — little Freddy Ingram — was horribly ill. The menacing symptoms had increased and now they all knew that Freddy had pneumonia. A trained nurse had been installed. And then another nurse was there for night duty. The doctor's car stood constantly in the Ingram drive. And on the third morning, ominous receptacles were in the upper hall; oxygen for instant use if need should be.

All the neighbors sent in things. Toys for Fiske who was convalescing but not yet able to go out, and who must be kept quiet. Prepared food to help out Katie O'Hara who had to cook for the nurses and was back and forth all day, answering the telephone. These people were so kind in time of trouble. They could not do enough. Not like city apartment dwellers, Gail reflected, who might call up and inquire, but would never walk three blocks with a bowl of soup and go up in an elevator to deliver it.

She touched John's arm as he went out of the porch door. He had stepped across to let them know how Freddy was, and for a breath of outdoor air. For two days he had not been at his office and he looked tired and white from sleepless watching.

"John! I'm so sorry —"

"I know, Gail." He stood woodenly, staring ahead

of him.

"I wish I could do something —"

"There's nothing to do ... It's just one of the things we have to get through somehow." The suffering in his eyes wrung her heart.

She slipped an arm about his shoulders. "I love Freddy too. I know how you feel, John."

He stood in that wooden way, staring ahead of him.

"No — you couldn't. Only somebody who'd had a child could know."

He did not even notice when she shrank away. Withdrew her arm. All he could think of now, she saw, was his baby girl for whom they were fighting in that upstairs room. He went down the porch steps, through the gap, never glancing back.

Three times Gail had been over, inquiring at the kitchen door. Katie O'Hara talked with her and once, Lucy, who had established herself in the Ingram house "to answer the telephone." Gail, begging Katie O'Hara for news, could hear the subdued southern drawl in the hall: "No, Mrs. Beech, no better. If she holds out through the night — Yes, of course we are awfully anxious. Thank you for calling."

If Freddy pulled through that night there would be hope. The doctor had given that promise. After dinner Gail trudged down to the bridge and back with Bill and then restlessly paced the house. She could not sit still, over here, and read, with John going through this torture. She had to do something — anything — just to be near John. Perhaps she couldn't understand as another parent would, but she had to let John know she suffered with him. Lucy wasn't a parent either, yet Lucy was over there, going through it all with John. Gail's blue eyes were dark with pain. It was her place. Hers! To suffer with John. Whether he asked her or not, she had to be there.

Katie O'Hara was in the kitchen, preparing a tray for the night nurse. She looked apathetically at Gail, her plump Irish face distorted with weeping. "Fiske is afther askin' for ye. The nurse said to sind ye up whin ye come in. The back room, mind, and be awful careful not to make no noise on the stairs."

Fiske was sitting up in bed eating milk toast. He beamed at Gail. He did not know how ill his little sister was, at the other end of the hall. Gail told him the story he instantly demanded — the one about tigers in the jungle. A nurse came in and smiled at her — then shook her head at the quick question in the visitor's eyes. "You'll come again, won't you?" she whispered, outside the door. "He's been asking Miss Lovelace to send you over to tell him a story. I suppose she forgot. He's a darling little fellow, isn't he?"

Why should Lucy forget a message from little sick Fiske? Lucy didn't want her over here. "I'll stay!" was Gail's instant, fierce decision. "It's my place, not hers. I'll stay until I have seen John." She had to see John and let him know that her heart, also, was breaking about Freddy.

From the foot of the stair she turned toward the library — John's special sanctum, where his piano was, and that picture of the blonde woman who had been Freddy's mother. Only one lamp was lighted and the room was so still Gail thought it must be empty. Then she saw John, leaning forward in a big chair, his head down on his arms that were crossed on the table. The light of the lamp streamed down on his hair.

And sitting on the arm of the chair — Lucy. Not talking. Stroking the bent head. She looked up and saw Gail in the doorway and put warning finger to lip. But John, sensing perhaps a third presence, lifted his head. He rose at once.

"Come in, Gail."

He tried to smile at her and the smile, on his haggard face, made her suddenly want to cry. "I couldn't stay away," she said. "I had to come —"

"Of course," John said. "Of course, Gail—" as though he took it for granted that nobody could bear it, staying away. He placed a chair for her. "Sit down, my dear."

Instantly the hysteria left Gail. Over here — near John — in this quiet room; with John, in spite of the grief and anxiety that looked out of his eyes, so controlled, she felt quieted herself, her own emotion stilled in presence of this patiently borne trouble. But she would not sit down.

"I've been up with Fiske," she said. "He wants to see you."

John lifted one hand and swept back the hair from his forehead. "I'll go now. Poor little tad, I've neglected him; but I didn't want him to sense things and worry himself sick again."

Gail turned to Lucy. "You'd better come home with me, then."

"Yes, Lucy," said John, "you go with Gail. There isn't anything anybody can do and I've got to be upstairs."

Lucy didn't want to go. "Not till I know about Freddy —"

John picked up her coat from a chair and wrapped it round her. "I'll telephone."

Gail would not let him walk back with them. She and Lucy walked single file in the narrow trail through the snow. Lucy chattered all the way about how much John's children meant to her, but Gail did not hear. She was looking up at the sharply bright stars. It looked so icily cold — up there — and so immeasurably far. Would little Freddy be going out, among those stars, tonight... and where? Who would come to get her and show her the way? If Freddy went, would she not be fortunate? There was so much to suffer, if you grew up. It wasn't worth it: all the pain...

It was impossible to sleep. Gail sat, wrapped in a thick doublegown, in the window of the back room, available now that Randolph Ormsbee had departed. With the leaves gone from the trees, she could see the lighted rear windows of the Ingram house. She wondered if Lucy also were keeping watch. Lucy's room over the study, had a window that looked out at the back. But Gail did not care what Lucy did; she was almost unconscious of Lucy. All her thought was concentrated on that distant, lighted house above which such trouble hovered. And all night, in spirit, she kept vigil with John. Immemorially etched upon her consciousness was the aspect of her garden that January night. There was no moon, but because of the pallid snow and the brilliance of the stars there was an eerie light — wan, like the beginning of dawn.

The hedges showed in black lines and gaunt branches of trees pricked up against the star-sprinkled sky. Now and then, in the ravine, a twig snapped in the intense cold. And once a little animal sped across the snow.

Through gnarled branches of apple trees in the Ingram yard she could see the lighted windows of John's home. The two windows of his library. Over them the windows of John's bedroom. A bathroom window where shadows came and went. And downstairs, the kitchen windows. So long as all those lights gleamed steadily conditions must be unchanged. Nothing sudden or dreadful had happened.

It was about four o'clock when John telephoned. Gail went down — so stiff from cold and from her long cramped position that she had to go slowly on the stairs. John's voice replied to her breathless "Yes?"

"That you, Gail? It's all right. She's going to pull through."

"Oh, John . . . thank God!" Gail felt the hot tears racing down her cheeks.

"The doctor's gone. She's asleep. I knew you'd want to hear. Did I wake you up?"

"No — I haven't been to bed . . . John, I'm so thankful!"

"I know, Gail. We all are. I thought I was going to lose her. It's all right now, though . . . And say, tell Lucy, will you?"

Gail tapped at Lucy's door and, getting no answer, went in. Switched on a light. The room was in its usual state of messy disorder and Lucy, snuggled under warm coverings, was fast asleep. She cried too, when she heard the good news. Sitting up in bed, with the curls tumbling over her shoulder and her cheeks rosy from sleep, she was extravagantly pretty and like a just-awakened little girl. She mopped her eyes with a corner of the sheet. "I knew John would call up. Precious little Freddy! It's been an awful night for all of us, hasn't it?"

CHAPTER XXVII

Two by the Fire

AFTER Lucy had gone, Gail thought, perhaps she would be able to get to work. First Lucy had delayed her start because of Freddy's illness. Now she was in bed with a wretched cold undoubtedly contracted, running back and forth through snow in thin slippers. It was one of those mean colds that make the voice thick and the nose red and the eyes bleary. Lucy cuddled in bed and Regina carried up trays. Another telegram had arrived from Georgia and a trunk almost completely packed stood in Lucy's room. But John Ingram had mentioned a possible business trip to Washington as soon as he felt quite safe about leaving Freddy with a nurse in charge at the Ingram house, and Gail suspected that Lucy was maneuvering to make part of her journey in his company.

Gail felt no inclination to work. Even the necessary newspaper copy was an effort. She could not seem to concentrate and found herself making foolish errors and senseless repetitions. Phrases would not form themselves without tremendous mental effort. Again and again her hands fell from the typewriter and she sat listlessly gazing out at the winter landscape. The passing of tense emotion had left her with a feeling of lassitude — an inertia that was entirely alien to her temperament.

She would get down to work. She must. She

would feel better when she had the house to herself. Just herself and Regina and Bill. No outside distractions... When Lucy had gone... And John also.

Unconsciously she was bracing herself for a climax. Before Lucy departed she would say something. Or John would. Or they would both tell her together. When she knew the worst she would be able to face it and accept it. And get to work. It was this waiting for a thing to smite that took all the heart out of one.

A fortnight of rain had followed the night of brilliant starlight. The January thaw had melted away the snow, only a few dingy patches were left in corners of the garden. Rain beat down on muddy beds and dripped from the roof of the porch. Dusk closed in gray and melancholy; there were no more gorgeous orange sunsets behind white-blanketed hills.

Lucy, sneezing and snuffling in bed, protested her grief about disappointing Freddy at story-telling hour. Freddy had milk toast too, now, for supper and after that there must be the story before she would go to sleep. "But how can I go over there with this beastly cold?" lamented Lucy. "That nurse wouldn't let me in the room." Gail was requested to telephone.

But Gail put on galoshes and raincoat and went, herself. Freddy must not be denied the bed-time story.

And Freddy, blessed baby, did not evince bitter disappointment when she beheld the visitor.

"Dail," she summoned peremptorily, "look at my new dollieth. Favver bwingth a new one evwy night." The four dolls sat solemnly at the foot of the bed. Gail earnestly admired them.

"How about a fairy story?" she said.

She sat in a low chair before the nursery fire with Freddy, bundled in a soft blanket, in her lap. Freddy's little face was pinched and she was pathetically light a weight. Her eyes, big in a white, small face, stared up at the story-teller. Gail hugged the little body close.

"Oh, Freddy!" she whispered. And her own eyes were suddenly wet, looking down at the child.

"What you cwyin' for?" demanded Freddy.

Gail winked back the tears and laughed cheerily. "Because I'm so happy, ducky, that you're all well again. We've got to build another snow man soon, haven't we?"

Freddy's hand stole up and stroked Gail's face.

"I love you, Dail!" she said.

Then her glance traveled beyond Gail, across the room, and she mentioned casually, "There'th favver."

He stood there, smiling at them. "Hello," he said. "So we have a real raconteur on the job today! If I'd known that I'd have been home earlier."

He walked back with Gail, holding his big umbrella over her old felt sport hat that had weathered many downpours.

"How's the book coming?" he asked.

She told him. About the publisher's letter. About the revising she had to do.

He stopped short in the mud of the drenched garden. "When was it finished?"

She hesitated. John's eyes looked so ridiculously indignant. "Of course this publisher had it some weeks —"

"'This publisher.' Has it been out before?" When she nodded, he demanded: "Why didn't you tell me when it was finished?"

She didn't answer. The little frown was back again between her eyebrows and her mouth was set in a straight line.

"Look here, Gail, that wasn't very fair to me, was it?"

Fair! He talked about being fair! "I rather thought," she said, "you had lost interest in the great event."

"Oh, you did, did you? After all the patience I've tried to show!"

Neither of them noticed that the umbrella had tilted and rain was pelting down on them. John looked distinctly belligerent and Gail (who so strongly favored directness) put now on the defensive, experienced the wholly feminine impulse to dodge.

"Aren't you glad my book is a success, John Ingram? You don't act so."

"Certainly I'm glad — but what has that to do with it? It's aside from the point."

They had come to the porch steps and she could see Bill's anxious, watching face inside the glass doors. "Oh, never mind," she said. "We can't talk, here in the rain. I'll show you the publisher's letter, next time you are over."

"You'll show it to me right now," said John. "And you'll explain why I was kept in the dark several weeks about that book being finished."

Several weeks! If John but knew that the wretched book had been on its journeyings since

November...

But somehow Gail felt inordinately cheerful... because John seemed so very mad.

She bade him light the living-room fire while she divested herself of hat and raincoat. When she came back she had the publisher's letter with her. John still looked belligerent — and a little hurt. But an editor is an editor: he who had once longed to write himself, knew what that letter must mean to any literary aspirant.

"You'll get to work at once, I suppose — and be buried again till Easter in that novel."

"Oh, I don't know —" The author's tone singularly lacked enthusiasm.

"What's the matter with you, Gail? You've worked too hard, that's what. I was afraid of it. Don't you suppose I've seen how thin and dragged you were looking? But I didn't interfere. I didn't say a thing... Did I?"

"No, John." Her voice was very low. She leaned forward and propped up a log on the fire. Rain beat against the windows. Faintly, from the kitchen, came sounds made by Regina, starting dinner preparation.

John was lighting his pipe — always permissible he knew in this house. "Sort of cosy," he remarked, sitting back and drawing comfortable puffs, "to be talking to you, for once, without a sweet southern background."

Gail sat rigid on the low stool — Lucy's pet ottoman, always in the fireside corner. Gail had dropped on it to mend the fire more easily. She looked across at John. A straight look. "I thought," she said, quietly, "that you were completely captivated by — my southern background."

"Who — little Lucy?" He smiled indulgently. "She's a cunning thing, isn't she? Bit of a chatterbox, though —"

"I had an idea—" Gail spoke through stiff lips — "that you intended to marry her."

He sat up straight. Stared.

"Are you crazy?"

"She's — she's so fond of the children," faltered Gail.

John laughed — shortly. "Very likely. But, great guns, a man wants a little more than that — in a wife." Then he frowned. "When did this bright idea strike you — pairing off Lucy and me? Did you think I coveted three immature companions at my dinner table, instead of two?" He looked at her, still frowning. "Have I ever given you the least reason to imagine I cared — that way — for Lucy?"

"Yes," said Gail. "You have." They were having it out now. No sense in quibbling. "I saw you kissing her — at the Christmas dance."

"Oh, you did!" John had knocked out his pipe, thrust it into his pocket. "I hope you also saw the mistletoe. When a cute little thing in pink ruffles puts up a face to be kissed under Christmas mistletoe what would be your notion of a he-man's behaviour? To draw himself up with a Galahad air and inform her in a dignified way he hoped he was not that kind of a fellow —? Of course I kissed her. Why not?" John's eyes twinkled.

"And," continued Gail, "she met you for lunch in town and neither of you said a word about it —"

John nodded. "You mean that time you sent her to the office and said I was to take her out to lunch—"

"I never said that —"

"It was what I understood. I was pretty sore about it, too. You know very well what Thursday is; — just before we go to press. I thought you might have shown more consideration. That's why I never mentioned it, I suppose."

Gail knew John. He always did preserve a dignified silence when he was annoyed with you. That might have been it, of course.

Aloud, she remarked. "So Lucy lied to you."

"Oh, come now, Gail. She told a fib maybe, because she wanted her lunch and didn't like to suggest the thing herself. She's a cute little dodger. She doesn't mean any harm. Those southern girls are full of tricks. What does it matter if I did take her out and feed her?"

Gail sighed. No man would ever see the full iniquity of a Lucy. Men might not take the Lucys seriously but they would always be indulgent toward anything so cunning and so pretty. She had one more incriminating fact and she produced it: "Well, how about your meeting, evenings, when the 5.57 gets in, and walking home together?"

John would have been angry by now if he had not seen the real trouble in the blue eyes that were so seriously arraigning him.

"Look here, Gail," he said, getting up and coming toward her, "you can't mean to tell me you resented my walking up the road with little Lucy Lovelace when she stopped at the station for me? I thought it was darn nice and friendly of her. Are you out of your mind?... Or am I a dumb idiot?"

Gail had risen too. Her face was rather white. Her blue eyes looked into his.

"I guess you are, John," she said. And laughed a little shakily.

He seized her by the shoulders; shook her slightly. "You're an exasperating woman. Here I have been, patient as the dickens for months: waiting for that confounded book to be done. I had to talk to somebody — if you wouldn't talk to me. I had to have some excuse for coming over here, hadn't I — to be where you were? Lucy Lovelace hasn't any romantic notions about me; she knows very well how much I think of you. She is fond of me as she would be of — of an uncle. And she told me herself she was considering whether she would encourage that young Bascome who is at Yale."

Very likely, thought Miss Ormsbee, unimpressed. The Lucy's always had second considerations up their sleeves.

John continued: "He is going down to Atlanta to see her, this summer."

"That will be nice," said Gail.

She said it absently. Her concentration was elsewhere. At that moment Gail was facing acknowledgment of one of the lessons of her life. She was not strong and efficient — as she had so fondly fancied. She was weak as any woman. She would have supinely given up because of oversensitive pride that could not bear getting itself hurt. And for all her vaunted assumption of superiority, her cherished fetish of forthrightness, she had been no bigger, no better poised than women she had held in contempt because of their lack of logic and their evasion of plain truth. A dozen words, courageously spoken, any time, would have saved her all this unhappiness — and her own obstinate feminine pride had kept her from saying them. Women were all alike. And she was one of them. Hereafter, she would be more understanding of all the rest.

John's hands were still on her shoulders. He looked as though he would like to shake her again. "There is only one glimmer of sense in the whole silly business and that is: it looks to me as if you cared." He bent down and tried to see her eyes. "Do you, Gail? Do I mean more to you than that book? Sometimes I've wondered. I've been pretty patient. I want my answer right now!"

The black lashes flashed up and he saw her eyes. Something in them made him drop his hands from her shoulders — reach for her with his arms ...

But she pressed both of her hands against him, pushing him off.

"Wait — !" She ran out of the room and in a moment was back, carrying something in her hands. It was the novel. She walked over to the fireplace and, stooping, laid the manuscript on the flickering logs.

"That's my answer," she said, straightening up.

"Gail —!" He started toward her. Stopped, and looked at the manuscript about which smoke was curling ...

But John had been for many years an editor. He seized the tongs and conveyed the bundle of manuscript to a place of safety on the hearthstone. It was slightly charred and some of the pages were curling, but a thick packet of bond paper does not ignite in an instant. He stamped on it vigorously until he was certain every spark was out.

"You precious little fool!" he said to her — but this was minutes later and they were sitting, very close together, on the sofa —"Did you think I'd let you do a thing you'd bitterly repent — and probably blame me for, ten years from now?"

She looked without acute interest at the scorched manuscript on the hearth — and snuggled closer into John's arm. Very firm it felt. And tender... Protective.

"In ten years," she said dreamily, "I might get at rewriting it."

"You'll rewrite it in less than ten years," he told her firmly. "We are going to make a go of this thing, Gail — God bless my girl!" He stooped to kiss her again — "But you are going to have your chance as well as I — and my constituents. Do you imagine I'd let you give up writing?"

"Oh, well —" her head lay back against his arm that was flung along the cushions behind her. "Does it matter?" she said.

And that was the way they left it.

John was full of plans; they had been simmering in his head, he confessed, while he had been waiting for her to finish the book. He could sell the other house and buy in this one from her — it had a better location, on the golf course. Then she could keep her garden. And he had an option on the ravine property... "We can put a garage back there and build out a wing on that side; make a library of it, with a big window looking right down into the brook. And it will give us extra bedrooms and bathrooms upstairs —"

Gail sat up straight.

"But, John, that would mean getting rid of some of my hedges!"

John's eyes twinkled. "Exactly what I have in mind, my dear; — getting rid of some of your hedges."

THE BEST OF RECENT FICTION

Virtuous Husband, The. Freeman Tilden.
Voice of the Pack, The. Edison Marshall.

Wagon Wheel, The. William Patterson White.
Walls of Glass. Larry Barretto.
Way of an Eagle, The. Ethel M. Dell.
Way of the Strong, The. Ridgwell Cullum.
Way of These Women. E. Phillips Oppenheim.
We Must March. Honore Willsie.
West Broadway. Nina Wilcox Putnam.
Westward to Paradise. W. D. Hoffman.
West Wind. Crosbie Garstin.
West Wind Drift. George Barr McCutcheon.
Wheels Within Wheels. Carolyn Wells.
Whelps of the Wolf. George Marsh.
When a Man's a Man. Harold Bell Wright.
Where the Waters Turn. Theodore Von Ziekursch.
Whispering Outlaw, The. George Owen Baxter.
White Wolf, The. Max Brand.
White Moll, The. Frank L. Packard.
Wild West. Bertrand W. Sinclair.
Window at the White Cat. Mary Roberts Rinehart.
Winds of Chance, The. Rex Beach.
Winning of Barbara Worth. Harold Bell Wright.
Wire Devils, The. Frank L. Packard.
Wishing Ring Man, The. Margaret Widdemer.
With Juliet in England. Grace S. Richmond.
Without Gloves. James B. Hendryx.
Woman Haters, The. Joseph C. Lincoln.
Woman of Knockaloe, The. Hall Cane.
Woman Thou Gavest Me. Hall Caine.
Women of the Family, The. Margaret Culkin Banning.
Woodcarver of 'Lympus. Mary E. Waller.
Wrath to Come, The. E. Phillips Oppenheim.
Wrong Mr. Wright, The. Berta Ruck.

Year of Delight, The. Margaret Widdemer.
Yellow Claw, The. Sax Rohmer.
Yellow Shadows. Sax Rohmer.
You Can't Win. Jack Black.
You're Only Young Once. Margaret Widdemer.
You're Young But Once. Louise Breitenbach Clancy.

Zeppelin's Passenger, The. E. Phillips Oppenheim.